Between Stone & A Hard

Between Stone and a ha

©Neil Hallam 2018

Published by Lauman Media and Publishing

1st Published 2016

2nd Edition 2018

Other titles by Neil Hallam

The Nev Stone & the Watchers novels
Between stone and a Hard Place
Stone, Paper, Bomb
Breath Becomes Stone

Loxley: modern day Robin Hood tales
Loxley: a dish served cold
Loxley: Swim, Bike, Die

Non-fiction titles
Rocking the Streets – a history of English youth culture

The Robin Hood 500

The Robin Hood Cycleway

Between Stone & A Hard Place

Neil Hallam is a freelance photojournalist based in Nottingham, England. A keen motorcyclist throughout his adult life, Neil contributes to motorcycle magazines in: Australia, USA and Great Britain.

Neil's love of adventure has taken him to many of the world's most interesting places, which find their way, via his imagination, to the pages of his books. Many of his adventures have been on expeditions to remote areas including the Himalayas and Mongolia.

For over twenty years, Neil has worked in a variety of roles across the Blue Light Services. He has an MSc in Disaster Management. The real life experience and advanced theoretical understanding add depth to Neil's plot lines and subject matter knowledge.

Between Stone & A Hard Place

Chapter 1

"Convoy checking in sequence".
The surveillance team of one bike and four cars checked in with control as they sped to the subject's last sighting.
"Nev", "Tom", "Suzie"," Jock", "Phil"
The vehicles left space between each other and regularly changed position to confuse the suspect they were following. Then biker Nev Stone spotted the van they had been tailing. Intelligence suggested the driver was an Al-Qaeda convert and the small van was loaded with explosives.
"Nev permission?" called Stone, asking permission to break Control's radio priority. "I've got eyeball, moving up to get video".

Nev Stone was powering his adventure motorcycle along Portugal's Algarve motorway. But his mind was drifting from the monotony of the motorway to his former life as a surveillance biker with Britain's Counter Terrorism Command.
Stone had spent the last three days lying on a Faro rooftop dressed in a camouflage ghilli suit. The wait was worthwhile as it gained Stone exclusive photographs of Team Farense footballer Sergio Silva leaving a city brothel.
The tip was part of the 1% bikers thank you for saving their English President's life in prison. The photographs had already been sent to his press agent and would pay some bills, but the job did not have quite the adrenalin of chasing Al-Qaeda across Britain. So Stone passed the miles remembering life in the British Police. He used to ride a powerful surveillance motorcycle as part of a counter terrorism team, with a pistol under his arm and a carbine rifle in his pannier.

Stone's life today was more sedate, but it would still be the envy of many. Home is a yurt in Portugal's Algarve National Park, close to the surfer's Mecca of Sagres. He had learned to surf and rode his adventure bike around the region's wilderness.

Between Stone & A Hard Place

He supplied his picture agency with a regular stock of surfing photographs. His earnings were often boosted when he got a tip from his biker brothers and turned his surveillance training to the art of paparazzi.

The Costa Vincentina National Park on Portugal's south western tip was where Stone had pitched his yurt a year ago. Building is strictly limited in the wild coastal area, but authorities turned a blind eye to the odd temporary structure or surfers' camp.
Dirt roads cut through scrubby vegetation, linking small copses of weather beaten trees. It was in one of these sheltered areas, a short walk from the beach, that Stone has made his home. His was a very eco friendly lifestyle; water came from a nearby stream, power and some hot water from solar panels and heating from a thick Portuguese jumper, or wood burning stove.

Stone's reverie was broken as he left the Tarmac at the tiny enclave of Ingrena and started along the dirt track to his yurt. Here the Triumph Explorer came into its own, picking its way across country. The trail wound its way through the many unofficial camp sites cut into the scrubby bush.
Most of the vans parked in the clearings were the small camper vans of the areas transient surfer community. A few others were the elegant motor homes of more affluent tourists.
Nev enjoyed the variety of his neighbours, who came from all corners of Europe and further afield on the international surf tour. Many of the surfers he knew well, while others provided an interesting distraction to his exile.
Taking the last turn towards his own secluded camp site, his police man's instincts started to alarm. A motor home and a black Mercedes saloon were parked in the next clearing. But the motor home was bigger than those used by touring holiday makers and was decorated in a way typical of Europe's Roma Travelers. Stone had rarely seen any Roma outside of the cities and holiday resorts. Playa de Luz was the closest he had seen them to the National Park. Years of

Between Stone & A Hard Place

police diversity training tried hard to keep Stone's mind open to the Roma, but he never quite trusted them. Stories of crimes from burglary to people trafficking seemed to follow in this group of travelers' wake.

The top of the range Mercedes had Eastern European plates, which also seemed out of place in his surfer's enclave, particularly considering the risk of damaging such an expensive car on the rough track.

Stone cut the engine of his motorcycle, dismounted and crept closer through the trees. His years as a surveillance officer helped his stealthy approach to the vehicles. Controlling his breathing, Stone slipped under one of the vehicle's windows, listening to the people inside. The voices of two men carried clearly from the vehicle. The language sounded Russian, but he could not understand the words, except for vodka, which seemed universal.

Beneath the loud voices of the two men was something softer, which Stone had to concentrate on to separate out the faint sound. It sounded like a child sobbing, but he still couldn't quite make it out.

Stone moved around the vehicle, trying to see inside. But the windows were either too high, or positioned so that his shadow would cast inside, giving him away.

Growing more suspicious, Stone pulled himself up on the camper's wheel arch to look through one of the high windows.

Seated at the table were two dark haired men. One was immaculately dressed in a dark Italian suit. His dress and Slavic features suggested he owned the Mercedes. The second, more casually dressed man had an appearance confirming Stone's suspicion that the motor home belonged to the Roma.

Then, a slight movement in the corner of his eye caught Stone's attention. There, curled in the corner of the van, Stone saw a young girl, no more than eight or nine years old. What struck Stone was the girl's curly blond hair, setting her apart from the two dark haired vodka drinking men at the

Between Stone & A Hard Place

table.
The girl did not look happy and the scene was not playing well to the former police man's suspicious mind.

Then the girl looked up. Her eyes, full of tears, connected with Stone's. He wanted to put a finger to his lips, but to keep his balance at the window the best he could do was shake his head. The subtle message did not work, as he then heard a soft English voice say "please".
This was enough for both men to follow the girl's gaze, straight to Stone's face.
Adrenalin instantly started to course through Stone's system. He dropped from his perch on the wheel, diving for cover to give him a little thinking time.
He didn't get much time to think as the Slavic looking man ran from the far side of the motor home. Stone expected to see a gun, but was relieved to see only a machete. He could improvise enough from the surroundings to even the odds a little against a blade. Quickly surveying his surroundings, he spotted a cudgel shaped branch and a longer, sharper looking stick. He picked up the cudgel and moved towards the man to gain some element of surprise. As he moved out of the bush he kicked the long stick into a position he could retrieve it from if needed.

"Hey you"! shouted Stone, as he walked towards the man. His expensive looking business suit looked very out of place in their surroundings. But Stone was sure the suit's designer never imagined it accessorised with a machete.
The man turned, raising the huge knife and shouted at Stone. He spoke a few European languages, but none from the former Soviet Union, where he thought the man's dialect originated.
Stone did not understand the words, but he understood their delivery and accompanying body language. They were shouting "threat" more clearly than any words could do.
Stone knew the advantage of confidence, so he walked towards the Slav raising his cudgel. They reached a stand off, a few feet from each other. The Slav waved his machete

Between Stone & A Hard Place

at Stone and continued to shout what he assumed were obscenities. Then he realised that some of the shouting was instructions to the other man, as he saw the Roma drag the girl away from the motor home and towards the Mercedes. The Slav had not been coming for him; he was creating space to get the girl to his car.

Instantly Stone made his decision to move. Rushing towards the Slav, his first swing of the cudgel was to the hand holding the machete, causing him to drop the blade. His second blow was to the Slav's head, knocking him to the floor.
Stone did not wait to check on the Slav, as the girl's cries had now turned into screams. The Roma and the girl had crossed most of the distance to the Mercedes in the time Stone had spent on the Slav, but Stone closed the gap even quicker.
It was then that Stone saw the gun. The Roma had one strong arm wrapped around the young girl's neck, pulling her across the clearing. But in the Roma's free hand shone the polished finish of a small pistol. Stone had heard plenty of jokes about taking a knife to a gun fight, but now faced the reality of a gun fight armed only with a heavy stick.
He reacted quickly, running towards the man. This sharp movement saved his life as the first shot rang out. The bullet found its mark, but only a glancing blow to Stone's left arm. The wound was running with blood, but adrenalin seemed to be taking care of the pain.
Stone went into a rolling dive taking him towards the Mercedes and out of the line of fire. Luck seemed to be with him as his roll landed him next to the sharp stick he had kicked out earlier. It was still hardly a gun, but gave Stone something more effective than a cudgel.
Knowing the Roma's aim would be affected by holding the girl, Stone went quickly on the attack. Feinting one way then the other, he forced the pointed stick into the forearm holding the gun. The Roma dropped the gun and recognising Stone to be a real threat to him, let go of the girl too.
The Roma was powerfully built, looking like a bare knuckle

Between Stone & A Hard Place

boxer. Stone was also in good shape, but his motorcycle clothing hid it well. The Roma must have thought the advantage was his, as rather than try to recover his gun; he went straight for Stone in a neck lock.
It had been a few years since Stone's last police self defence training, but the prison gym and his new outdoor lifestyle kept him fit and the repeatedly trained moves came automatically. Stone stamped down hard into the Roma's shin, then used body leverage to throw him over his shoulder. Both men fell to the ground and were rolling across each other trying to gain advantage.

While Stone fought the Roma, he neglected the Slav who had now regained his feet. Stone felt the cold gun barrel against his neck and a calm but forceful instruction in words he could not understand.
Stone felt the Slav push harder with the barrel, indicating he should lie in the dirt. Knowing he had no chance with a gun at point blank range, Stone did as instructed.
By now the powerful Roma had caught the girl and was dragging her back towards the car. The Slav joined him and while keeping the gun trained on Stone, opened the car boot to put the girl in.
It was then that the biggest surprise happened. The tiny girl had managed to pick up a large stone and swung it straight at the Slav's head. She could not put much force behind the blow, but it was enough for the pistol to move away from Stone.
Stone reacted instantly, jumping to his feet, picking up his sharp stick and rushing at the Slav. But Stone had not taken account of the blood he was losing from the bullet wound and his movements were becoming slower. The Slav had time to again turn his gun towards Stone. His only option was to strike out with the stick. It was a poorly aimed blow, but by chance hit the most vulnerable point available. The point went deep into the Slav's throat. With a sickening gurgle, the Slav fell to the floor.
Dealing with two powerful adversaries in his weakened state was too much for Stone. The big Roma kicked out at him,

sending an explosion of pain through his ribs.
Doubled up and fighting for breath, Stone could do nothing as the Roma threw the girl he had been fighting to save into the Mercedes and drove away.

Stone ran the few hundred yards to his motorcycle. He tried to give chase, but weakened by blood loss and the beating he had taken, he could not ride quickly enough. The weight of luggage from his trip added to the weight of the 1200cc bike and the Mercedes was out of sight by the time he reached Tarmac and the first road junction.
Rather than blindly choose a turning, Stone returned to see if he could get any information from the Slav.
He rode back into the clearing finding the Slav lying where he had left him in the dirt. Stone had been sure the branch could not have inflicted any real damage. Training again kicked in and he quickly searched for a pulse. Finding no pulse at his wrist, Stone turned to find the pulse in his neck. This was when Stone saw the extent of the damage his stick had caused to the Slav's throat. No one could have survived such an injury.

Stone's thoughts first turned to the young girl. He had lost the trail of Mercedes the Roma had driven her away in. Now the only other source of information was dead. Stone started to look around the clearing for anything that would help find her.
It was then the consequences of taking a second life hit Stone. A momentary loss of control lost Stone his police career and led to a manslaughter conviction when he shot a terrorist suspect. Now Stone was faced with explaining his actions in killing the Slav.
Panic set in as Stone began to relive the long months of investigation and trial that ended his police career. Stone dropped to his knees beside the Blood soaked body. He tried to think logically and work through his story for the Portuguese police. He knew that this time deadly force was justified, but his only witness was in the fleeing Mercedes and any prosecution would rely on similar fact evidence. His

Between Stone & A Hard Place

mind drifted from that logic to the day he last shot a gun.

Between Stone & A Hard Place

Chapter two

The Midlands Region Counter Terrorism Unit had been working on Operation Trefoil for several months. Like all their cases it began as a single strand of intelligence, developed by the detectives, before growing into a job for the Ops Team.
Nev Stone was one of the most experienced officers in the team of five police officers. His Sergeant, Jock Miller was a recent transferee from the Metropolitan Police SO15 Counter Terrorism Unit. The other three constables in his team were all younger local officers.
His team were all trained in surveillance photography, firearms and advanced driving. Stone had ridden motorcycles from the moment he was old enough for a licence. His commanders snatched at this experience and trained him as a surveillance motorcyclist. His job when the team was deployed on mobile surveillance was to cut through traffic and get an early visual contact, or "eyeball".

Operation Trefoil started for Stone in the same way as all operations, with an early morning briefing at their covert police building.
He had already been to the garage and checked over the mechanics and video equipment fitted to his high powered motorcycle. He had visited the armoury and drawn out his Glock pistol, which now sat comfortably in a pocket of his leather jacket. A Heckler and Koch short carbine rifle also nestled in its specially adapted pannier case.

Briefings were always late, so Stone occupied himself by studying the latest intelligence bulletins and photographs circulated through the unit's secure intranet system. The rogue's gallery was often much the same from one day to the next, but today he saw several new profiles had been added to their watch list. The new subjects were all connected to Nottingham, rather than Birmingham or Leicester which was more usual. This interested Stone as Nottingham was his patrol area before transferring to the

Between Stone & A Hard Place

Counter Terrorism Unit, so he spent extra time looking over their new subjects.

Eventually the unit's Detective Inspector arrived to brief the team on their tasking for the day. DI Tony Jones, or Jonah as he was usually known, had been with the Counter Terrorism Unit forever. It was simply known as Special Branch when he joined and he had outlasted all of its force and regional incarnations.

Jonah was not one of the modern breed of politically correct managers. Command viewed him as something of a dinosaur, but he got the job done more effectively than any of the younger Inspectors.

His briefing started as always, with the sort of joke which would land anyone else in hot water. Stone remembered being at a post mortem when Jonah cracked a joke comparing Morris Dancers with pricks. The pathologist's young assistant ran from the room trying to stifle her laughter, before the pathologist said "I'm a Morris Dancer". Thankfully today's joke was a little less risky and Jonah soon moved onto briefing their operation.

Operation Trefoil involved the Nottingham based terrorist cell Stone had just read about. Other specialist teams had been shadowing the four men for several months. Government Communications Headquarters, or GCHQ, had first flagged the cell for the Midlands Team's attention when they started buying explosive precursor chemicals. A mix of static surveillance and traditional detective work had kept up with their efforts to produce a large quantity of explosive.

Jonah briefed Stone's team on the players, where the explosives were stored and what vehicles they were likely to use. But no target had yet been identified. This could only mean that the Trefoil cell had not been told the target and some more senior AQ leaders would provide instructions at the last minute.

Command had considered raiding the cell's safe house in rural Nottinghamshire. But, as they appeared to have a hierarchical structure of separate cells, there was a risk that

another cell could be tasked with the same target. So an unusually risky decision had been made to let the terrorists run and maintain mobile surveillance.
This was where Stone's team came into play. As soon as the static observation point saw the explosive packed van move out, the mobile team would follow and intervene before it could be detonated.

DS Jock Miller led his team out to their standby positions near Newark. Radio etiquette demanded that the static obs point had radio priority, as they had the "eyeball". At regular intervals the obs point would give a "stand by, stand by". This was just to let everyone know the radios were still live. Occasionally a more detailed update would be given as the terrorists moved between the farmhouse and their vehicles. Once they were seen wiping down the farmhouse the team knew they were "game on".
Then the radios came alive again. "Off off off". "It's right right, A46 towards the city".
This was the team's cue to move out from their standby positions. Their five vehicles had been spread across the possible routes out of the farm. Now they had a direction of travel they had to quickly move up and follow the terrorist's van.

"Convoy checking in sequence", said Jock as a prompt for his team to check in. "Nev", "Tom", "Suzie", " jock", "Phil", replied each of them, indicating their order in the small convoy.
Stone was riding the only motorcycle among the five surveillance vehicles. Luck had placed him in the direction of travel taken by the van, so he was at the head of the convoy as they sped towards the van.
Then he spotted the van and keyed up his radio. "Nev permission?" called Stone, asking permission for radio priority. "I've got eyeball, moving up to get video".
He opened up the 1400cc Kawasaki to close the distance between him and the small van, overtaking the van to allow his rearward facing camera to film the occupants.

Between Stone & A Hard Place

As he passed, Stone looked to his left and caught a good view inside the van. "It's Bravo and Delta" he said. The four subjects had been code named Alfa, Bravo, Charlie and Delta. But only two of them were in the van.
Now that Stone had been up close with the subjects, he would have to get clear to avoid making them suspicious. But he had to wait until the next car in his team came within sight.
Steve Jones had lost his first name very early in his police career. Despite his scouse accent sounding nothing like Welsh, he had always been known as Tom.
As Tom's Mondeo came into his mirrors, Stone powered away to find somewhere to duck out of sight. He spotted a farm entrance and pulled behind the hedge.
Jock tasked Suzie Best to meet Stone so that he could change his jacket and the bike's number plate, giving him another shot at getting close to their subjects. Suzie was far too young to appreciate Jonah's humour in allocating her an Audi Quatro car. She just thought the old DI gave her a nice car because he fancied her. Jock and Nev were just old enough to remember the rocker Suzie Quatro, and they hadn't quite ruled out Jonah imagining Suzie in tight leather trousers.

Team members often took a gamble getting ahead of a subject vehicle, as the whole convoy following would soon be noticed. Knowing their subjects had Nottingham ties, Stone sped through the back roads to come out on the A52. Today his gamble was correct as he heard Tom Jones call out "it's A52 towards the city".

Now the team had an expected destination, DI Jonah Jones began work with the intelligence cell to predict likely targets. An American trade delegation was being hosted at the Council House in Nottingham's Old Market Square, but road closures made this an unlikely target for a vehicle borne improvised explosive device, or VBIED.
The English Defence League was holding a demonstration at a mosque on the edge of the city. Jonah at first ruled this

Between Stone & A Hard Place

out; thinking it unlikely Islamic fundamentalists would explode a bomb near a mosque. But when Jonah looked more closely at the plans he realised the demonstration had only been allowed by moving it from the mosque and closer to the nearby Salvation Army building. Jonah thought this had to be the target; EDL supporters and a Christian building in one hit. So Jonah made a call to the City Division Commander calling out as many uniforms as they could muster at short notice.

Back on the A52 traffic was light and the surveillance team had to spread out to avoid being spotted by their subjects. Jock had taken position two cars back from the van. Stone pulled out of a lay-by just ahead of the van and began heading towards the city.
But as he passed the entrance to the National Watersports Centre at Holme Pierpoint, he saw in his mirrors that the van, closely followed by Jock, had turned right into the centre's access lane. Stone turned his bike around and followed them into the lane. Jock must have kept his car behind the subjects for too long, because as he took the turn, the van sped off at the first blind bend. Jock and Stone accelerated to catch up, but reaching the first junction they could not see which fork the van had taken.
Talking quickly through the car window, Jock sent Stone left towards the slalom course, while he headed right to the regatta lake.

Urgent radio messages had passed the information back to Jonah. Either Jock had been spotted earlier than they thought, or they had the target wrong. But what could be the target at a Watersports Centre? Jonah and his intelligence cell began working all of their contacts for ideas.

Stone started to methodically move through the car parks looking for the van. Two gleaming Ducati sports bikes caught his eye, and then as he approached the slalom course he spotted their riders watching the kayaking from a bridge over the course. The two riders wore pristine racing leathers and

Between Stone & A Hard Place

looked much cleaner cut than your average biker; one of them was more noticeable with his ginger hair. They were both flanked two older men wearing two piece bike leathers, who somehow looked less aristocratic than the young bikers. As they walked towards him, Stone thought the younger men strangely familiar. Then recognition hit him and he called Jonah up on his radio. He asked "are we expecting a royal visit, cos I'm sure William and Harry are here on bikes".

Jonah did not know of an official visit, but making a call to his contact at the Met's Royalty Protection Team provided information he should have been briefed about. Princes William and Harry were conducting a low key and unpublicised visit to support Harry's Paralympics soldier charity at Holme Pierpoint.
Prince William's love of his Ducati motorcycle is well known. Younger brother Harry kept his motorcycle licence quiet, as it gave the young Army Officer a chance of anonymity with a helmet covering his ginger hair. The Princes had ridden across from Sandringham with a minimal security escort and only planned a flying visit.

This put the team on full alert. If the Princes were the target and not the EDL as thought, then the terrorists must have excellent intelligence sources. Jonah started to coordinate the surveillance team into the slalom area.
He also started to recall some of the uniforms from the city centre, but knew it would take time to move them through city traffic. His small team would be without back up for a while.
As Stone watched the Princes, Jock, Tom and Suzie pulled into the car park. Jock spotted the small van moving from behind a delivery truck. The van drove to a position close to the Princes and a small group of injured soldiers. Stone saw the two suspects get out of the van. He reacted instantly, laying down his Kawasaki and quickly closed the gap on foot drawing his pistol as he ran.
Stone began shouting "armed police, on the ground". Then as he got closer he shouted towards the princes "move,

Between Stone & A Hard Place

there's a bomb in the van ".

The terrorists initially froze, but then started to run away from the van. Stone got within range of one of the men and running high on adrenalin, fired two shots at the man's head. Two shots, or the double tap, is a standard military tactic. But the police are expected to use minimal force. A first, let alone a second shot, must always be proven necessary. Stone realised that as the man was running, he would have some explaining to do about taking the shots.

Jock was there seconds after Stone had taken his shots. "Shit Nev" "it wasn't a Kratos" shouted Jock. Operation Kratos was the police plan for dealing with suicide bombers. Where there is real risk of a terrorist triggering a suicide device, it is the only time firearms officers can use what would otherwise be excessive force. The need to prevent detonation overrides restraint and allows for multiple head shots. This was how Brazilian Jean Charles DeMenez was thought to have been shot so many times. The officers mistakenly believed they had been given authority for Operation Kratos.
Jock knew this was not a Kratos operation and a running suspect reduced the prospect of a suicide device being detonated, so he was now worried for his colleague.

The two protection officers had first thrown the Princes to the ground, but now turned their attention to the second man from the van. Drawing their own weapons they chased, caught and arrested the terrorist.

After requesting an ambulance Jock went straight to Stone. As Sergeant his responsibility was to preserve the scene, the body and Stone's weapon until Professional Standards or PSD arrived.

Between Stone & A Hard Place

Chapter 3

However justified the circumstances seem, any police shooting demands an investigation. The local PSD would be first on scene, but they would soon be followed by the IPCC, or Independent Police Complaints Commission.

Despite their friendship, Jock had to take control of Stone and treat him as a crime scene.

First he made safe Stone's pistol, unloading it and sealing it in an evidence bag. Then he lined the back seat of his car to create a forensically clean area for Stone to sit. He knew that Stone's clothes would be taken from him as soon as they reached the police station.

"How's it look?" asked Stone as he took his place in the back of Jock's car. 'I don't know" replied Jock. "It was a big bomb, but you double tapped someone running away".

The Princes had been spirited away in a fast car to a nearby hotel. And all they could do now was sit and wait for the circus to arrive. It did not take long for Forensics to start taping off the scene and uniforms to cordon off the area.

No one was sure who the on call PSD officer would be, they had their preferences, but it could be any of the senior ranks. The Head of Department was their last choice, but it was Superintendent Chambers turn for the call out. Chambers was a fast track candidate who had little experience of ops work. He was reputedly a meticulous detective, but lacked any knowledge of firearms or counter terrorism.

Supt Chambers slowly walked around the scene, taking in the positions of the van, dead terrorist, Stone's Kawasaki and the general lay out of the area. He then instructed Jock to take his team to the City's ops base to go through PIP.

"More bloody TLAs" said Stone. He always complained of the bosses' use of jargon and Three Letter Acronyms, which he ironically shortened to TLA.

Post Incident Procedure, or PIP, was where his team would be quarantined to surrender their weapons and clothes. Their cameras and vehicle black box recorders would be downloaded and they would give their first accounts of the

Between Stone & A Hard Place

incident.

"Great job Nev". "You'll be fine Nev". "Good luck Nev". By the time Stone reached the Riverside complex news of the terrorist attempt on Princes William and Harry had reached the cops stationed there. The good wishes kept coming as many knew that Stone faced months of trying to justify his kill

The briefing hall at Riverside had already been commandeered for the Post Incident Procedure when Jock and Stone arrived.
Other PSD officers had been called out by Supt Chambers and were starting to arrive. Most operational cops called their internal investigation department the "Rubber Healers" on account of their reputation for sneaking up on other cops.

Representing Stone and his team were the "Feds". The Police Federation is the closest thing to a Trade Union that the police are allowed, but they could often cause problems being too keen to take on the establishment.

Refereeing all this was the Post Incident Manager or PIM. This was Chief Inspector Jim Henson, a very experienced Firearms Silver Commander. His job was to take control of all the involved officers, go though a checklist of post shooting actions and also pick up the welfare of the team. Jim Henson being appointed was the first good news Stone heard since taking his shots.
Henson's name had earned him the nickname "Muppet", although he was anything but a Muppet. Henson had been running firearms ops in Nottingham since the dark days of the 90s when the city gained its title of Shottingham. If anyone would be fair to Stone, it would be Chief Inspector Henson.

Muppet Henson's first duty was to take possession of the weapons from Jock Miller, then outer clothing from the two officers. Stone had taken responsibility for both shots, but a thorough investigation demanded that all of the armed

www.neilhallam.com

officers' clothing is examined for gun shot residue. That way the investigators can cross reference all the accounts with the physical evidence.

"Tell them nothing for 24 hours" advised the Feds. The official process allowed for a very brief initial statement to be given through the Feds, then after 24 hours give a detailed statement.
Stone decided he would waive his right to a delay and speak openly to the investigators. He was also keen to give his story before the IPCC arrived to take over. So he sat down at a computer and typed up everything he could remember into his initial account.
He just finished typing in time for the Commission's investigator to arrive. Despite Stone asking for an early interview, the IPCC insisted on the 24 hour delay.
After a sleepless night he found out why they had delayed. Muppet phoned and said "the IPCC want a criminal interview, they think it's unlawful". The Feds had arranged for a solicitor and Stone had to report to HQ later that morning.

"You do not have to say anything" began investigator Russ McCready. Stone absently watched the cassette tapes turning as McCready ran through the formal introductions.
"It's all in there" said Stone handing over the statement he typed the previous night. The investigator droned on in his monotone, reading the statement onto the tape, while Stone examined the cassettes again.
Then the real interrogation started. "This tells me what you did Nev, but I need to know what you were thinking".
Every action in Stone's statement prompted questions about his thought patterns. The cat and mouse questioning progressed steadily through the day's events. But the pace slowed as Stone got to the part where he recognised the Princes. Now every few words brought a barrage of questions, "what were you thinking", "what were your options"?
"Did you see a gun?" asked the investigator. "No" replied

Between Stone & A Hard Place

Stone, "but I knew there was a big bomb".
"Why the head shots"? asked McCready. "To prevent a detonation and save the heirs to the thrown" replied Stone.
"Tell me about proportionality Nev" said McCready.
"Proportionality" replied Stone. "I'm looking at a bloody great IED, William and Harry were there, it could have been triggered any minute. Of course it was bloody proportionate",
Then came McCready's hard line. "He was running away, there was no detonator!"
"I was making quick decisions. I thought the Princes were in danger and I took the shot" said Stone.
"You took two shots" replied McCready. "The double tap" "you're not the bloody SAS!"
Twenty minutes of questions about the shots went round in circles before Stone's solicitor finally interjected. Then suddenly the investigator said "interview terminated" as he turned off the tape. "We'll be in touch when a charge decision has been made" he said, gathering up his file.

Almost a year of suspension from duty had been hard for Stone.
First the uncertainty of where the case was heading. Then, learning he was to be charged with manslaughter, the seriousness of his situation hit home.
Muppet Henson had been Stone's only official link with the police. As his welfare contact, Muppet visited regularly, trying to keep him upbeat and prepared to defend himself. Colleagues had been warned not to visit, as being a suspected criminal, Stone was a Notifiable Association and a risk to the force's reputation. But the counter terrorism officers had years of tradecraft to rely on and most managed regular visits without their bosses finding out.

Eventually, despite the efforts of Muppet and his remaining friends, the process finally wore Stone down. It was the hardest day of Stone's life when after 20 years in the police, he tendered his resignation and entered his plea. "Your Honour, this doesn't come easy to me" said Stone. "I took those shots with the best of intentions and would possibly do

Between Stone & A Hard Place

the same again. Prince William and Prince Harry are alive, but a man is dead. I accept that I made a mistake and the bomb wasn't about to be triggered, so I plead guilty".

Stone had been free on bail throughout the investigation and walked into Nottingham Crown Court a free man on the day of sentencing. Judge Davis had appeared sympathetic towards him, even extending the time for pre sentence reports to allow him longer with the file. But despite a friendly judge, Nev had little illusion that he would walk free from court that day.

A 20 year police officer, Stone had multiple commendations for bravery and was noted for his lack of nerves. But waiting for Judge Davis to begin summing up was giving stone an uncomfortable feeling in his stomach.

"You have pleaded guilty to Manslaughter on grounds of gross negligence" began the Judge. In some respects I would have been interested to know a jury's take on the matter. But I must now sentence you. I will take account of the circumstances, your exemplary police career and I will give credit for an early guilty plea".

"I have heard about large quantities of explosives packed into a vehicle,"

"The prosecution has acknowledged that your subject was armed and that you did not know the target".

"A significant amount of forensic work has been done on the bomb to determine its trigger mechanism. However, there is no way you could have accounted for this information in your decision to shoot".

"The prosecution believes that you were negligent in not following the police firearms policy. Your guilty plea acknowledges that you accept the policy was not adhered to".

"But I for one would not like to have been in your position. The Heir and spare are alive. It is difficult to say what would have happened without your intervention".

"I have considerable latitude in passing sentence for manslaughter. You have taken a life and the family will expect me to pass a custodial sentence". "This I will do and consider three years to be appropriate". "I discount this by a third for your guilty plea and sentence you to two years imprisonment". "If, as I expect, you will, serve your sentence with good behaviour, you should serve less than 12 months".

Judge Davis ended by saying "I hope you find some way of turning your time in custody into a positive experience". Neither the judge nor Stone could imagine the way his life would be changed by prison.

Chapter 4

A dark shadow passing overhead shook Stone from his memories. Looking up he saw a flock of Griffon Vultures circling overhead. These huge birds were a regular sight in the Algarve on their migration to North Africa. But it was their liking for carrion that brought Stone to his senses. There could only be one reason for the scavengers' interest, the body of the Slav and the increasing pool of blood. "Time to go to work" thought Stone, as he began to prioritise his actions.

His first job was to bind the bullet wound in his arm, but Stone still had some decisions to make. He should really wait for the Portuguese police. He was no longer a cop, he had killed someone, but more importantly, there was a young girl in very real danger.

Stone hated the thought that running may hamper a police investigation, but he was caught between a rock and a hard place. He could not entrust his own liberty and the girl's life to the local police, so rapidly turned his mind back into investigator mode.

"Evidence" he told himself, heading for the motor home. By going inside Stone knew he would leave his own forensic trace, but he needed evidence to have any hope of finding the girl. So despite knowing his forensics would strengthen any future case against him, Stone started to work the scene.

He could not take anything away, as he knew that would be seen as tampering with a crime scene. So he worked only with his camera. He began with general shots of the scene, taking in the Slav's body, the motor home and tracks left by the Mercedes which had taken the girl.

This led into a search of the vehicle. He had to balance thoroughness against getting away before the police arrived. Any documents he found were photographed and returned where he found them. Most of the documents were printed in Eastern European Cyrillic script, so would need to be translated later.

He checked in the wardrobe for clothing labels, to give clues about where their owners had been. The man Stone had chased off did not live alone; the wardrobe was stocked for a woman too. Most labels were Spanish or Portuguese, but some had Arabic labels. Even the food cupboards got attention so he could plot the vehicle's travels. Tinned food was all locally bought, but the Roma obviously had a sweet tooth judging by the drawer full of chocolate and Turkish Delight.

Checking his watch regularly, as he was afraid of the time his search was taking, Stone turned his attention to the body. A quick search produced two passports. Both had the Slav's photograph, but showed different details. The older one was Romanian, but the newer was Bulgarian. "EU membership" said Stone, thinking the Bulgarian passport could have been obtained for travel within the European Union, as Romania was not yet a member. He photographed both passports.

Stone's last task was samples. He was not sure how he could get them to a lab, but old habits die hard. He collected cotton buds and food bags from the motor home's cupboards and used them to swab blood for DNA. Then spotting different coloured dirt in the Slav's shoe tread, he sampled that too, scraping some into another food bag.

Between Stone & A Hard Place

Happy that he had everything he could harvest from the crime scene, Stone returned to his motorbike. The walkie talkie he used to communicate with the MC and their security staff could also pick up police frequencies. What little radio talk there was came from Sagres, where there was a problem with a group of drunken surfers heading for the beach. While local officers were tying to prevent a drowning, he knew they were not heading towards him and could not have heard the shots.

This gave Stone time to visit his nearby yurt and pack an extra holdall with   changes of clothing to supplement the surveillance kit he had worn for the Faro assignment.

There was a safe buried in the dirt floor of his yurt, covered with rugs. Stone recovered his cash, passport and other papers from the safe and replaced the rugs.

Then, strapping the holdall across the pillion seat of his Triumph, Stone picked his way along the dirt track towards Ingrina. He had made a good choice in the rougher of the two trails, as reaching the road he saw the GNR, or National Guard of The Republic turn their police car onto the better track. He could tell through his radio that this was the only police patrol in the area, so rode steadily towards Lagos and refuge at the Watchers MC clubhouse.

Stone often chose the more scenic coast road to visit his MC Friends. But today he chose the N125, as this good quality road would get him to safety much faster. The road's many roundabouts passed quickly as he skilfully manoeuvred the big motorcycle. Each town brought traffic control which turned signals red if the speed limit was exceeded, but where he was able, Stone used all of the bike's 1200cc.

Soon he reached the old walled city of Lagos. The Watchers had found an ideal location for their clubhouse, just inside the magnificent stone walls. The building had been a car showroom, with a night club on the upper floors. The Watchers had the security contract for the nightclub and when the owner went bust owing them money, they took over the building.

Recognised instantly on the CCTV monitor, the roller shutter

www.neilhallam.com

to the downstairs garage raised to give access to Stone's bike.

Working the doors were two prospects, who Stone had not met before. The prospects were probationary members of the Motorcycle Club, or MC. They wore the same sleeveless leather vest as the full members, but they had only the word Portugal on their backs. Only after proving absolute loyalty to the club would they be awarded the other two patches for their backs.

Full members had a top rocker with the name Watchers and a centre logo of a watchtower with searchlights.

Barely had Stone put down his helmet when a familiar voice boomed across the garage. "Nev, my brother, how was Faro?" The Watchers' President, Skull Murphy, grabbed Stone in an embrace typical of all biker greetings.

Christened Tim, Murphy gained his nickname when he lost his hair while still in his twenties. Years of body building had pulled Murphy's skin tight across the angular bones of his face. The loss of his hair just emphasised his skeletal appearance and the name Skull soon stuck.

"Faro went like clockwork, but I hit a spot of bother back at the yurt" "let's get a drink and I'll fill you in. I think I'm going to need some help with this one".

Skull pulled them each a draught beer from the bar and they settled into the armchairs for Stone to tell his story.

"Anything I involve the MC in needs a vote" said Skull. "They won't turn you down, but I need to keep things right".

1% bikers pick and choose which laws to obey, but they never step outside of Roberts Rules of Order in the democratic running of the club's business.

"Mandatory Church" barked Skull into his phone as he started calling in members for a vote. Church is what the bikers call their formal meetings to decide on club business. Skull needed six of the chapter's ten full members to commit the club to Stone's cause.

Skull Murphy was a founder of the Watchers MC, their International President and the only Englishman among the

Between Stone & A Hard Place

Portuguese and Spanish members of the Lagos chapter. He moved to this quiet corner of Portugal with his friend Nev Stone, the man to who he owed his life.
The two friends had helped consolidate the clubs control of security contracts across the Algarve's tourist resorts. In doing so they had made the members wealthy men and earned their unconditional respect.
"Lagos are riding, Derbyshire and London will be on planes within the hour" Skull only needed six local members for a quorum, but wanted the expertise from the two biggest and longest standing English chapters.

While Skull was working his phone, one of the Prospects finished dressing the bullet wound on Nev Stone's arm. The MC would not involve a doctor unless absolutely necessary and the wound did not go deep. He was often reminded how different this 1% MC world was from the motor cycle clubs he had known before. Mainstream clubs used an extra letter in their names, calling themselves MCC. These are said to represent 99% of the world's motorcyclists. The remaining 1% consider themselves outside of society and outside of the law; they would quite literally die for each other.
He could not be a full member of the MC without going through the Prospect phase. But his relationship with Skull Murphy was too close for him to spend a year as a probationer, where he would effectively be treated as a slave by the fully patched members.
Despite not being a complete insider, Stone knew he could count on the club's support. He just had to be patient while they played out their democracy.

Soon the roar of big bike engines echoed around the old town as the Lagos Watchers returned to their clubhouse. Big international clubs, like the Hell's Angels, insist their members ride American Harley Davidsons. When the Watchers formed in England, they decided to adopt European motorcycles. Most rode big Triumphs, or Italian Moto Guzzis, but a few had customised BMWs and a selection of other European bikes.

Between Stone & A Hard Place

Always the showman, Skull rode the world's biggest production bike, a 2300cc Triumph Rocket III.
The first two bikes to join them in the clubhouse garage was a pair of identically customised Triumph Thunderbirds. At 1700cc these were big bikes, but looked tiny against Skull Murphy's 2.3. Their riders were as identical as their bikes. Twin brothers Paulo and Pedro Da Costa had been founders of the Lagos chapter and were both officers of the club. They were respectively Secretary and Treasurer, but in reality shared the two roles.
"How do you tell them apart?" Stone asked the twins, mocking the most regular question they get asked about their bikes. "Sometimes we are not sure" replied Paulo. "But the different number plates help" added Pedro. The three men hugged each other in turn, slapping each other on the back with an "ola". This was the traditional greeting of these men, who even without a blood tie considered themselves brothers.

It did not take long for the remaining four members that Skull had called in to arrive.
Joao Alva, rode in on his Moto Guzzi California which was modelled on an American Police bike, but painted with the Watchers' logo. Joao held the rank of Sergeant at Arms, a mountain of a man; he was responsible for discipline and security within the chapter. Sergeant at Arms is a traditional rank within the 1% MCs, but there was little for him to do among the watchers members. Being quite senior in their security careers, they all had reasonable self control and security of the club house was covered by all of them. Joao was most often called into role with their junior employees, as most joined the company as bouncers and worked their way up.

The pair riding in together had been friends since school. They stood out by riding cafe racers, rather than the cruiser style bikes favoured by most of the members.
Rui Cal rode a very loud customised Ducati. He was a fan of all things Italian, wearing their sharp suits for work and

Between Stone & A Hard Place

driving an Alpha Romeo sports car when not on his bike. Miguel Cuba was chapter Vice President. He had lived in England for school and university, falling in with the Watchers and going to prison with Skull Murphy. On their release he helped found the Lagos chapter.
In homage to his years in England, he rode a Norton Commando cafe racer.

Last in was Andre Felix. Like Rui Cai, he held no specific rank in the chapter, but as with all full members he was a director of their companies.
Andre rode a belt drive 800cc BMW in a custom chopper frame. The bike was decorated with murals of his namesake Felix the cat.

With Skull, that made seven full patch members present and enough for their decision making. The bikers moved through to their conference room, which they knew as chapel. Only fully patched members were allowed through here, so Stone was left in the bar with the Prospects and a few employees. The voting did not take long as they only had two major decisions to make.
First was whether to commit club and company resources to finding the girl. This was soon agreed, as the right thing to do. But they also knew that Nev Stone would be able to spin the whole episode into an exclusive media story for which the MC would take a cut.
Second was whether or not to cover for Stone if he became a suspect and wanted by the police. This would mean breaking the law by assisting a suspect, or possibly obstructing the police. But it was a line they were happy to cross for their friend.

Stone was starting to drift off. His weekend on surveillance had been a sleepless one. The beating he had taken from the Slav and the Roma took even more out of him. Adrenalin had been keeping him going, but safe in the Watchers' hands Stone was losing focus and slipping deeper into the settee.

Between Stone & A Hard Place

Chapter 5

The bed Stone woke on through his dream was much less comfortable. His dreams were back in prison serving his manslaughter sentence. Just as Judge Davis predicted, Stone was keeping his head down and steadily gaining credit towards an early release.

His police career had demanded regular workouts and even in prison the habit drew him regularly to the gym.
Two big tattooed men were in the gym at every opportunity, pumping the largest weights.
"The Red Skull and Zorro" thought Stone to himself. He would not risk a fight by saying anything aloud, but silently compared Skull Murphy to the Captain America villain and Miguel Cuba with the Latin American hero.

 Despite regularly sharing this space, the men had little to do with Stone, or anyone else. They tolerated Stone and some of the older inmates in their space, but kept to themselves. This changed whenever any younger street gang members tried to use the gym and the men became deliberately intimidating, driving the youngsters out.
As spring turned to summer the sweat tops gave way to vests or bare torsos. Stone had guessed the men's tattoos were gang related, but now, without their shirts, he could see exactly what bonded the men.
Their backs were tattooed with the three part logo usually seen on the jackets of outlaw bikers. A curved top rocker read "Watchers", while it's mirror image below read "England". Between was a caricature of a watch tower.
Stone could not help wincing at the thought of how long they had spent under the needle.

Stone had ridden motorbikes throughout his adult life. He had also been a member of several motor cycle clubs, but his knowledge of the 1% MC world only came through his police work. He had often done surveillance of organised crime elements within the Hell's Angels and Outlaws MC, but

Between Stone & A Hard Place

had never come into real contact with the Watchers.

The morning which was to change the direction of Stone's life started much the same as every prison morning. "Send down the twos" shouted one of the Prison Officers, indicating that landing two should be let out to conduct the business of the day.
Each of the five landings were let out individually. "It makes sense" thought Stone. "This lot would stampede if five lots of 80 prisoners were let onto the stairs at once".

Together with the other prisoners on his landing, Stone shuffled slowly along the landing and down the stairs. They always tried to prolong this brief period between inactivity and organised activity. Those who had become friendly chatted, although Stone generally kept himself to himself. "Come on, move it along, stop the chat"! Shouted the officers, although without conviction, they knew they had to give a little to keep order.
They were heading down for sowsh, or social time. The many drug addicts among the population would be making straight for the hatch and their methadone prescription. Stone used this as a chance to leapfrog the breakfast queue.

After breakfast Stone would always go into the exercise yard for his wing's permitted daily hour.
Waiting in line to be searched was frustrating as the sun shone through the open door. Two prison officers patted down the prisoners, looking for weapons or drugs. It took Stone some time getting used to constantly being touched by the officers. Pat downs were just a part of life in prison. Finally in the sun, he started to jog around the perimeter of the yard. The bikers were, as always, taking advantage of the sun. Skull and Miguel were together in the centre of the yard with other members of their MC doing body weight exercises, such as press ups and sit ups. They acknowledged Stone as he jogged by, but true to form, did not engage on conversation.

Between Stone & A Hard Place

After exercise, most prisoners returned to their cells, but those wanting to do Workshops queued beside the yard gate.

Workshops were at the far side of the exercise yard. Here the prisoners could earn a few pounds doing a bit of menial assembly work.

Only a limited number of trusted prisoners were allowed Workshops time. Stone always did his best to be front of the queue, as he found the repetitive work relaxing.

It was rare for the bikers to want Workshops. Stone noticed they only seemed interested if the street gang members were in the queue.

If the bikers did join the line, they would bully their way towards the front to be sure of their places. Today was no different, except that Senior Officer Fulton intervened. "We're only having two of you lot" he said, allowing Skull and Miguel Cuba to the front, but sending the other two back to the wing.

SO Fulton did not seem so particular with the gangbangers, as they were harder to identify than the back patch tattooed bikers. Stone thought he could identify six of the young street dealers in the queue. He made a mental note to keep clear as there was obviously some animosity between the gangs.

Once the correct number of prisoners was chosen for Workshops and the remainder returned to the wing, two Officers walked them crocodile fashion across the yard. Inside the Workshop looked something between an aircraft hanger and a factory. The walls were bare brick and the floor painted concrete. Large tables filled the floor, around which the prisoners sat to do their work. Today's task was putting together sets of plastic cutlery for ready meals. "Good thing they don't give this lot the metal stuff" thought Stone.

Workshops provided opportunity for an extra shower. The building had a rudimentary shower block, which the prisoners were free to use. They were paid for the work they completed, so most worked as long as they could. Stone did

Between Stone & A Hard Place

not need extra money, so valued another shower.

Stone had seen Skull and Cuba head towards the showers a few minutes before him. He had missed the four Gangbangers who went before them.
The bikers had a problem; they were backed into the wall, surrounded by the youths. Stone knew the bikers could handle themselves. But spotted a flash of metal in a hand moving towards Skull. Instinct and training switched in and Stone swung a high kick into the knifeman's kidneys.
The bikers reacted punching and kicking at their assailants, backed up by Stone who continued until the knifeman hit the floor.

By now the Officers had moved in and all six were restrained and taken to the Seg, or Segregation Unit.
After being strip searched, Stone sat in solitary, worrying that his remission time would be removed and he would spend longer in prison. He had all night to worry, until he was led to the conference room for Daily Adjudication. There was trouble in the prison so often, that the governor held a mini court each morning to deal with prisoners who spent the night in Seg.
"I deny the allegations" replied Stone, in answer to the charge of assault.
On the Governor's table Stone recognised the weapon he had kicked from the gangbanger's hand. It was a nasty makeshift prison weapon. Two parallel rows of razor blades were melted into a toothbrush in place of its bristles. A cut from such a knife was difficult to stitch and left a horrible scar.
"It's alright Nev" said the Governor. "We've fingerprinted the blade, and your story matches Murphy and Cuba's". The Governor instructed that Stone be returned to his cell, letting slip that the strip searches had found knives on all of the street gang members.

"Nev isn't it?" asked Skull. It was the first time Stone had heard Skull speak to anyone outside his group.

www.neilhallam.com

Between Stone & A Hard Place

"I owe you big style" he said. The biker knew much more than Stone, it was clear that he had an inside track from the staff. Stone's distraction had come at the instant that Skull's crew were to be knifed. His first kick gave the bikers the upper hand and saved his life.

As the days passed, Stone was invited to work out with the Watchers. They told him how Skull, Cuba and a few others had taken to night club bouncing while at college. Their love of fast motorbikes took more money than the student grants could fund.

He learned the root of their problem with the drug dealers. Skull's younger brother Pat had moved away from their parents to join his older sibling's adrenalin fuelled life. But the long hours in the night clubs led Pat into amphetamines and cocaine, a lethal cocktail which ended his young life.

"If the dealers have a gang, then so should we" said Skull. Not for them the trappings of the street gangs though. Their choice was the outlaw biker route. Bonded together as brothers, with a love of bikes and a common enemy.

Fuelled by their hatred for the dealers and their drugs, the Watchers expanded, forcibly taking over security contracts on bars known to tolerate dealing.

The more their business expanded, the bigger their MC grew. From their small group in Derbyshire, chapters branched out into other cities and eventually into London. The Hell's Angels and Outlaws MCs took interest in the Watchers growth. Normally they would only tolerate a new MC if it was a puppet of their own bigger empire. But the Watchers anti drug stance gained favour with the big clubs, not through altruism, but they approved of the Watchers taking down the competition for them. Under the big clubs' noses the Watchers had grown to a size no one wanted to go to war with.

The biker's release date came a few months ahead of Stone. As the day approached, Skull made an odd request. "Join us for chapel in the morning Nev". Stone had not used the prison chapel throughout his incarceration. "Never have taken you guys as religious", replied Stone. "We're not, but

Between Stone & A Hard Place

neither are the dealers who use it as a market place".
The chapel sat at the hub of the prison, linked to the wings like spokes of a wheel. It was the only place that prisoners from all wings could meet.
Sunday came and Stone joined the Watchers in Chapel. Their very presence was enough to intimidate most of the dealers and Skull took the chance to offer a way of repaying his debt to Stone.
Skull explained they needed a Security Licence to operate their business in Britain. With their GBH convictions they would not get their licences renewed. But Miguel Cuba's family lived on the Algarve, where the Portuguese authorities were not so particular. They planned to open a Watchers chapter on the Portuguese coast, along with the security business they always ran alongside their club.

"Join us in the sun Nev, I'm sure we can find work for a man with your skills" offered Skull. He described how they took over security contracts for pubs, clubs and hotels. They were more than just bouncers. Skull Murphy and Miguel Cuba had met in college studying electronics. They built CCTV and alarm systems, as well as providing the muscle. He wanted Stone to use his police background to professionalise their image in the holiday area saturated with British tourists.
It was a better offer than Stone would get as a former jailbird back home, so two months later he left East Midlands Airport for the Algarve.
The formula worked a treat. Stone fronted their approach to the British owned businesses, while Cuba handled the locals. Skull used the MCs Europe wide network to bring in technicians and muscle.
They started with the smaller resorts of Lagos and Sagres, then moved on to the bigger developments. Within a year they controlled most of the security contracts from Albuferia to the Cape.

Between Stone & A Hard Place

Chapter 6

Stone's time in Portugal began with him sleeping in the Watchers' Lagos clubhouse. But he was soon drawn to the more relaxing life of his yurt among the surfing community. He still spent many nights on the Watchers' settees when he was in Lagos for work or parties. So it was no surprise that he had drifted into a dream filled sleep waiting for the Watchers vote.

Stone was woken by Skull shouting "The club is behind you Nev" as he walked back into the bar. "Paulo is sorting some false papers, so you can get out and about. Felix will get you new wheels". The Watchers ran a bike and car dealership, to provide a supply of vehicles for visiting members. The changing stock was also useful to their security business and would help Stone keep ahead of the local police. "Papers will take until tomorrow, so you can't risk leaving the clubhouse until then", said Skull. He added "give me the ID details you got from the Slav and the motor home, I'll get Cuba busy with our contacts".

So Nev Stone fetched his camera from his motorcycle pannier and began to download the photos he had taken after killing the Slav.
All of the pictures would need careful examination for anything Stone had missed in his hasty scene examination. But that would have to wait until he had printed out copies of all the documents he had photographed.
"Here you go", said Stone, handing a bunch of paper to Miguel Cuba. "Romanian and Bulgarian passports for Blagoy Cvetkov. VRMs for the Merc and motor home. There's driving docs and passports in three different names for the Roma".
"Este certto", all right, replied Cuba. "I'll see what I can do".

"Now that's all in play, let's deal with Faro" said Skull. Stone's paparazzi job in Faro had already gained him tabloid sales for Team Farense footballer Sergio Silva's

Between Stone & A Hard Place

indiscretions at the Faro brothel. But there was a deeper reason for the Watchers providing Stone with the information and help with the job. Faro was proving a tough city for the Watchers to take over security contracts. A foreign criminal gang operated what was effectively a protection racket in the city and would not allow in any competitors.

The Watchers felt no guilt in strong arming competition when necessary, but they preferred to use brains before brawn. A common tactic was to discredit competitors, either with their clients or the police. This was the real motivation behind Stone's assignment.

The brothel marketed itself as a high class sauna and massage. Its wealthy clientele would be very unhappy to think their reputations were at risk through tabloid publicity. So this had given the Watchers a perfect tool to hurt the gang with.

Now that Stone's first shots of Sergio Silva had whetted the tabloid's appetite, he and Skull needed to pitch a follow up story that would fatally damage their competitor's business.

Looking through the photographs and surveillance notes with Skull took Stone back to the beginning of the assignment which led him into the crisis he now faced.

The Faro job started when a cleaner at the brothel got drunk at a Watchers' party and said more than she should have done about her employer's famous clientele. A footballer using her place of work was a big deal to her and thinking she was among friends, told the MC about Sergio Silva's regular visits.

Knowing this was just the thing to embarrass the owners, Skull asked Stone to plan a surveillance operation.

Stone slipped into Faro in the small hours with one of the Watcher's technicians. Together they hid small wireless CCTV cameras around the brothel to send back pictures of clients arriving and leaving.

The film showed what the cleaner had told them. Silva always visited on Saturday evening, to celebrate his team's performance.

Between Stone & A Hard Place

He always used the same VIP room, fitted with a hot tub. This they knew from the cleaner who helped decorate the hot tub and bed with Team Farense football scarves. But they could not see inside the room and they could not rely on a cleaner to fit hidden cameras.

Disguising himself as a variety of tradesmen, Stone hunted the area for vantage points he could use. Only one position gave him a view of both the entrance and the VIP room window. This was from the flat roof of an office building, but was far from ideal as it was overlooked by several higher buildings.

"How can I work this?" thought Stone. "The window glass is painted over". "Pictures of Silva going in will embarrass, but will hardly do the damage we need for a takeover". Pretending to service the rooftop air conditioning units, Stone went through his options on the office building's roof. Suddenly it came to him. "From this range I won't need much paint removing to use a big lens and a laser microphone ", thought Stone.

The plan relied on the cleaner as an insider, but she was terrified of the brothel's foreign owners. If she was caught, she would end up forced to service their clients as punishment.

Skull had anticipated this and once they got the girl boasting of the famous footballer's indiscretions, he recorded the increasingly colourful stories. The call girls talked freely to her and she excitedly retold it all to her friends the Watchers. The recordings were the girl's undoing. Scraping paint from the window risked her being caught, but Skull's recording promised certain exposure. She had no choice but to take the risk and play her part in Stone's plan.

The vantage point could only be accessed during office hours and Stone needed to be there on Saturday evening. He considered abseiling in from surrounding buildings, but the business district was too busy, even at the weekend. His only option was three nights on the roof.

Between Stone & A Hard Place

The watchers called in a team of their technical staff to play the part of surveyors at the office building. They had gained access by offering the building owners a free security survey, looking for vulnerabilities. Stone would need more kit than he could risk carrying up to the roof himself, so the extra hands were vital to him.
Over several days the team secreted supplies around the rooftop. Packets of concentrated food, bottles of water and a sleeping bag were hidden among the machinery. By Friday afternoon the technical equipment Stone would need had also been put into place.
Stone had been spending his time putting finishing touches to his urban ghilli suit. This was his own adaptation of the camouflage suit originally used by Scottish gamekeepers and adopted by military snipers. The suit, covered by flaps of cloth and foliage, broke up the wearer's silhouette while stalking deer or enemy soldiers. Stone's version used colours which would blend with the brickwork and felt roof of the office building, allowing him to hide in plain sight.

Late on Friday afternoon Stone slipped in with the maintenance crew, carrying the last of his equipment. While his crew and the office workers left for the weekend, Stone lay motionless in his ghilli suit. He would have to stay there until the light faded and he could move closer to his vantage point. As darkness drew in, Stone got lucky. The light went on in the VIP room and he was able to test his camera and other equipment. The cleaner had done as instructed and cleared just enough paint from the window to afford a glimpse of the hot tub. Once Stone was happy with his kit, he rolled out his sleeping bag and settled to a few hours sleep. He knew the following day would be long and tiring. Before first light Stone had packed away his sleeping kit, dressed in his ghilli suit and was in position at the edge of the roof. He had a long wait until the afternoon's football was over. Through his earpiece Stone heard that Team Farense had won their game, meaning Sergio Silva would soon arrive for his post game celebration.
The brothel keepers must also have been listening to the

Between Stone & A Hard Place

radio as Stone could see the team scarves and lion mascots being put in the VIP room.

Silva unwittingly helped Stone by not being very subtle. He parked his very distinctive Porsche in the street immediately below Stone. The motor drive whirred as the camera followed Silva's progress along the street and to the brothel entrance. A skimpily dressed hostess met the footballer at the door and Stone's Nikon captured it all.

He trained his laser microphone through the window and began to listen. The media has speculated that US Special Forces used this type of microphone to eavesdrop on Osama Bin Laden in his Pakistan compound. The Watchers had used their security contractors to obtain a powerful unit for Stone. The device relied on there being a vibrating surface in line with the window. Usually it would be a glass fronted picture that would be set vibrating by the pressure waves from voices inside the room. In this tackily decorated room, Stone had a huge mirror on which to train his laser.

"You play with one ball, I play with two balls" said the female voice inside the room. Stone's long lens captured tantalising glimpses of the girl undressing Silva and the two of them moving to the hot tub.

The floor to ceiling mirror did more than help Stone focus his laser microphone, its reflective surface dramatically increased the coverage of his camera lens. The quality was not great, but he could clearly pick out Silva's distinctive physique being bathed by the naked girl.

The footballer boasted constantly of his successes that afternoon. Stone allowed himself a smile as the conversation flowed into his recorder. "The tabloids will love this" thought Stone, "but I doubt his wife will be so happy".

On the hours went, with the girl flattering Silva and the footballer exercising his ego by comparing the girl with the many other hostesses who had serviced him at the brothel. They moved back and forth between the bed and hot tub, with Stone wondering how long the testosterone fuelled sex would last.

Eventually Stone's earpiece went quiet, as the rhythmic sounds of the bed faded and the couple sunk back in the

Between Stone & A Hard Place

bath. Before long Silva was dressed and at the front door. This time a sharply dressed older man was there to see off the wealthy client. Stone zoomed in to capture this new image.
"Unlikely to feature in my story" thought Stone, "but he looks important enough for Skull to be interested". He knew the Watchers wanted to damage the brothel's owners and this man looked the part. He was too old to be security and looked too comfortable to be a client. So logic put him as either owner or management.
Stone's motor drive spun again as the hostess gave Sergio Silva a long, lingering kiss goodbye. As the footballer walked off to his car, Stone slid across to the roof's shadows and went to work with his laptop. He downloaded his cameras and congratulated himself as he reviewed the results. "A good night's work" he thought. "I'll have no trouble pushing one through my agent tonight and a cracking follow up in a day or two ".

"Nice one Nev", said Skull. Stone could not email off his picture without checking with his friend. Both Stone and the Watchers had an agenda in this assignment. So, while still hidden in the shadows of the plant room, Stone phoned the Watcher President and shared some of the more graphic photos by e-mail. Together they agreed on the words and pictures they would use as an appetiser for Stone's press agent to give the tabloids. They would first release only photographs, holding back the more damming voice recordings for later.
If Stone worked quickly, he could get them out just in time for the Sunday edition. But the risk was too great as he could not get out until Monday morning. So he agreed with Skull to hold off publication until he was safely off the roof.
Knowing he had all day Sunday to work on his story, Stone backed up his photographs and audio files through a 3G device to the Watcher's server, then grabbed a few hours sleep.
Feeling more refreshed from his sleep, Stone got to work on his photographs. He had chosen a set of four that he would

www.neilhallam.com

Between Stone & A Hard Place

send to his agent, but they first needed editing. The set needed to suggest Silva in a compromising position and suggest location to those in the know, without giving away the premises to the paper's readers.

The tactic in editing the way they agreed was calculated to give Skull leverage with the Faro businessmen, who bought their security from the Watcher's competition. Sergio Silva would be harmed by their first publication, but given that he was cheating on his wife, they viewed this as acceptable collateral damage. The brothel owners would not initially be harmed, but letting all the local business owners know that more photographs existed would be a powerful threat. "If we can do this to the brothel, what can we do to you?" thought Stone, knowing how Skull would use his work.

Stone spent the rest of Sunday on his laptop, editing the remainder of his photographs. As the light started to fade, he zipped into his sleeping bag and slept until Monday morning. He was awake well before the buildings early morning cleaners arrived, as they were to be his cover to get out. Stone had one of the cleaners' uniforms to wear and he could carry his equipment out in plastic bin bags. As efficiently as he expected from the Watchers, as soon as Stone hit the street, a plain van pulled up to collect him.

They had a short drive to one of the MC's storage units in another part of Faro. Here Stone e.mailed his captioned pictures to his press agent, loaded his Triumph Explorer and started the ride back to his yurt where he found the motor home and his current troubles had begun.

Between Stone & A Hard Place

Chapter 7.

"Print some of the old guy" said Skull. "I've a feeling we should find out who he is". In order to gain any bouncing and security work in Faro, the Watchers needed leverage against the East European crime gang's strangle hold. "He's a bit Ruski looking, so he could be Red Mob" added the Watchers' President.

As the printer was warming up, Joao Alva, the MC's Sergeant at Arms shouted them over. "Boss, you had better come look at the news".
Sky News was running a piece on a young girl missing from an Algarve village.
Stone was instantly stunned as a photograph of a pretty blond girl playing on the beach filled the TV screen. "That's the kidnapped girl" he eventually managed to get out.

As the girl's picture looked out from the screen, the newsreader's voice told of nine year old Lucy Varley who was last seen making the short walk from the resort's restaurant where she had eaten her breakfast to the family's bungalow.
With mum at the restaurant and Grandma and Grandad at the bungalow, they thought nothing of allowing the bright girl to make the five minute walk alone.
The family was starting their second week in the tourist village of Pedralva when disaster struck and Lucy disappeared, on what was a regular walk through the village.
The reporter followed her route, starting at the small restaurant, with its thatched canopy. She moved along narrow cobbled streets, through the beds of well tended bushes and single story, white washed buildings.
"It seems inconceivable that anything bad could happen in such a quiet and traditional resort", said the reporter. "But happen it did. Young Lucy hasn't been seen for over ten hours now".

Family and friends had spent most of the day searching the

Between Stone & A Hard Place

village and surrounding fields. Now, as evening drew in, the police had declared a police incident and flooded the area with officers.

Stone had passed though Pedralva many times, both mountain biking and on his off road motorcycle.
The village had received huge injections of development money in recent years from a variety of big investors. The pretty village was tucked into a wooded valley accessed by a twisting mountain road. That was the only Tarmac access, but there were several dirt roads leading through the valley and over the surrounding hills.
The restaurant where Lucy had last been seen was a regular haunt for Stone. He had spent many hours on their terrace drinking freshly squeezed orange juice and chatting with his friends.

The screen faded to a press conference. The scene was a standard one in such situations, with police and relatives sitting behind a table, against a police logo backdrop. Stone recognised the girl's mother before the caption appeared on screen. The attractive blond woman looked very much like the girl he had seen taken. The reporter's voice announced Lucy's mum as 35 year old single mum, Trudy Varley. Next to her, looking to be in her early sixties, was the grandma, Joan.
Completing the trio at the table was the senior police investigator, Ricardo De Sa. Chief Inspector De Sa had been sent to take command by the Department of Criminal Investigation in Portimão, explained the reporter. She went on to describe him as one of the Algarve's most experienced senior detectives.

Chief Inspector De Sa was first to speak. Stone guessed he must have already said his piece in Portuguese for the local news channels, as he now spoke to camera in fluent, but accented English.
De Sa explained what they knew so far. The restored inland village of Pedralva was well away from the tourist hot spots

of the coast and suffered very little crime. Mum and Grandparents had felt safe letting Lucy walk the cobbled streets alone. She had got to know the streets of the small village well. Five miles from the coast, Pedralva was surrounded by forest and farmland, but Lucy knew not to stray from the village on her own.
The Chief Inspector said the police were treating it as a missing person enquiry and asked for anyone with information to contact his incident room in Villa Do Bispo.

Stone was amazed at how calm the two women had remained as the policeman spoke to camera. Soon it was Trudy's turn to speak and emotion began to take over. As the cameras turned towards her, Lucy's mum broke down. It seemed an age before she was able to speak, but Stone knew it would have seemed an eternity to Trudy. With tear filled eyes, Trudy praised the police and local people for what they had done so far. She repeated Chief Inspector De Sa's plea for information, adding a personal plea for her baby to be returned

Thinking back to his own career in the police, Stone remembered how often guilty relatives had pleaded their way through similar press conferences. It almost seemed part of the investigation to watch how the next of kin would handle themselves on camera.
But having witnessed the Roma man making off with Lucy at the botched handover, Stone felt comfortable that mum's emotion was genuine.

Nev Stone was slowly burning up inside. Trudy Varley had come across as a pleasant and genuine mother. The story the news reporter and the Chief Inspector had painted was of a close and loving family enjoying an active holiday in the area he had grown to love.
Stone had always avoided working on child abuse enquiries during his police career. He admired the officers who could work every day amongst such horror and yet remain calm and professional with the perpetrators. Even on terrorist

operations, Stone's quick use of force had cost his career and his liberty. He was glad to have never been put close to such monsters.

But the voice of reason was still working for the former policeman. "It looks like a kidnap, but we know nothing of the family". "Assume nothing, believe nothing, check everything" said Stone to himself, repeating the mantra drummed in to recruits during CID training. Stone had to find Lucy, for his own sake as well as her's, but he resolved to do the work logically and professionally.

All of the bikers had gathered around the clubhouse TV to watch the news report. "Bastard" said Skull Murphy. "How could anyone do that?" The other Watchers all added their agreement to their President's outburst.

"Not so quick" said Stone. "Everyone is a suspect until we prove differently, even mum and grandma".

"No", shouted Chapter VP Miguel Cuba. "The family wouldn't be involved. Could they?"

"I hope not" said Stone. "But I remember the Shannon Matthews case a few years ago in Yorkshire. Her mum staged a kidnap of their little girl for charity handouts and media payments". Stone had not worked on the case, but he vividly remembered the upsetting case which had dominated the British news at the time. It involved a large dysfunctional family, from one of Dewsbury's sink estates. A mum of seven, her jobless boyfriend and the boyfriend's uncle had conspired to hide nine year old Shannon while milking the media frenzy. Thankfully Shannon was found unharmed and her mum, the boyfriend and uncle got eight year sentences. "These seem very different people to the Matthews', but I'm ruling nothing out yet".

While Stone talked with Cuba, his attention was away from the TV. He quickly turned back to it when Joao Alva shouted up "hey, you're on again Nev".

A different Sky reporter was now standing close to the clearing where Stone had killed the Slav.

"Police have confirmed that the body of a man has been

removed from the clearing behind me. They are treating the death as suspicious, but are not releasing any more information until the body has been identified and next of kin informed".

Although the news crew had not been allowed through the police cordon, Stone knew the area well and instantly recognised where the reporter was standing. As the camera panned around the scene, he could see that the motor home was still parked where he had searched it earlier that day. The reporter turned his attention to interviewing the senior police officer at the scene. Inspector Luis Enes looked older than Chief Inspector De Sa. Unlike the more senior officer, who had been dressed in a sharp business suit, Inspector Enes looked more traditionally Portuguese in corduroy trousers and leather jacket. All that was missing was a corduroy flat cap, but Stone imagined this had been taken off for his interview.
Something about the casual looking Inspector reminded Stone of his old boss DI Tony "Jonah" Jones. "I hope he's half the cop that Jonah is, I need someone bothered enough to look beyond the obvious", thought Stone.

Inspector Enes made what Stone recognised as a standard police holding statement, when there is little to go on.
"The body of a middle aged man has been removed from the area behind me" began the Inspector. "His injuries are of a type which we are treating as suspicious, so I am appealing for any information about activity around the Ingrena area today. We particularly need to speak to the driver of a black Mercedes which was seen being driven quickly along the coast road".
"That's a relief", thought Stone. "It doesn't sound like my bike was spotted, but it can only be a matter of time before they link me through the yurt and my DNA."
Any delay was a bonus for Stone. He needed to find the girl before a serious manhunt began for him. With his manslaughter conviction, Stone knew the police would take the easy option and try to prosecute him for the Slav's death.

Between Stone & A Hard Place

The Inspector went on to explain the scrubby area within the National Park was a haven for surfers and artists who lived unofficially in camps among the trees. The police would soon be sending out teams to visit the camps, interview the occupants, and where necessary, search the camps. "That's all I need", thought Stone. "They'll be in my yurt in no time at all and without me in residence, they'll have to start hunting."

The news report about the body was much shorter than the one about the missing girl. It also appeared that the police were not linking the two incidents.
Serious crime was rare at the western end of the Algarve. Stone knew the local police, the National Guard of The Republic or GNR, would have to call in assistance from bigger law enforcement agencies across Portugal. Chief Inspector De Sa's appointment had been the start of this influx. As Senior Investigating Officer he would have authority to bring a wide range of specialist teams into his investigation.
Stone had seen this happen during the days following the disappearance of Madeline McCann. Although three year old Madeline was much younger than nine year old Lucy, it was easy to imagine the investigations would begin on similar lines. This was bad news for Stone, as it meant the possibility of UK liaison officers being sent over. A police officer being jailed for shooting a suspect was a big deal in Britain, any officers sent over would soon connect him to the Slav's death.

Stone had a decision to make. If he gave the police the information about the Roma and the Slav, it could help find Lucy. But it would also link him more quickly to the killing. He needed to work out the best way of passing the information anonymously. The MC would help provide the cut outs to separate him from the tip off, but it would only be a temporary reprieve. There were far too many factors which would connect him to the dead Slav: his yurt, his tyre tracks, DNA from his wounded arm, not to mention any possible witnesses.

Between Stone & A Hard Place

He could only hope that he was not also made a suspect in the kidnap enquiry. If the police made that lazy assumption, they would be chasing up a blind alley which would never lead them to Lucy.

"What do you think Skull?" asked Stone. "Do we tip off the police now, or wait until we have more to give them?"
Despite it being Stone who had been a police officer, the MC President had worked in private security for decades and Stone valued his friend's council.
"You've always talked of the Golden Hour Nev, where the most vital work is done early in the investigation" replied Skull. "Besides, if Lucy gets killed, you have no witness."
Stone thought about the biker's observations, and then added "we can't hit the ground as fast as the police, we're still waiting for your team and my fake ID".
The two men agreed a reluctant witness was the best option. The police already knew about the black Mercedes, so an anonymous phone call could put Lucy in the car and describe the driver. That would give Chief Inspector De Sa a start on Lucy's last sighting, but would delay involving Stone.

Rui Cai rolled his Ducati out of the clubhouse garage and powered away from Lagos. They had considered making the anonymous call from a pay phone, to give the police nothing to trace. But, using one of the Watchers' stock of disposable cell phones would allow the police to locate where the call was made by using GPRS. This is a process of triangulating the phone signal, using the three closest mobile phone masts.
By getting close to Ingrena, Rui Cai's call would have the authenticity of being made from the right location.
As one of the few sport bike riders among the Watchers Rui was among the least conspicuous, once he removed his club emblem, or colours.
The public tended to view all MCs as Hell's Angels and expected them all to ride customised choppers. But Rui's bike was more similar to those ridden by weekend bikers, so he slipped unnoticed into the coastal village of Ingrena.

Between Stone & A Hard Place

To the few people who passed him on the quiet road, Rui Cai looked like an ordinary motorcyclist parked at the roadside to smoke and take a phone call. He was in fact playing the reluctant witness, talking to the police incident room in the nearby town of Villa Do Bispo.
"I saw that girl Lucy today. She was in that black Mercedes they talked about on the news". Rui was sticking to a script Nev Stone and Skull Murphy had prepared. Every difficult question was met with "I don't want to get involved, I worry for my family".
Rui gave the detective at the incident room a rudimentary description of the Roma who had driven the Mercedes. He hoped the police could identify him from the documents Stone had photographed and left inside the motor home.
His task complete, Rui Cai started the big V twin engine and headed back to Lagos. His only remaining task was to throw the pre paid cell phone over the highest point on the cliff top road.

Between Stone & A Hard Place

Chapter 8.

While Rui Cai had been out passing their information to the police, the remaining Watchers had been working the phones, calling in favours from contacts within the security industry and the Portuguese underworld.
The MC operated in a grey area where their businesses were, on the surface, legal and respectable. But when it suited them, they were comfortable using less legitimate methods. This meant they had a huge range of contacts, from respectable business men, through to some very unsavoury characters.

It was through a mix of these sources that the Watchers started formulating a theory of how a man with Romanian and Bulgarian passports was involved in a Portuguese kidnap plot.
Nev Stone and Skull Murphy had heard plenty of stories about former Russian KGB agents moving into crime when the new post Soviet Russia had no need of a secret police.

The Portuguese members had also been taught to fear their home grown version of the KGB, the PIDE, or Polícia Internacional e de Defesa do Estado.
Reputed by those in the know to be one of the world's most effective intelligence services, the PIDE was set up by the dictator Salazar in 1933.
Salazar originally followed the Nazi's example of the Gestapo in setting up his secret police. The model served him well throughout the Second World War. Portugal remained neutral in the war, creating an exile haven for a pot pori of people including Ian Fleming and the Spanish Royal Family. The cross fertilisation of nationalities gave the PIDE a big intelligence gathering advantage over their competitors.
In 1945, following the end of the war, Salazar remodelled his secret police, moving away from the Nazi model and following Scotland Yard's example of an investigative agency.

Between Stone & A Hard Place

Through the remaining years of the dictatorship, fear of the PIDE intensified as they involved themselves in colonial wars and in the taking of political prisoners at home.
When the dictatorship fell in 1974, the Carnation Revolution, as history remembers it, was almost bloodless. The only four deaths during the coup resulted from PIDE gunfire.
So despised was the PIDE that Portugal managed without an intelligence agency until 1984.

Miguel Cuba told Stone what he knew of the PIDE and explained what happened to many of these agents of the dictatorship. Attempts were made to bring them to trial, but only seven were charged and none faced jail. With no home market for their espionage skills, many descended into crime.
Forty years on from the Carnation Revolution, any remaining PIDE Agents are in their seventies, but they have become very proficient in their ruthless brand of organised crime.
Cuba knew they specialised in drug trafficking and protection rackets. He suspected they were at the heart of the Watchers' problems gaining a foothold in the Faro security business.

The key players in Faro were Eastern European, but the MC suspected a deal between the former KGB Russian mafia and the former PIDE gangsters. Only such a deal would allow the foreigners to operate.
During the Cold War, fascist Portugal and communist Russia were poles apart. But in the new regimes, where cash is king, Miguel Cuba was convinced they had buried former rivalries.

As Stone and Cuba discussed the PIDE and KGB links, they heard the distinctive exhaust note of Paulo De Costa's Triumph Thunderbird ride into the garage below. The MC's Secretary had returned with the false papers Stone needed in order to leave the clubhouse.
The Watchers were mostly legitimate businessmen, but they would often admit to "fracturing the occasional law". When it

suited them, they would deal with a variety of underworld contacts. Their only red line was drugs, if you dealt in drugs, you did not do business with the Watchers.

One of Paulo De Costa's personal contacts was a master forger who plied his trade from the oldest part of Lagos' old town. Hugo Franco copied old masters for pleasure, he usually had a Rembrandt or Picasso on his easel. But it was his printing which earned his living. Hugo ran a perfectly legal print shop, but for trusted clients he could reproduce almost anything.

The old forger was Godfather to the De Costa twins and had known them since they were young boys. In their devoutly catholic community, the status of Godfather was important and he would drop everything when the twins asked for a favour.

Hugo had prepared an impressive ID package for Stone in record time. He had: passport, driving licence, EU reciprocal health card and papers for the new motorcycle which was on its way to Stone.

Nev Stone had chosen to keep his first name. He knew from his covert life that he could easily be given away by someone recognising him and calling his name.

"Hello Nev Shaw", said Stone, examining his new UK passport. The forger Hugo had manipulated Stone's photograph to turn his jet black hair into a salt and pepper, greying colour. "This chap looks lots older" said Stone. "Don't worry Nev" replied Skull. "One of the girls is a hairdresser; she has popped out for some dye".

Things were starting to come together now for Stone. The new bike the Watchers had obtained through their motorcycle dealership arrived next. They knew Stone would need to present a very different profile than his Watchers' identity. The police would be looking for his adventure bike and would know of the MC's distaste for Japanese motorcycles. Skull had sourced a Yamaha for him. The FJR 1300 model they bought is used by many of the world's police forces, so would be a good workhorse in the weeks to

Between Stone & A Hard Place

come.
"I'll miss my Triumph" said Stone. "But you've found me a nice machine, thanks".

Stone had barely had time to admire his Yamaha when the hairdresser returned with dye and equipment from her nearby salon. Before long, ten years had been added to Stone's appearance and he would be ready to get amongst the investigation.
He changed from his usual denim and leather outfit into more mainstream casual motorcycle clothing. Kevlar armoured canvas chinos replaced his denim jeans. His well worn black leather jacket was replaced by a smart fabric bike jacket. He also had to say goodbye to his favourite open face helmet, as he would be too easily recognised with his face on show. The Watchers had got him a plain white helmet, with a full dark visor to hide behind.

Stone, Skull and the De Costa twins were about to leave the garage when
Paulo's cell phone rang. It was the old forger "Olá filho", "hello son. You should come back to see me. There are things you should know and bring your English friend". Paulo knew the old man disliked phones, so made no attempt to question him further. "We're on our way padrinho", replied Paulo to his Godfather.
Stone's new identity needed a lower profile than he could have with the larger than life bikers. So he was first to leave the clubhouse garage on his new Yamaha.
The three outlaw bikers soon followed, but took a different route. The twins on their identical Triumph Thunderbird's followed their President.
Pedro and Paulo agreed Nev had made a wise choice riding alone. There was nothing low profile about Skull Murphy's Triumph Rocket III. He rode the world's biggest production motorcycle. It was fitted with a custom exhaust which sounded out every one of the bike's 2300 CCs.

Both routes brought them to Hugo Franco's studio at the

same time. They used a discrete entrance located up one of the old town's many alleyways.
While Pedro made coffee at the stove, the old forger began to speak.
"You already know you may be going up against the PIDE".
"None of you remember the last years of Salazar. As the dictator's grip on Portugal and his African Empire waned, the PIDE became ever more ruthless."
"I was an artist. They didn't like artists, thinking us all communists". Hugo told how so many of his contemporaries had simply disappeared". "But I was lucky" he said. "They needed my forging skills, so I stayed alive".

All Portuguese people knew how the suddenly unemployed PIDE intelligence agents became a mafia. Again Hugo found favour with them and avoided paying the "protection" demanded of many small businessmen. Hugo's trade off was in providing the fledgling local mafia with papers and counterfeit cash with which to fund their criminal enterprises.
"We knew not to refuse an offer from the PIDE", said Hugo. "You either did business with them, or you disappeared, so I printed for them".
The old forger went on to explain why he had never told his twin Godsons about his secret life.
"You boys were always against drugs. Your mother encouraged you in that view, even though I, her uncle, was involved in the PIDE's trafficking". "Your father earned his living legitimately as an engineer and knew nothing of my connection to the PIDE". It was your father, who despite your mother's reluctance wanted Uncle Hugo to be your Godfather".

After their parents died in a car accident, Hugo honoured his niece, their mother, by protecting them from the criminality. He thought that protection wasted when they chose the outlaw biker life. But was overjoyed to find the Watchers were one of the very few 1% Motorcycle Clubs to adopt an anti drugs stance.

Between Stone & A Hard Place

Hugo continued, explaining how the former intelligence agents had first opened hashish smuggling routes from Morocco into Portugal's Algarve ports. Then when South America had a surplus of cocaine, they took advantage of the Portuguese being among Europe's poorest citizens. They had no shortage of willing mules to smuggle the narcotic into Lisbon airport from Mexico and the USA.
The forger provided passports, identity cards and shipping manifests for most of the drug routes.

"Now you boys and your friends are in danger and I must help you" said Hugo.
"You have heard of O Lobo?" he asked. "The Wolf?" replied Stone. "I thought he was just a legend".
"He is very real" said Hugo. "There are very few left alive who knew him as Carlos Lobo. I have not heard his first name used in over 60 years".
Carlos Lobo was a young PIDE agent when Hugo Franco first met him. The young agent's ruthless streak quickly brought him into the Dictator Salazar's closest circle of body guards. His temperament so closely resembled that of his name sake the wolf's, that before long his first name ceased to exist.

O Lobo had become so close to the dictator, that after the Carnation Revolution, he was the best placed of the PIDE to benefit from Salazar's secret networks and hoards of cash. Hugo warned the bikers, "O Lobo is now over 80, but I still fear him, and so should you".
The Wolf had used the dictator's hoarded wealth to build a narcotics empire across Southern Portugal. So ruthless were his methods that few were brave enough to even speak the psychopath's name, let alone inform on him to the authorities. As four decades rolled by, O Lobo's empire grew, the hashish flowed across the ocean from Morocco and the cocaine flew in from the Americas.
The Wolf needed legitimate businesses to launder his drug profits. Bars and massage parlours under his control appeared across the Algarve, all cleaning O Lobo's dirty

Between Stone & A Hard Place

money.
The same rural poverty which provided the Wolf with his cocaine mules provided a stream of pretty young women to satisfy the desires of affluent foreign tourists.

"Now things are changing", said Hugo. "O Lobo has foreign partners; I am printing papers for Russians, Romanians and Bulgarians". "The papers are for girls. Many of them are girls, not women, too young to be selling their bodies. Because they came in with my forged papers, they don't exist. Those who don't please their masters disappear over the side of O Lobo's hashish smuggling finishing boats".

"Is this why Lucy was taken?" asked Stone.
"I know nothing of your Lucy, save what I have seen on television", replied Hugo. "But I fear the Wolf's paw in this. If what you have seen can hurt him Nev Stone, then you are a dead man walking".

The old forger decided he had said enough. His conscience was torn between his love for the De Costa twins and his fear of the Wolf.
Stone and the twins had a long list of questions for him, but Hugo would not answer any of them.
Eventually he did add "the Good Shepherd Sisters might help. A lot of the girls will talk to them".
"Who are they", asked Stone. Pedro De Costa was able to answer that question. "They're nuns", he replied. "They specialise in missionary work with the sex workers".
That was the last they could get from Hugo and decided not to push their luck any further. The bikers left Hugo with the emotional goodbyes usually reserved for other bikers.

"Cuba was nearly a monk", said Skull as they left. "I'll see if he's heard of the Good Shepherd Sisters".
Skull had met his Chapter Vice President Miguel Cuba at university in England. Miguel and his sister had been sent to a Benedictine monastery school in York by their deeply religious parents. Miguel had lost his faith and turned away

Between Stone & A Hard Place

from the church, but Skull was sure his sister had followed a theological path.

Following up the lead to the nuns would have to wait though. Stone wanted to visit the abduction scene at Pedralva before the police had chance to connect him with the Slav's death. The De Costa twins returned to their clubhouse with Skull. The extrovert bikers would attract too much attention among the heavy police presence at Pedralva. Stone hoped his more mainstream image would blend in better.
He powered his new Yamaha out of Lagos, following the southern Algarve coast. At Villa Do Bispo he turned north along the wild west coast. Stone could not help contrasting this road with the A38 back home. Both were long single carriageways, running along their countries western edge. But the Portuguese version was a much quieter route, passing through pretty villages, rather than the big towns of the English Midlands.

The mountain road to Pedralva ran off from the west coast. Stone had ridden it often, but still enjoyed the ride. Before long Stone had parked his FJR1300 outside the police cordon and walked into the village. He had modelled his new image on motorcycling celebrity and actor, Ewan McGregor's motor biking persona. Stone hoped this would be low profile enough to avoid attention.

Between Stone & A Hard Place

Chapter 9.

Dressed in his khaki coloured motorcycle jacket and tan chinos, and with his hair newly speckled with grey, Stone walked through the tourist village of Pedralva. He had decided to start at the village restaurant. It was a risk, as the staff knew him, but his connections to the MC usually avoided loose lips or difficult questions. It was a risk Stone had to take, as the restaurant had been the last place young Lucy Varley had been seen.
Like most police officers, it had always been Stone's practice to begin an investigation by visiting the scene. All his trains of thought and potential hypotheses would flow from his impressions at the crime scene.

Two police cordons were in place. The first prevented vehicle access, where Stone had left his motorcycle. The second was staffed by an officer of the National Guard of The Republic (GNR), with a clipboard logging people in and out.
The GNR could not completely close down Pedralva, as it was the height of the tourist season and tourism was the village's only income. But they needed some control and the Agente with his clip board was their solution.
This was to be the first test of Hugo Franco's forgery skills. Stone presented the passport identifying him as Nev Shaw. With a cursory examination, his false name was added to the log and Stone walked into the centre of the village.

Officers of Portugal's various law enforcement agencies were hard at work. Police Judiciaire technicians, Portugal's CSI, were taking photographs, fingerprints and samples. Dog handlers from the National Guard of The Republic were following their sniffer dogs around the village. The dog handlers stood out from the arid landscape in the bright green overalls of the GNR Special Operations Unit.

They had placed a junior GNR Constable, or Agente, near the restaurant with the task of speaking to tourists. Stone

Between Stone & A Hard Place

remembered the British police giving Community Support Officers this task back home. There was always a wealth of information in the community which could easily be lost if no one was engaging with the public.
The Agente looked bored, as few people other than the police were about, many locals and tourists had spread out to assist with the search.

The senior investigator, Chief Inspector Ricardo De Sa, had been on scene earlier to brief his team. Chief Inspector De Sa was known for his long hours, regularly opening the incident room at 6am and being the last to leave at midnight. So the young Agente had a good idea of what was happening. She was excited to be part of a big case and lost no time in telling Stone all about it.

The Agente explained that the disappearance of a child must be reported as widely as possible, on the national as well as on the international level. All the Portuguese police were already on high alert, as well as their counterparts at Interpol.
The National Guard, supported by the civilian population, had started to organise searches, which were continuing today.
Of course Stone already knew all this from the news, but he let the Agente talk on.
She told Stone that the Spanish customs service has been asked to increase vigilance at the two ports maintaining links with Morocco, Tarifa and Algecira. They had also set up a control post on the Guadiana Bridge at Portugal's border with Spain.
Stone filed this information away, as it would be useful if he or the Watchers needed to travel.
The Agente was also excited about a team of analysts at the incident room, who were going through the register of all paedophiles present in the region. The Agente explained they were looking for actual links to the case and creating diagrams of the connections. Again Stone expected this to be standard practice and took comfort that if the police were

looking for him, they were also looking wider.
In all the Agente had told him, Stone had not featured once, so he felt safe that he had not yet been connected to the case.
But then came the news he did not want to hear. The first English police officer had arrived at the Villa Do Bispo incident room. Glyn Towers was attached to the UK Embassy as police liaison officer to Portugal. His brief was to facilitate communication between the police forces of both countries.
Mr Towers would be arranging for other British officers to come out, "maybe even from Scotland Yard", she added. Stone knew the first officers out would be from Lucy Varley's local force, but he left the young Agente with the impression that the Metropolitan Police were on their way.
It had not yet been released where the Varley family lived. Stone hoped it would not be a midlands force, where the officers would know him.

The last piece of information Stone got from the Agente was the most useful of all. Lucy's mum, Trudy Varley had taken to sitting in a quiet area at a well, just outside the village. The distraught mother found it easier to cope away from the bustle of the investigation. Stone needed to see what information Trudy could give him.
It did not take Stone long to find the well. All of the local farms had their own wells, but there was only one which was obviously accessible to the public. To give himself an excuse to be at the well, Stone had picked up a discarded water bottle, which he had in his hand as he scrambled down the hillside from the track to the well.
Stone could see the blond hair of Trudy Varley as he approached. She was sitting with her back to him, leaning against the well and looked to be reading a book.
"Sorry, I didn't mean to disturb you" said Stone. He did not let her know that he recognised her. "Thirsty work riding a motorcycle around in this heat. I've just come to top up my bottle".
"Please do" replied Trudy. "I like the view down the valley

Between Stone & A Hard Place

from here and the water is always fresh and cool if you drink it straight from the well".

Stone immediately liked this friendly, attractive woman. Less than 24 hours from the kidnap of her daughter and she was able to engage, somewhat tearfully, in pleasantries with a stranger.
"Sorry, I haven't introduced myself" added Stone. "I'm Nev. I'm out here for a couple of weeks riding my motor bike".
By feigning no knowledge of the kidnap, Stone was able to ask her about the police operation. Despite her obvious distress, Trudy appeared comfortable with Stone and had soon told him about Lucy's disappearance.
Trudy also told Stone a little about herself. She had been a single mum since Lucy's dad left three years ago. The family lived in a village on the outskirts of Coventry, where her parents helped with child care so that Trudy could continue her nursing career.

Getting witnesses to open up had always been one of Stone's strengths as a detective. Trudy gave him much more detail than the news reports had told.
The family were creatures of habit. The grandparents ate quite simply and took most of their meals in the bungalow. But mother and daughter both liked to try the European dishes at the village restaurant. Inevitably the nine year old would get restless after eating and would run back to the bungalow ahead of Trudy. Stone realised this would have given the abductors ample opportunity to observe and plan, making a spontaneous kidnap less likely. It also raised the possibility that the Roma would have been seen around the village.

Stone changed tack and worked the motor home into the conversation. "I'm looking to stay a little longer next trip, so I might bring my motor home. It doesn't look easy to get one along the mountain road though".
"Oh, there's another road", said Trudy, pointing down the valley. "That dirt road leads out to Budens. It's more suited to

Between Stone & A Hard Place

4x4s, but I've seen a few campers crawl along it. We had a really fancy one here for a couple of days last week".
Trudy described the same ornate motor home in which Stone had encountered the kidnappers and Lucy. Now he was certain this was part of a planned abduction. He just needed to work out the who and why, in the hope that would lead him to Lucy before any harm came to her.
"I've got a few biker mates out here, I'll see who I can round up to help search", said Stone as he said his goodbyes to Trudy. "I'll leave you to your book, but try not to worry, there are so many people looking for Lucy".
With that, Stone walked back to his bike and rode back across the mountain road. His first impressions of Trudy Varley from the TV press conference were reinforced by meeting her. Stone hoped he was right about her not being part of the plot, as he had taken a liking to the attractive intelligent woman. He was certainly impressed by the calm way she was dealing with the kidnap, obviously distraught, but not making a nuisance of herself to the investigators.

As he rode, Skull Murphy connected with Stone through his helmet's blue tooth equipment. "Head back to the club house" said Skull. "The UK guys are here.
Stone turned his bike towards Lagos. Being an international club, anything this big would need involvement of the Watcher's mother chapter from Derbyshire.
The club had humble beginnings in the market town of Ripley. Skull, Cuba and a few others started bouncing at local pubs and clubs, before gradually taking over contracts in the surrounding cities.
Skull Murphy still held the post of International President, but the other International Officers were from English chapters. Stone knew that Skull would have briefed the English members before he arrived, but he would still have to convince them that helping find Lucy was a good thing for the club.

As he rode the Yamaha into the Lagos clubhouse garage, Stone noted there were no new bikes parked. This meant the English members must have been collected from the airport by car. They either planned a short visit, or wanted to keep a low profile, as it was rare for a Watcher to be without a motorcycle.

Stone knew all the English visitors and was greeted by all four in turn with a traditional biker bear hug.
Bill Thomas was the Derbyshire President and international VP, so other than Skull he was the most senior of the MC Officers. He was one of the founder members and had been in prison with Skull and Cuba when they first met Nev Stone. Standing out from the group was the slim, dapper looking, Tony Smart. He was Secretary of both Derbyshire and International Boards and the only Watcher likely to wear a suit. He had a clean criminal record, being an experienced Solicitor. He joined the club through his love of bikes and for employment as the company's senior lawyer. Smart kept his involvement mostly to corporate matters, to distance from much of the unlawful activity. Stone was surprised to see him in the Watchers' bar with someone likely to become a fugitive. He was sure the lawyer would not be stopping long.
Jack Tate was the London VP. He is a computer expert and the company's IT Director. Tate was an unlikely looking computer geek. His shaved head and gym toned muscles were not the usual hallmarks of a computer specialist.
Former Royal Marine, Steve Butler was both London and International Sergeant at Arms. The stocky commando was shorter than the other Watchers, but far more deadly than most.
As well as by necessity a very tough man, Butler was also a technical surveillance expert. The Watcher's employees and enemies alike could never be sure if he had a bug or camera watching them.
Stone knew this was a very capable group. As well as being senior figures in the MC, they were all senior directors in a successful international business.

The bikers had already held the formal meeting they called church while Stone was riding back from Pedralva. The

Between Stone & A Hard Place

English members were happy with Skull's explanation; they just wanted to greet their friend and countryman.
With lots of work to do, the group did not open up the clubhouse bar. But they did make sure one of the prospects kept the expensive coffee machine in constant production. Caffeine would be needed to fuel the long hours to come.

In an age of 24 hour news reporting, each announcement of a new bulletin drew the bikers' attention.
Mostly it was the usual fare of celebrity gossip. But, while the bikers discussed events so far, Stone's photograph filled the screen.
It was an old photograph, taken outside the court on the day he was sent to prison. But it heralded the police knowing of his involvement.
They listened as the reporter described how a disgraced British policeman had come to live in a yurt close to where the body of the dead Slav had been found.
The reporter explained the police wanted to speak to Nev Stone because distinctive tyre tracks matching his Triumph Explorer motorcycle had been found at the scene and his yurt appeared to have been hastily cleared of personal belongings. Apparently a witness had also described the adventure bike being ridden quickly away from the area.
They did not reveal how they thought Nev Stone was connected to the incident, but the reporter did say that they were awaiting DNA testing of blood found at the scene. Stone knew some of that blood would be his and that would open a whole new aspect of the police investigation.
The report went on to detail the eye witness evidence which Rui Cai passed to the police about seeing Lucy in the black Mercedes. They gave the Roma's description and said that both Nev Stone and the dark haired man were urgently sought by the investigating officers.

"That's earlier than we had hoped" said Skull, worried about Stone being named in the news report.
"I'd like to say the new identity had been tested, but the young cop at Pedralva was a bit of a newbie" replied Stone.

Between Stone & A Hard Place

The De Costa twins quickly reassured him that their godfather's work had never let them down yet.

With that, Skull turned his attention to his Vice President, Miguel Cuba. He told his friend the slightly cryptic message the old forger had given them about the Good Shepherd Sisters.
"That's my sister's order", said a very surprised Miguel.

Between Stone & A Hard Place

Chapter 10

"It's always been a bit of a family joke that being a nun, Barbara is more than just my sister, she's everyone's Sister" said Miguel Cuba.
"Our parents were always travelling on missionary work for the church, so Barbara and I were sent off to boarding school".
Cuba explained their deeply religious parents were torn between wanting the best for their children and fulfilling a sense of duty to their God.
So, rather than regularly uproot two young children as they travelled around the developing world, they sought out what they saw as the best option for a catholic upbringing.
Their parents chose Ampleforth College at York, in Northern England. This is a catholic boarding school run as part of a Benedictine monastery. The Cubas knew that becoming fluent in English would be important for their children and the school had an excellent academic record. But it was their sport and athletics program which attracted young Miguel and in fact was all that kept him regularly in school.
For their parents, guilty at boarding the siblings, the co educational policy of the school was the most important factor. Keeping brother and sister together was important to them, so separate monastery or convent schools were never an option.

"I lost my faith mid way through senior school" said Cuba. But I stuck with Ampleforth to be near Barbara and because I enjoyed the sports activities".
Cuba's sister was two years younger than him, so he stayed in sixth form to remain with Barbara until she turned 16.
"I started an engineering degree, met Skull and the rest is history" said Cuba. "But Barbara's faith had grown with the monk's teaching. As soon as she was old enough she became a novice nun and later, Sister Barbara".

"I knew that prayer and contemplation would never be enough for Barbara", said Cuba. "She started looking for a

Between Stone & A Hard Place

higher purpose and found it in The Congregation of Our Lady of Charity, The Good Shepherd. Which usually goes by the simpler title of, The Good Shepherd Sisters."

"So how does that help with our search for Lucy", asked Stone.
"They are dedicated to working with prostitutes and trafficked women", replied Cuba.

Cuba told his friends about his sister's catholic order. "We call prostitution the world's oldest profession" he said. "Barbara's order had been working with the women for a very long time. They were founded in 1835 by Saint Mary Pelletier, in France. On top of the standard vows of poverty, chastity, and obedience, the Sisters of the Good Shepherd take an extra vow; to labour for the conversion of fallen women needing refuge from the temptation of the world".

Part of their order has become a None Governmental Organisation, or NGO, associated with the United Nations. They have offices in Geneva and New York. Sister Barbara Cuba's British education got her posted to the New York office, working directly with the UN.

"I might not share Barbara's faith" said Cuba, "but I'm proud of her work". Miguel Cuba had been searching his iPad while he spoke to his friends. He was looking for a news clip that he had proudly saved to his device and watched repeatedly. The clip was of a news conference at the Vatican. A parade of international dignitaries, including the Pope and the British Home Secretary spoke about the evils of modern slavery and sex trafficking. The conference was being orchestrated by the head of the Vatican Gendarmerie, and at his side was a beautiful dark haired nun, of Mediterranean appearance. Stone did not need telling that the nun at the centre of the proceedings was his friend's sister.
Throughout the news report, they returned to a single memorable sound bite from Pope Francis "Human trafficking is an open wound of contemporary society. A scourge upon

Between Stone & A Hard Place

the body of Christ. It is a crime against humanity".
The message of the conference was one of a joined up, international campaign against sex slavery. At the heart of the campaign was Barbara Cuba's Good Shepherd Sisters.

"Can Barbara help us from New York" asked Stone. "Oh, she's closer than that" replied Miguel Cuba. 'Barbara's taking a sabbatical at their Portuguese convent on her way back from the Vatican".

It is not always easy to telephone a nun inside her convent. But Barbara Cuba's UN role meant that, outside of prayer, she usually had her mobile phone to hand. Miguel reached his sister on his first attempt and was soon catching up with news of her big new project.

Eventually Miguel was able to tell Barbara about young Lucy's kidnapping and their belief that it was linked to people trafficking. He held back the detail of Stone's involvement, as that was not something the Watchers would discuss over the phone.

Miguel obviously gave enough to pique his sister's interest, as she offered far more help than he was expecting. "Chief Inspector De Sa is part of our law enforcement network. I'll go and offer him some consultation" said Barbara. "Give me a couple of hours to find Ricardo De Sa and I'll come to your clubhouse, we're long overdue a catch up".

Stone then set about guiding the Watchers through turning their clubhouse bar into the type of incident room he had regularly used during his 20 year police career.

He allocated one wall each to the kidnap at Pedralva and the handover of Lucy at Ingrena. Then he dedicated another wall to the key players. Meticulously going through his notes and recollections, Stone pulled together everything they knew so far about everyone of interest to his investigation.

Photographs of Lucy and her family were printed from the internet and pinned to the wall, along with the information Stone had gleaned from Trudy.

They had no photograph of Carlos Lobo, the Wolf, but they

Between Stone & A Hard Place

were able to pull together a small amount of known facts and a lot of rumour about the former PIDE kingpin.

Stone's search of the Roma's motor home had produced a wealth of information from his photographed documents, but they could not be certain all were genuine. The documents showed the Roma couple who owned the motor home to be; Ferko Mordecai and his wife Chavali Mordecai.

The Slav killed by Stone had now been named by the media. Blagoy Cvetkov was named as a Bulgarian businessman, who owned tourist businesses in Bulgaria and Portugal. One internet source speculated that Cvetkov's businesses had grown from the KGB run Intourist organisation. The name and photograph for the Slav matched the information brought back by Stone, so he too went on the wall.

The last wall was reserved for links and associations. Today's police analysts use sophisticated computer software to keep track of the people, places, mobile phones etc, which are important to a major investigation. But Stone was an old school cop, he preferred to see printed photographs, with the connections physically made with string.

Steve Butler, the London and International Sergeant at Arms, was helping Stone sort through photographs for his links and associations wall. Among the pile of photographs were the ones Skull had asked him to print of the man at the Faro brothel.

Butler picked up the close up photograph of the old man, flanked by brothel hostesses, waving off footballer Sergio Silva.

"I know him, or rather knew him. It's been over 10 years, but I wouldn't forget him", said Butler.

Steve Butler was a former Royal Marines Commando and a lifetime mountain sport enthusiast, who had climbed and skied in most of the world's high places. Between leaving the Marines and joining the MC, Butler had worked for an adventure holiday company.

"One of our walking destinations was Bulgaria. I spent weeks

Between Stone & A Hard Place

protecting our local contractors and clients from this guy and his gorillas." Butler's former employers operated an Eco Tourism model, where they used local businesses to operate their holidays. Particularly with new destinations, they would send a London representative as a company liaison. Often this liaison was Steve Butler.
Bulgaria was a new destination at the time, the troubles in the Balkan Peninsula had settled and low prices were attracting tourists to the former Soviet Block countries. Bulgaria's Rila range boasts the Balkans' highest peak, so the low prices and the mountainous country's varied ranges made an attractive walking destination.

Butler found a tourism company based in Bulgaria's capital of Sofia. They were already offering a wide range of traditional and active holidays, so they seemed an ideal local partner. Their first expedition to the 2925 meter high Mount Musala went well. The collapse of the Soviet Union left a very obvious mark on Bulgaria's tourist areas. A lot of money had clearly been spent on hotels and infrastructure, providing attractive destinations for the Eastern Block's more affluent citizens. There were also a big variety of hostels for the holidaying workers. But all around were part finished projects, where the flow of money had dried up with the end of Russian influence.
All the locals were eager to please the tourists, but there was something underlying which seemed wrong to Butler.

Butler soon discovered the Bulgarian company was little more than the former KGB sponsored Intourist company. They were now rebadged and independent of their former Soviet masters, but were still in the same mould.
The customer care from Butler's new partners left much to be desired. They were more skilled in exercising fear than negotiation.
But it was their shady business practices which brought them quickly into conflict with Steve Butler and his employers. They began with adding last minute surcharges to clients, as local expenses. Then with a week to go until

Between Stone & A Hard Place

their biggest ever group of walkers arrived, the Bulgarians tried to increase the contract price, on threat of cancellation. Butler salvaged the trip through a mountaineering contact. His climbing friend had married a Bulgarian girl and the couple were well known among the mountain's hotel owners. They put together an alternative walking holiday for the clients, which enraged the former spymasters.

Butler spent the whole of that fortnight keeping their thugs away from his new holiday leaders and their clients.

"He was the ring leader", said Butler. "Always ahead of us when we moved resort, ferrying his thugs about in an old Mercedes".

Butler described arriving at each change of hotels with his group, to find the hotel had received a visit from the former KGB heavies. None of the hotels turned them away, but it cast a shadow over each night's stay. It was on the walks, away from witnesses that Butler was most concerned. Each time their route came within easy reach of a road, the same group would be waiting. They did nothing more than chain smoke and stare at the clients, but Butler needed to be constantly on his guard.

"He's years older and more expensively dressed, but I couldn't forget him in a hurry".

"If he's still using the same name, it's Georgi Dimov", added Butler.

"That's starting to piece together", said Stone. "The guy I killed, Blagoy Cvetkov, runs a Bulgarian tourism company. It's too big a coincidence to ignore, so Dimov is a suspect too and he goes on the wall."

"Skull, can you rattle his cage a bit with the footballer photos?" asked Stone. "We'll see what sort of reaction we can provoke."

It had taken several hours for Nev Stone and Steve Butler to complete the painstaking work of putting everything of interest to the investigation onto the clubhouse walls. They were just putting in the final detail as they heard the garage roller shutter working.

Between Stone & A Hard Place

Every member of the security conscious MC looked up at the CCTV monitor. Walking away from a Harley Davidson Sportster was a girl in figure hugging leathers with long black hair hanging from the back of her helmet.

Only one of the bikers recognised the woman. "She's here", shouted Miguel Cuba, as he ran downstairs to greet his sister.
Without her helmet, Stone immediately recognised the attractive nun he had watched in the Vatican video clip.
"I don't think I have ever met a motorbike riding nun before" said Stone.
Barbara Cuba explained that her older brother Miguel had taught her to ride his motorcycle when she was still too young for a licence. She started to ride again when she began her NGO work with the sex workers. "It's a great ice breaker and I seem more approachable to the women than if I was in a car", said Barbara.
"It's just a shame she rides a Yank", said Miguel, referring to his sister's American Harley Davidson. "I wish you would find a different way of saying that", replied Sister Barbara." it's an innuendo which doesn't sound very nun like".
The Watchers had a policy of riding European motorcycles. But Barbara had spent a lot of time in the US working with the United Nations, so had developed a liking for the iconic American motorcycle.

Stone and Skull were anxious to know what Barbara had found out from Chief Inspector De Sa, but it had been over a year since Miguel and Barbara had last seen each other. So they had to be patient while the siblings caught up on family news.
Before long Miguel had managed to steer his sister onto the kidnapping. Barbara's briefing was a mix of what the police had told her and her own knowledge from the Good Shepherd Sisters.
The police were not much further ahead than Stone and the MC. His own thoroughness at the scene had provided a wealth of information. The conversations with Trudy Varley

Between Stone & A Hard Place

and the young Agente at Pedralva had brought them to a similar point to the police.

All the key players who now featured on the clubhouse wall also featured in similar charts in the police incident room at Villa Do Bispo. The big difference though, was that Ricardo De Sa considered Stone a suspect in both the Slav's death and Lucy's kidnap. He was planning to make the announcement at the next press conference.

Barbara Cuba threw her own ideas into the mix. The Good Shepherd Sisters had been fighting a people trafficking route from Eastern Europe into Spain and Portugal. Poverty in parts of the former Soviet Union meant that offers of work in the Iberian tourist industry tempted many away from their homes. Some of the job offers genuinely led to hotel work. But many found themselves in brothels, working off their debt to the traffickers.

Once here, their debt would increase with living costs and interest added by the gangsters. The women would take years to repay their debt, with violent enforcement for those who did not cooperate.

"That fits with what we know about Georgi Dimov and Blagoy Cvetkov, they are both former KGB gangsters and run tourist businesses" said Stone. "But it doesn't explain a kidnapping. Lucy Varley isn't a trafficked East European, she's English".

Between Stone & A Hard Place

Chapter 11

Barbara Cuba had a theory about the kidnapping. "I think it must be to do with the girl's age", she said. "Their phoney job offer scam only works if the women are of working age." "The gang I have been working against only seems to abuse young adult women. Children would be a new departure for them, but there can be big profit if they have found the right customers".
"So", replied Stone, "we think Georgi Dimov and his KGB crew are the Balkan connection and this Wolf may be the Portuguese end. But figuring out who might buy a nine year old girl could be the key to finding Lucy".

Stone's hypothesising was cut short when they were again called over to the TV area of the Watchers' bar.
Joao Alva, the Lagos Sergeant at Arms, had continued to monitor the news channels for anything of interest to them. The familiar backdrop of the police incident room at Villa Do Bispo was again on the screen. The News Channel reporter was interviewing Chief Inspector Ricardo De Sa, the Senior Investigating Officer for the kidnap.
Absent from the press conference this time were Trudy Varley and her parents. But another man, who Stone did not recognise, sat alongside De Sa.
The Chief Inspector was just providing a brief update to satisfy the press pack which was growing in size on a daily basis. De Sa began by thanking the hundreds of tourists and local people who had been searching the forest around Pedralva for any sign of young Lucy. They had not found Lucy, but his officers were sifting the forensic evidence and other clues to identify lines of enquiry.

"It doesn't sound like they have much at all", said Skull. "We're further ahead with one ex DC and a bunch of bikers". "Don't underestimate them", replied Stone. "Chances are they will be holding more back than they are giving away". "De Sa will only release enough to keep the press machine on side and to keep the public phoning information to them".

www.neilhallam.com

Between Stone & A Hard Place

Then Chief Inspector De Sa introduced the man sitting alongside him. Glyn Towers was a British Police Inspector, attached to the UK Embassy as Police Liaison Officer to Portugal.
Stone had heard about Glyn Towers' arrival at the incident room. The young Agente he spoke to at Pedralva had talked about the English police man.
Towers was there to aid communication between the Portuguese law enforcement agencies and the UK forces. He would pass on any requests for help through the complicated diplomatic channels. Stone knew that Towers would have to communicate across the Foreign and Commonwealth Office, for them to request that the Home Office release their police resources. Towers was too professional to speak about the red tape tying his hands, but he had made some headway, which he shared with the cameras.
"Family liaison and our concern for what Trudy, Judy and Jim Varley must be going through are important to us" said Towers. "The Midlands Region Major Crime Unit have released a senior police officer to lead on the family's welfare".

Then came an announcement which was a real surprise to Stone. He had been hoping an officer from his own force would not be appointed, as he feared they would assume guilt based on the terrorist shooting which forced him out of the police.
But what he heard next could not have been better news.
"Chief Inspector Jim Henson has been released from his role with the Midlands murder team to look after the Varley family", said Towers. "We are expecting him to arrive later today".
"Brilliant", said Stone. "I couldn't have wished for anyone better than Muppet". Chief Inspector Jim Henson was the Post Incident Manager, who took charge when Stone shot the terrorist suspect who threatened the lives of the two princes.

Between Stone & A Hard Place

The name he shared with the creator of the Muppet Show earned his slightly disrespectful nickname. But all who worked for him knew Muppet to be an experienced and fair commander.
Although he would know of Stone's past, he knew the whole story and would not jump to hasty conclusions.

The news camera turned back from Glyn Towers to Ricardo De Sa. What came next was much less welcome news.
"We previously asked for information about a motorcyclist seen near Ingrena, close to the time Blagoy Cvetkov was killed." Said De Sa. "Forensic evidence at the scene suggests this may be Neville Stone, an English motorcyclist who lives in a tent near to the murder scene". "Stone's yurt has not been occupied since the incident and there is evidence that he recently collected belongings from the yurt".
"An eye witness placed a girl matching Lucy Varley's description in a car making off from Ingrena at around the same time, so we are potentially linking the two incidents".
De Sa announced that he was formally declaring Stone arguido, or suspect, in both the kidnapping and the death.

The legal position of an arguido in Portugal is much the same as formally declaring someone a suspect in Britain.
It is legally impossible to take statements from someone as a witness if the police could later turn their statements against them. As soon as the police realise that a witness could himself be involved in an illegal act, he is considered arguido. Thus, from then on, he has rights and duties. Contrary to what has been written in the press, the arguido is protected and acquires the right to silence, which would not be the case if he were being treated as a witness.

Chief Inspector De Sa continued "Stone is linked to a death several years ago in England. He should therefore be treated as dangerous".
"What a croc!" Said Skull.
Stone replied "it's a tough call for them. I know what evidence there is and I thought from the start they might

Between Stone & A Hard Place

suspect me. That's why I didn't go to the police".

As Stone and Skull were talking, Stone's mobile phone rang. The Watchers' technicians had set up a sophisticated divert, so that Stone's traceable personal phone was several miles away at a safe house. Any calls were re-routed to regularly exchanged prepay phones. They had done this in readiness for Stone being treated as arguido, as one of the investigators first actions in a homicide or kidnap would be to triangulate suspects' phones.
Very few people had Stone's personal number. He had a second phone for business which was widely known, but it was his private number which was ringing.

"You've got yourself in another pickle, haven't you Stone lad!" said a familiar voice. It took Stone a few seconds to register why the voice he had only heard occasionally in the years following his imprisonment sounded so familiar. Suddenly the voice registered "Jonah!" exclaimed Stone, "I've not heard from you in ages".
Tony "Jonah" Jones had been Stone's Detective Inspector on the Counter Terrorism Unit. Despite the two rank difference, Stone had always been close to the old DI. Jonah had been one of the few colleagues who stayed in contact through Stone's investigation and imprisonment. When Stone left Britain to live in Portugal, they stayed in telephone contact, but it became less frequent. Time had slipped by and it was at least six months since they had last spoken.

"Have you got any news I don't know? asked Stone. "I managed to work out that I'm in trouble all by myself".
"I'm at Faro airport", is that news enough?" replied Jonah. "I'm retired now, so thought you might need some help".
"Fantastic! I'll get one of the guys to collect you", replied Stone.

As soon as Stone was off the phone, Skull urged caution. "I know he's been a friend, but he's still a cop. I'm going to need some safeguards before he comes here".

Between Stone & A Hard Place

Skull dispatched Stone to a house owned by the Watchers on the outskirts of Faro.
Then, most of the Lagos chapter headed out in a series of nondescript cars and vans. Crucially, two of the cars were identical. This would all play a part in the Watchers' sophisticated anti surveillance plan,

Andre Felix drove a plain van to the airport pick up area. The rear of the van was windowless and Skull Murphy could not be seen from outside, which, considering his frightening appearance, was no bad thing.
Felix pulled the van alongside Jonah, but before he could move to the passenger door, Skull had pulled him in through the side door. As soon as Felix drove off, Skull was busy with a selection of electronic detectors. He needed to be sure that Jonah was not carrying any bugs or tracking devices.
Next he emptied Jonah's suitcase into a large empty holdall he had brought for that purpose.
Only when he was satisfied did Skull speak to their passenger.
"Sorry for the rough welcome to Portugal", said Skull. "The local police think Nev is a suspect, so we need to keep him safe until he can clear his name. We've got a couple of vehicle changes to make, so just do as you are told".
"Where are we going?" asked Jonah. "That's need to know and you don't", replied Skull. "Just somewhere safe that you can talk to Nev".

Once away from the high security area of the airport, Felix expertly drove the van at speed through the narrow streets of Faro's old town. He executed a series of manoeuvres designed to lose a tail. Often he would drive twice around a roundabout, before returning along the route he had just driven.
On several occasions Felix reversed into a driveway, allowing him to watch the passing traffic, before setting off in a random direction.
Then, suddenly, he came to a halt outside a small bar. Skull

Between Stone & A Hard Place

grabbed Jonah in one hand and his holdall in the other. He quickly pulled the retired cop through the bar and into its rear car park. Here the identical De Costa twins sat ready in identical Peugeot saloons. Skull and Jonah jumped in the car driven by Pedro. Then Paulo and Pedro shot out of the car park in different directions, with Paulo acting as a decoy.

Before long Pedro had dropped his passengers off at the door of an Intermarche supermarket. The two men were now wearing the uniform of middle aged Portuguese men. They had put on dark brown flat caps and brown leather blouson jackets. The Watchers held the security contract for this area's Intermarche chain. With the former KGB and PIDE gangsters controlling the pub, leisure and tourist businesses in Faro, retail was the only sector open to the Watchers. But it enabled Skull to utilise his employees as counter surveillance operatives.
Jonah and Skull moved around the supermarket, while his guards watched the car park and CCTV for signs of surveillance. Once they were sure they were clear, they moved to another car driven by Rui Cal, who drove them another circuitous route to the Faro safe house.

"Sorry about the cloak and dagger stuff", said Stone to his old DI. "But we had to be certain you hadn't brought a tail".
"Only three certainties in life Nev lad", Jonah replied. "Death, taxes and student nurses".
Jonah was notorious for his tasteless jokes, which had often landed him in trouble with his police bosses. Stone usually tried not to encourage him, but quietly hoped he didn't know any jokes about nuns, which might offend Barbara Cuba.

"It's good to see you Jonah. How did they get you to retire?" asked Stone.
"It's a long story", he replied, "but I was pretty much forced out".
Detective Inspector Tony Jones had survived the cul of older officers under Regulation A19. This was a method by which officers with 30 years service could be made to take their

Between Stone & A Hard Place

pensions, allowing forces to cut their workforce and wages bill. Jonah's specialist skills were too difficult to replace and he was allowed to work longer than the standard 30 years. "After avoiding A19, I thought I was pretty safe. But then we got a new whizz kid Chief who wanted rid of the dinosaurs", said Jonah. "He'd missed the boat for compulsory retirement, so decided to transfer me. I ended up as a Community Policing Inspector. I tried my best, but after nearly 30 years a detective, I was rubbish at it. So I gave in and retired".
Jonah went on to explain how he had pulled together a small group of retired detectives into a private investigation firm. They specialised in surveillance, with clients coming from both the business sector and private clients.

Stone and Skull talked with Jonah for an hour or so, satisfying themselves that he was really retired and not tasked to find Stone.
They still exercised some caution, they gave Jonah use of the safe house and the car Rui Cal had driven him in. Both house and car were among a number the Watchers kept pre prepared with bugs and cameras. The car too had a tracking device as well as the hidden cameras and microphones. If Jonah did make any move against them, they would know about it.
Stone left his former DI with an intelligence file to read, then headed off with Skull, promising to collect Jonah when they were ready to move.

Back at the Watcher's Lagos club house, Jack Tate, the London VP and the club's computer expert was monitoring the bugs and tapping into the house's internet Wi-Fi. Jonah was busy researching the case information Stone had given him. All his internet searches fitted the right pattern. The bugs caught Jonah's half of phone calls to a broad range of contacts across various law enforcement agencies. He was pulling in favours for information on the sex trafficking business. Jonah's contacts were walking a fine line in talking to a retired cop about operational matters, but he was a

Between Stone & A Hard Place

master at offering some of his expertise in return.
Jack Tate had found nothing to suggest Jonah had any hidden agenda. The Watchers would not let down their guard, but they felt safe in bringing Jonah in closer to the investigation.

It was proving to be a nostalgic day for Nev Stone. As Glyn Towers had earlier announced, Jim "Muppet" Henson was not long in arriving. The News Channel's hourly bulletin featured the now familiar Villa Do Bispo briefing room. This time Muppet sat at the table alongside Chief Inspector De Sa and Trudy Varley. Clearly nothing new had happened with the case, as the pleas for information were the same as earlier in the day. Although De Sa still asked for information about Nev Stone, the message was softened by a plea from Muppet for Stone to call him personally.

Between Stone & A Hard Place

Chapter 12

Stone's day began with granting Muppet Henson's request to call him. Stone had been driven out into the rural area north of Lagos; where it would not matter if the police were able to GPS locate his pre-pay phone. With a Watcher driving the 4x4, Stone was able to talk while they moved around the network of dirt roads criss crossing the mountains.
Stone had decided to be open with Muppet about what had happened at Ingrena and how Blagoy Cvetkov had been killed. If they found Lucy, she would confirm his story. But until then, he was sure Muppet would do his best to convince the Portuguese police of his honesty.
Stone gave Muppet the same number which Jonah had used to contact him. The Watchers complicated system of re routing the calls would prevent the police from finding him through the call.

The clubhouse was again busy. Some of the Watchers had been there all night, monitoring police radios and the TV news bulletins. Most had grabbed a few hours sleep. Those closest to Lagos had gone home; others had crashed at the clubhouse.
Sister Barbara Cuba had gone home with her brother Miguel. They had little sleep as they were late going to their rooms with so much to catch up on. But the ride back to Lagos got their adrenaline flowing and set them up for the day. It was the first time Miguel and Barbara had ridden together. The outlaw biker was an expert at riding his Norton Commando around the Algarve's twisting country roads. But he was impressed with how his sister handled her much less sporty Harley Davidson, he was holding back very little to allow her to keep up.

The Watchers had voted to allow Stone into their church, or meeting room, as long as they were only discussing the investigation. So their day began with Stone and the MC's officers holding church to discuss tactics for the day.
Events had moved on so quickly that the hidden CCTV

Between Stone & A Hard Place

cameras were still in place around the Faro brothel. Stone had used them to confirm the footballer Sergio Silva's visiting habits. Now the cameras had a more serious use in tracking the movements of Georgi Dimov.

Dimov had been spotted by Stone during his paparazzi assignment at the brothel, but it was the London based biker Steve Butler who had linked him to Lucy's kidnap. They suspected the former KGB operative was now involved in the protection rackets and prostitution ring operating under cover of a tourist agency.

The cameras had recorded Georgi Dimov arriving at the Faro brothel in the early hours of the morning and he had not yet left. The bikers agreed that following Dimov when he left was a good place to start. Their hidden cameras would capture him leaving, then a series of cars, bikes and vans would follow Dimov to his destination.

By the time Stone came out of church, Jonah had already been collected from the safe house. He sat in one of the bar's booths with a group of the bikers and true to form, he was telling one of his tasteless jokes. "So, Mother Superior and two novice nuns are at heaven's gates. They each have to answer a religious question to gain entry. The novices answer their questions on the Garden of Eden, but Saint Peter says Mother Superior must have a harder question. What was the first thing Eve said to Adam after they ate the apple? asked Saint Peter. As Mother Superior thought of an answer, she exclaimed, "oh, that is a hard one!" Then Saint Peter opened the gates".

Jonah had not seen Barbara Cuba slip onto a bar stool behind him as he began his joke.

Stone walked over to the booth and said, "Jonah, have you met Sister Barbara? She's our contact from the Good Shepherd Sisters". Barbara had put on her nun's wimple headdress, she did not always wear it, but could not resist as Jonah began his joke about nuns.

In the 20 years Stone had known Jonah, it was the first time he had seen his old DI lost for words. Barbara could not keep a straight face for long and soon the whole group were rolling about laughing.

They did not have long to enjoy their moment of humour at Jonah's expence, as Georgi Dimov was spotted on the hidden CCTV camera.
This was where the Watchers showed that they were much more than just a Motorcycle Club. The MC members were the senior executives of a security business spanning many countries. Their employees crossed a wide range of security skill sets; from bouncers, through computer and video technicians, to private detectives. The Watchers had brought in their most skilled operatives to help in the search for Lucy.

The hidden cameras captured Dimov leaving the brothel. His exit was with almost as much flair as witnessed by Stone watching the footballer Sergio Silva leave a few days earlier. But Stone's trained eye caught subtle differences. Although the hostesses seemed to be lavishing attention on Dimov as he left, it somehow did not seem as genuine as the attention they showed to Silva.
Georgi Dimov turned out of the brothel entrance and walked down the street towards the black Audi saloon the Watchers had already identified as Dimov's car. He surprised them by not getting into the drivers seat, rather he reached into the back seat for an overcoat. With his coat draped over his arm, Dimov continued to walk away from the brothel.
Stone thought it unusual for a gangster of Dimov's status to be walking anywhere, particularly without bodyguards.

The Watchers had to scramble quickly to deal with the unexpected turn their surveillance had taken. Drivers from some of the vehicles scattered around the area quickly getting out on foot and closing in on Dimov. The first of them arrived on the street just in time, as the gangster turned up a narrow alleyway and out of the hidden camera's view.

The surveillance team were now using the system of parallel alleys and narrow streets to get ahead of Dimov, but they had only made one change of follower when they learned

Between Stone & A Hard Place

why Georgi Dimov had not used his car. The Bulgarian gangster had only walked a few streets, to a shabby looking house in a narrow back street. After the grandeur of the main street brothel Dimov had left, this seemed an unlikely destination.
The back street was too narrow for the Watchers' operatives to remain unobserved for long and they had no immediate access to any surrounding buildings. This made continued surveillance difficult as the operative would be easily spotted. The Watchers countered this problem with a technical team they had ready in the area. Hidden cameras were quickly secreted to watch the ordinary looking house, while the Watchers' team melted quickly away.

Stone and Skull decided they needed to be in Faro to see where the new development with Georgi Dimov took them. They had the safe house where Jonah was staying, to use as a base and sent the technicians who had placed the hidden cameras, to meet them them with monitoring equipment.
Skull, Miguel and Barbara flew out of the Watcher's garage on their motorcycles. The convoy of Triumph Rocket III, Norton Commando and Harley Davidson Sportster travelled west towards the Faro safe house.
Stone took one of the Watcher's cars and travelled with Jonah to join the surveillance team in checking out the back street house that Georgi Dimov had been followed to.

Jonah had moved seamlessly into work mode. His usual jokey manner had been replaced with the professional consideration of scenarios you would expect from a seasoned DI.
"Ok Nev lad, what do we know so far?" said Jonah. Stone knew this was a rhetorical question. His former boss had spent almost a full 24 hours studying the evidence, their intelligence, photos and internet sources. The old DI ran Stone through all the information he had memorised about Georgi Dimov, and then moved into his most likely hypothesis. "Got to be business Nev lad, or a mistress. We

Between Stone & A Hard Place

think he's brothel management. The house is too small for gangster money, so unlikely to be his. So, either he keeps a woman there, or it's connected to business. Given proximity to the brothel, I'm guessing business".
"I'm not so sure", replied Stone. "It's down market compared to the flash looking club they run as a brothel".

The drive to Faro passed quickly and soon Stone and Jonah were debriefing the surveillance operatives who had tailed Dimov to the back street house. Then, dressed in the typical dress of middle aged Portuguese men, they walked through the network of alleyways.
They slowed passing the house, to take in as much information as they could, Jonah concentrating on the upstairs, Stone on the ground floor. It was Stone who spoke first. "Check out the carving on the door, top left. I've seen that before, but thought it was just the Jack Wolfskin logo". Jack Wolfskin is the brand name of an adventure clothing company. They use as a trademark a stylised wolfs paw print. Stone had just made a connection to the old forger Hugo Franco's comment about "fearing the wolf's paw in this".
All of the Watchers led adventurous lifestyles and were used to seeing equipment company logos on buildings and vehicles. But Stone now saw this was different as it wasn't a sticker, the paw print was subtly carved into the same corner of the door he had seen on other buildings.
Stone asked Jonah, "Do you think the mark could put the building under O Lobo's protection?"
"I've seen similar ideas in other countries", replied his old boss. "It certainly fits what we're seeing so far Nev lad".

Stone and Jonah had just passed the door as it swung open. Georgi Dimov was first to leave, turning the opposite way to them, so Stone quietly passed instruction to the surveillance team to follow him.
Closely behind Dimov, three young women came out of the house and turned to follow Stone. They were chatting loudly and took no notice of the two men walking slowly along the

street. They slowed their pace and let the women get ahead. "Language?" asked Stone. "East Europe" replied Jonah. "Possibly Bulgarian, but could be Polish or a dozen others for all I know".

The women were not the least bit surveillance conscious and Stone had no difficulty tailing them without the help of a large team. They followed them to a nearby Intermarche, then to a pavement cafe for espresso on the way back to the house. Dimov also took little effort to follow, as he made the short walk back to the brothel.

With all their subjects inside and the exits covered by cameras, Stone and Jonah returned to the technical team's van. From here they called Skull to compare notes.

They were now drawing heavily on Jonah's expertise in scenario analysis. The old DI had already suggested two possibilities; that either Dimov kept a mistress at the house, or it was connected to the brothel in some way. "Well Nev lad, with three of them either Georgi is a very busy boy, or it's accommodation for the working girls. With the Eastern Bloc accents, I'd say the latter".

Barbara Cuba joined the conversation. "You brought me along to get close to the girls. Get me out there and I'll see if I can catch them at the cafe or supermarket" said Barbara. The team quickly agreed this as a good idea and sent her out with one of the girls from the technical team. Barbara did not take her Harley Davidson, as she thought her nun's clothing would be more suited to the task in hand.

Later the camera operators spotted two women leaving the house. They were much more elegantly dressed than before and the Watchers realised they could be right about them working in the brothel. The hostesses they had seen at the club door appeared high class, not the typical prostitute image.

Unexpectedly the women turned left away from the brothel and a foot team was quickly after them. It did not take long to find their destination, as the two women took a table at the pavement cafe.

"I've seen this pattern before" said Barbara. "At the house and club they will be watched and controlled. Any chance to be alone is treasured. The women will be enjoying a coffee together before going into work".

Soon Sister Barbara took a seat at the next table to the women. The crucifix and rosary they each held gave Barbara the connection she needed. Most of Eastern Europe is either Catholic or Christian Orthodox, both are more formal branches of Christianity than Protestantism and more receptive to a nun.

The two women, Silvija and Tanja, easily got into conversation with Sister Barbara. Their stories were familiar to Barbara, tricked into travelling for offers of work and now trapped in a cycle of debt to the traffickers. The fall of the Soviet Union brought greater freedom for her citizens, but the loss of Russian finance hit the smaller countries badly. Silvija and Tanja were both from Bulgaria, their fathers teaching in Sofia's university. But his wage alone could no longer support their families and the older daughters had jumped at the chance to send some Western wages back home.

But the reality was very different to their dream. The hotel jobs they were promised were really as hostesses in Georgi Dimov's brothel. They thought of running, but the gangsters had shown them photographs of their parents and siblings back home. Silvija and Tanja were told that their families would suffer if they did not cooperate and please the customers.

A newspaper headline gave Barbara the opportunity to steer the conversation to Lucy Varley, in the hope that the women may have heard something. "We not see Lucy, all club girls adult", said Tanja. "But sometimes talk of children. Sold to foreigners, Morocco they say".

Barbara could get no more from the women, as they dare not be late for work. But they went to the cafe the same time most evenings, so Barbara promised to see them again.

Stone, Jonah and Barbara headed back to the Lagos club house to debrief the new developments. The Watcher's teams were still in position and ready to react should

Between Stone & A Hard Place

anything happen.

True to character, Jonah immediately took a lead in the debrief. "Morocco is only hearsay from the girls, but it fits with other pieces. We know the Wolf's drug network extends to Morocco." Then Stone added "don't forget the clothing and Moroccan Turkish Delight I found in the Roma's motor home".

Between Stone & A Hard Place

Chapter 13

With the new information the Watchers' had uncovered, Stone put in a call to Chief Inspector Muppet Henson. Muppet was attached to the Portuguese investigation team as UK Liaison Officer. Despite their long friendship, he was still a serving officer and Stone used the complicated system of re routing his phone call.
"I've fed in all your intelligence Nev" said Muppet. "But they are still treating you as prime suspect. With your history, they don't believe it was a coincidence that so much happened near your yurt".
"But what about O Lobo and the KGB connection?" asked Stone.
The Chief Inspector's reply was simple, "they view the Wolf as untouchable and see you as a way of getting to him".

All the MC's key decisions were made democratically in their "church", so Skull called the members together with Stone to plan the next move. Stone had already sought Jonah's view, as he would not be allowed into the MC's private meeting room. The old DI had counselled Stone to look deeper into the Roma connection, as so far they had very little to firmly link them with the former spies.
The Watchers' meeting room was packed, with the local Lagos Chapter members and their English guests. All agreed the Roma connection needed to be followed up, but they could not decide how to resource the rapidly growing investigation. "Just like being back on the Force", thought Stone. "Never enough people to do the job".
Eventually they agreed to leave their surveillance and technical employees on Georgi Dimov and the brothel. The bikers themselves would handle the Roma camp.

The Roma or Gypsies had a semi permanent camp on the outskirts of Lagos, on the road towards Aljezur. The Portuguese Police had already visited the camp. Gypsies were historically thought of as child stealers, but this was no longer a popular view in politically correct Europe. The

authorities, fearful of criticism, forewarned the elders of their desire to search the camp. The Roma cooperated, allowing a voluntary search of their tents, caravans and motor homes. Nothing incriminating was found, but this didn't surprise Stone in the slightest.
"If they are part of it, they won't be keeping Lucy there", said Stone. "Especially when the Police were nice enough to warn them off. But we need a way of getting information, which won't be easy as outsiders".

It was Andre Felix who came up with a plan. Felix, like all of the MC members, was a director of their security companies. But he earned a sizeable second income from professional cage fighting. He knew there were always bare knuckle boxers among the Roma communities and with a big enough purse; they would not resist a challenge. Felix was straight on the phone to his fight promoter, the Gypsies' fights were never the highly promoted flashy events Felix was used to, but he was sure he would have a contact. There was big money to be made gambling on the underground fights and Felix's promoter was a regular attendee. He jumped at the chance of pitting his star fighter against one of the Gypsy champions.
Their Balkan champion was in the Algarve and a fight was arranged for the next day. Felix was pleased about the underground nature of the Gypsies fights. As one of his own cage fights would have needed weeks of promotion and publicity, much too long for the Watchers' current needs.

Miguel Cuba provided the next element of their plan. "If a Roma family settles long enough in one country, they usually adopt the local religion. So there's a good chance some of these are catholic. Why don't Barbara and I go in under the Good Shepherd cover?"
So, with Miguel stripped of his biker regalia and Barbara wearing her nun's habit, they set of for the camp ahead of the afternoon fight.
Catholicism is a faith rich in symbolism, the Cubas found it easy to spot which of the caravan owners followed their

Between Stone & A Hard Place

religion.
"I still can't believe the doors that clothing opens", said Miguel Cuba as he and his sister walked unchallenged through the gypsy camp.
Before long they had found an obviously catholic family sitting outside their caravan and slipped easily into conversation. The setting up of the fight ring in the middle of their camp gave Barbara a topic of conversation. Her work with the United Nations NGO had taught her the fine line between criticising a lifestyle and offering spiritual guidance. The risk to the fighters gave Barbara her spiritual hook and the family talked freely about the fighters and their travels around Europe to fight.
Barbara and Miguel left, promising to return later for the fight. But Miguel had left a listening device in the deck chair he had been offered and cameras under two of the caravans they passed.
Other bikers had been moving into the shrub covered hillside around the camp. Their binoculars and long range microphones, together with Miguel's bugs, would give the Watchers a good idea of anything that happened in the camp.

As the time for the fight approached, the Watchers had to decide how best to play their hand. "The best cover for most of us is plain sight" offered Skull. "The whole of the Algarve fight scene knows Felix is a Watcher. We might as well ride him there in convoy, and then put a few of the staff to work while the camp is distracted."
"Sounds like a plan", replied Stone. "Jonah and I will lead the sneaky team and leave you to run the circus", he added, knowing Skull Murphy would miss no opportunity to grandstand.

Loan bikes had now been brought in from the MC's motorcycle dealership for the four English Watchers. Together with the Lagos member's bikes, they were being cleaned and polished by the Prospects, in readiness for a grand entrance.

www.neilhallam.com

Between Stone & A Hard Place

Stone and Jonah had already slipped away to make a stealthy approach on the Gypsy camp. Miguel and Barbara Cuba were on their way, still in character as Catholic missionaries.
Then, what Stone always referred to as The Circus, came to town. The convoy of loud customised motorcycles thundered out of Lagos riding two a breast. As Chapter President, Skull always rode his huge 2.3 litre bike in front right. At his side was the star of today's show, the fighter Andre Felix on his BMW chopper. The remainder of the Watchers followed on in order of seniority, with the prospects and hang arounds taking up the rear.
The bikers' loud entrance to the camp provided the distraction they hoped for. The whole camp came out to watch as the big motorcycles were arranged in a semi circle on the challenger's side of the fight ring.
Skull continued in his role of ringmaster in making a big show of Felix's entrance. His big audience cage fights usually demanded bright clothing, more akin to a costume. But today's bare knuckle fight would be fought in jeans, boots and bare chest, saving Felix the need to change. He still wore his MC colours though; and his vest would be the last thing he handed to Skull before the fight started.

While Skull's larger than life character was drawing the crowd's attention, Stone, Jonah and two of the Watchers' investigators crept into the back of the camp from the surrounding undergrowth. Once the fight started they would search and bug as many of the caravans and motor homes they could enter unseen.
The Gypsy champion's entrance was with much less theatre than Felix's arrival, but it had much more impact on Stone. Walking across the field from an ex-military tent was Ferko Mordecai, the East European Roma who had taken Lucy. Ferko's forearm was wrapped in tape; Stone recognised this as being where he had caught the Roma with his sharp stick, saving himself from being shot.
"If he's tough enough to fight with that injury, we might have another King of the Gypsies" said Stone. As a young

constable, Stone had helped break up one of Bartley Gorman's illegal Gypsy bare knuckle fights. Gorman, who reigned supreme for 20 years, had told Stone that his title King of the Gypsies had been "earned in blood, snot, sweat and gore". Stone expected his friend Andre Felix would experience all of these in the 10 rounds to come.

Miguel and Barbara Cuba had rejoined the catholic family they befriended earlier, but this time they were ringside, awaiting the start of the fight. Barbara was attracting almost as much attention as the bikers did when they thundered into the camp. The sight of a nun sitting ringside for a bare knuckle boxing match was not an everyday thing. She was playing her role expertly, avoiding any mention of the Good Shepherd Sisters or her work against people trafficking. Today Barbara was simply clergy and was skilfully keeping the conversation focused on the group's family relationships and where the group had travelled.
The family confirmed what the Watchers suspected. There were two extended families in the group, one originating from the Balkans, the other from Iberia. Both families were linked by marriage. Ferko Mordecai was married to the daughter of the Portuguese head man. The group told Barbara of their travels across the whole length of Europe between Bulgaria and Portugal, although they remained tight lipped about any business other than fights. In keeping with the Moorish history of Southern Iberia, the clan also had family links with North Africa and Barbara filed that information away as confirmation that Morocco must play a part in their trafficking business.

If Felix could hold his own, Stone's team would have, at most, an hour to complete their work. But a lucky punch could end the fight in the first round, so they needed to work quickly. The two investigators moved efficiently round as many caravans as they could, planting bugs and taking photographs. Stone and Jonah concentrated on the tent Ferko Mordecai had come from. As they hoped, it was his temporary home. He had not yet replaced the motor home

Between Stone & A Hard Place

he left at Ingina and such possessions as he had left were easily accessible in the tent. Years of working together had honed their teamwork and they quickly and expertly searched the tent. As they expected, with the police having previously searched, they found nothing. They did leave bugs though, which they hoped would capture unguarded conversation. As they left the tent Jonah spotted something. "Nev lad, didn't you mention Turkish Delight in this fellow's motor home? He's got another stash over here". Stone saw that it was the same Moroccan brand he had seen before and replied "looks like Mordecai has been back to top up his stock already, or someone has been for him".

The fight was still underway when Stone and Jonah slipped back into the undergrowth. Andre Felix was barely holding his own against the Balkan champion, although both were showing the damage that relentless bare knuckle pounding inflicts. Both men had blood trickling down from eyes and lips. Felix was having difficulty opening one eye, due to its swelling. But, with one round to go, he started to turn the tables on Ferko Mordecai. The Roma had been blocking Felix's punches well, but his luck turned when he accidentally offered his injured arm as the block. Felix took full advantage, driving home a blow so severe, that it opened up the wound on Mordecai's arm. With blood trickling down the Roma's arm they went into the final interval, of which he would need every second's rest.

Ferko Mordecai's corner team had barely redressed the wound as the bell rang for the final round. "Ask not for who the bell tolls Ferko" taunted Felix as he landed the first of many punches. Mordecai was not giving in easily and had recognised the quote, coming back with "it tolls for you cat boy". But pain was weakening him and Felix could tell the punches were no longer coming with the same power. So, putting everything into one last blow, Andre Felix ended the bout by landing the Balkan champion in the dirt.

The Watchers knew this group of Gypsies were not the sort of good sports to host any sort of party as losers, especially with the money they lost betting on their champion. So the

Between Stone & A Hard Place

bikers collected their winnings and as quickly as they arrived, the convoy of bikes left the camp.

Stone had used his secure phone system to arrange a meeting with Muppet Henson. He knew the Chief Inspector would be at Villa Do Bispo, in the police incident room, so he bounced Muppet around a series of false locations until he could be sure there was no surveillance. Stone and Muppet were old friends, but he could not rule out the policeman being ordered into setting a trap. Stone quickly brought Muppet up to date on what they had found so far, and then just as quickly rode his borrowed Yamaha away through the town's warren of narrow streets.

Stone's escape was cut short, not by any road block, but by seeing Trudy Varley. Lucy's mum had been working with the detectives and needed to walk and be alone. Stone stopped his bike and began to introduce himself with the Nev Shaw identity he had used when he first met Trudy at Pedralva. "I remember you Nev Stone, I recognised you at the well" she said. "I'm a nurse, we have to watch for many changes in our patients, so dyed hair and different clothes did not fool me". "The Portuguese are convinced you are guilty, but the English cop, Mr Henson doesn't seem so sure and neither am I". Stone filled Trudy in with some of what he was doing to find Lucy. He did not mention the Watchers' help and he was especially careful not to let slip his friendship with Muppet Henson.

Always conscious of his need to keep moving when so near the police investigation, Stone took Trudy's mobile number and with a promise to keep in contact, he sped the big motorcycle away from Villa Do Bispo.

Between Stone & A Hard Place

Chapter 14.

Stone missed riding the Triumph Explorer he had stored while he was wanted by the police, but the ride along the coast road to Lagos on his borrowed Yamaha was clearing his head nicely. Before long he was back at the Watchers' club house, checking in with the bikers and catching up on progress of the investigation
"Georgi Dimov is on the move again" said Skull. "The Faro team have followed him onto the motorway, heading this way. I have sent Jonah out with Joao Alva and a couple of the English guys to pick them up".

Because of the bare knuckle fight and surrounding operation, Skull had left a skeleton team on the Faro brothel and the girl's house. With Dimov on the move in a car they needed more vehicles to switch the tail and avoid being spotted. So the four drivers leaving Lagos had to push hard to join the convoy heading towards them.
Joao Alva had taken position on one of the bridges crossing the motorway; he saw Dimov's black Audi pass under him and alerted the other cars to join the motorway. Georgi Dimov never drove quickly; he gave the impression of someone reluctant to attract police attention, so he was an easy subject to follow.
Dimov surprised the Watchers by leaving the motorway and passing by all of the big towns where they thought he could have business. But he surprised them more by taking the turn for Ingrina. There was still a small police presence guarding the scene where Stone had killed the Slav a few days earlier and it did not seem a place the gangster would want to be seen.

The narrow roads to Ingrina presented the Watchers with difficulties in following Dimov unseen, but Joao Alva's local knowledge took him quickly up a track to a hill top water tower where he could watch with binoculars.
Suddenly Alva realised where Dimov would be heading. "Big white house with high walls on the road to the beach" said

Between Stone & A Hard Place

Alva into the surveillance radio, directing the team to the most expensive house in the surfer enclave.
Planning permission to build or extend within the coastal national park was very strict. But Joao Alva knew the locals were suspicious of how much this particular house got away with. No one was sure who lived behind the high walls and gates, but they suspected either a politician, or someone with the money to buy a politician.
Jonah was first to get his car within sight of the house. "He's got a zapper for the gate Joao lad", said Jonah as he watched Dimov open the automatic gates and disappear into the grounds. "I m moving out before I'm spotted" said Jonah. "Best put one of the vans in lad; it will fit in better among the surfers".

Jack Tate and Steve Butler from the Watchers' London chapter had an old Volkswagen van which they were able to park in one of the regular camping spots close to the big house. Their English appearance fitted the cover they needed to maintain as holidaying Brits.
Jonah and Joao withdrew and left the Englishmen to their watch. It was getting late and the team assumed this would be where Dimov would spend the night. But, less than an hour after letting himself through the gates, Dimov was driving back through them and towards the main road.
Joao Alva decided to leave the VW van in position and used the remainder of his team to continue the tail. Dimov made their task easy by driving directly back to the Faro brothel, where they had enough cameras in place to watch discreetly.

"Time for a run" said ex Marine Steve Butler. "That track round the hillside will give me a look at the back of the house".
"Knock yourself out Steve", replied Jack Tate. The computer expert had no interest in running and was happy leaving his athletic friend to the military stuff.
Butler often ran through the National Park's huge network of trails. His practiced eye picked out a route around the hill

Between Stone & A Hard Place

which would give him a clear view over the high walls of the house. You never lose the fitness gained in Commando training and Butler had soon crossed the valley from their van.

As he began to jog up the hillside he started to feign shoe problems, this gave him the cover to drop to a crouch at a viewpoint below the house. Pulling a small scope from inside his clothes, Butler quickly scanned the rear aspect for detail which his skilled memory would later recount.

Skull Murphy had already sent one of their operatives to join Jack Tate in the van, so that Steve Butler could return to the clubhouse and brief him.

As he entered the clubhouse bar, Stone and Jonah were updating their briefing wall with maps and photographs of the big white house.

Grabbing a set of marker pens, Butler began to brief the other Watchers. "We've seen no lights or movement since Dimov left, so pretty sure it's unoccupied. There's good cover for approach from; here, here and here", marking arrows on an enlarged aerial photograph. "Alarm is a system we use, so we should be able to bypass it. Physical security looks good on doors, but the windows look easier, probably these two at the rear", drawing the rear layout from memory.

"Ok" said Skull, "Butler is proposing a forced entry, any thoughts?"

"It would be useful", replied VP Miguel Cuba. "But we risk tipping our hand to O Lobo with such an obvious intervention".

Stone suggested a solution. "Barbara should be able to get the right paperwork from the police incident room. If we leave the correct notices it will look like a search warrant. "

"No, Nev lad", replied Jonah. If this Wolf has corrupt officials in his pocket, he would soon know that no warrant was sworn. What about leaving something we took from the Gypsy camp, we can leave the crooks to fall out among themselves".

Ok" said Skull, "I like Jonah's plan, let's vote it". A unanimous sea of watchers' hands raised and they began the process of planning the raid.

As dusk arrived, Stone led his small team across the hillside towards the white house. Only four of them would enter the grounds; Miguel Cuba was with him, along with two technicians to deal with alarms, cameras and computers. "Looking clear Nev lad", said Jonah over Stone's earpiece. Jonah was realistic about his age, so despite wanting to back up Stone at the house, knew he was better coordinating the raid. He had joined Jack Tait in the surveillance van and was watching the house and grounds through an image intensifier.
"No infra red or laser", whispered one of the Watchers' technicians. Their first job was to check for magic eye beams on the wall and grounds. Given the number of wild animals in the National Park, they did not expect the owners to use a system which would false alarm so often. But their mission would be over quickly if the alarm was raised before reaching the house.
Stone's team slipped easily over the high wall and used cover of the garden's trees and bushes to approach the house.

Only one camera covered the alarm panel which the technicians needed to access. They had come with a technological solution to show the camera a recorded loop, but Cuba spotted a simpler method. "Wait, I can do this with that tree", said Cuba. He threw a weighted length of para cord around a nearby branch, and then carefully pulled it across the camera's field of view. "There, no risk of technical malfunction."
The two technicians moved across to the alarm box. It was a sophisticated system, but this helped Stone's plan. The alarm's controlling computer had more scope for manipulation than a simpler system which was either on or off. The technicians were able to bypass individual sections of the system without triggering any alarms.
One technician hooked up a portable terminal into the alarm system's computer, expertly manipulating the complicated

network of alarms and CCTV cameras. The other technician quickly defeated the locks securing the rear window and the remaining three climbed into the house.

They worked methodically through one room at a time, with alarms and cameras bypassed as they moved from room to room.
It was a very male house, what ornaments there were came mostly from travel. "Doesn't look much like a home, more an office" observed Stone. "Portrait of the dictator Salazar confirms a PIDE link. I've seen a few wolf's paw logos. The travel memorabilia is what we'd expect, East Europe and North Africa. But nothing very personal."

"Secret room,'" said Cuba, calling over Stone and their technician. He had found a man size safe door hidden behind a tapestry. "Quick, get it open", said Stone to the technician.
The technician went to work, but Stone could see the uncertainty on his face. The Watchers employees were among the best the security industry could offer, but Carlos Lobo had almost limitless funds. The sophistication of the alarm and CCTV played to their advantage, because they had learned to manipulate that particular system. But it was a different story with the safe. "Sorry Nev, we're still working on that model. It's new, the best you can buy".
"Ok", replied Stone. "Carry on, we'll just have to hope someone's been careless and left something out of the safe.

They continued their search into the bedrooms. "Still not very lived in", said Stone. The three guest rooms looked comfortable, but only contained functional furniture and nothing of a personal nature. The master bedroom was little different. "Couple of changes of clothing in the closet, but all brand new and locally bought." said Cuba. "It looks like his people have set the house up for occasional use and then most likely as a meeting place" added Stone.

Returning through the open plan living area, Stone thought

of something and went back to the room's ornate desk. "Let's try low tech for a change" he said to the others. Stone's kit bag was the product of many years of covert operations, some of the contents were much less sophisticated than the technical kit their employees used, but often no less useful. Stone pulled out a stubby, soft leaded pencil. Leaning over the desk's blotter, he gently began to rub soft graphite onto the blotting paper surface. "Bingo" he said. "Hotel address in Morocco". The pencil lead had revealed The Four Seasons Hotel in Marrakech.
After photographing the blotter in situ, Stone went back to the desk drawers. He found a replacement paper for the blotter and he bagged the sheet which had the address, placing it in his pack. He also removed an item from his pack, a small ornately engraved copper bracelet.

"Time to go" said Stone. Crossing the room towards their entry point, Stone dropped the bracelet close to the safe door.
Stone had found the bracelet when he searched the fighter Ferko Mordecai's tent at the gypsy camp. Mordecai had worn a bracelet with the same pattern when they fought at Ingrina. He had seen the same pattern on carvings and embroideries in both motor home and tent. Stone guessed that the pattern had some significance and took the bracelet to research it later. But for now, its only significance was to incriminate Ferko Mordecai's clan with the Watchers' burglary.

Stone's small team climbed back through the window and the two technicians went to work on the security system to cover their trail. "Ok, we've got 30 minutes to get clear. All trace of our entry is wiped, except the damage to the window. Then in half an hour, the cameras fail and the alarm sounds. It will look like that's the time of entry and we'll be well clear".
With that, the team worked their way back through the garden towards the high wall. On the way Miguel Cuba retrieved his cord from the tree, once again allowing the

Between Stone & A Hard Place

CCTV camera sight of the house.

"Ready to come out Jonah, how are we looking?" asked Stone over the radio. "Nothing moved on the road while you've been in there", replied Jonah. "And you've an hour before the beach bar closes".
Stone and his team slipped over the wall and across the bush covered hillside to their vehicle. The Ingrina area has lots of ad hoc camp areas used by the itinerant surfing community. Stone himself used one of them for his yurt. It was one of these that provided cover for the Watchers' vehicles, there was nothing suspicious about a van left in one of the many clearings. As soon as Stone was clear, Jonah and Jack Tait drove away from their clearing to join the others at the Lagos clubhouse.

By the time they arrived at the clubhouse Skull Murphy had already pulled together the full patch members and all the technicians who could be spared.
Jonah and Stone went to work on their incident wall, adding the information and connections from the raid on the white house. As they pinned up the photographs and added the string markers, Stone new that Morocco was now looming large in their investigation. They had no hard lead to Morocco, but too many circumstantial pieces kept dropping into the puzzle.
"The forger first linked O Lobo's drug network to Morocco" said Stone. "We've found Moroccan stuff in Ferko Mordecai's motor home and tent. The brothel girls have overheard mention of Morocco. Then we found the hotel information in a house connected to Georgi Dimov and probably Carlos Lobo".
Jonah, the retired DI, brought in his usual note of caution.
"Nev lad, none of that adds up to a smoking gun. Back in the police we'd have been hard pressed to take that much further without some local intelligence". Then turning towards Skull, Jonah asked "have the Watchers got a North African presence?"
"Not a full chapter" replied Skull. "But we've got a couple of

Between Stone & A Hard Place

English members out there freelancing. There are lots of ex pat entrepreneurs opening factories over there and most feel more comfortable with body guards."

Skull made calls to the two Watchers in Morocco, asking them to put out feelers about child smuggling, the Roma and the former PIDE gangsters. Barbara Cuba was also on the phone to her UN contacts. She was cleverly using Silvija and Tanja, the Bulgarian girls from Dimov's brothel as cover. By using their story as her current case, Barbara was able to draw on the resources of her religious order and their UN sponsored NGO, without drawing attention to her connection with Stone and the Lucy kidnap.

Between Stone & A Hard Place

Chapter 15

Suddenly the clubhouse activity was brought to a halt by a huge bang. The prospect who was watching the outside CCTV would be in trouble, but in reality he did not have time to warn of the truck which reversed rapidly towards, then through their garage doors.
All eyes were now on CCTV monitors as the Watchers saw men in black, with automatic weapons swarm into the garage and towards the stairs leading to their bar.

The Watchers were always ready for trouble with criminal gangs. The nature of their security business meant that they often took lucrative contracts from gangsters. But worse was the Watchers' attitude to drugs, wherever they could, the bikers disrupted the narcotics trade. The drug lords took any disruption to their cash flow badly and several gangs had hit back at the Watchers over the years.

A successful raid on their clubhouse had never happened before, but the bikers regularly practiced drills for such a raid.
They were careful not to be too blatant when they did break the law, so kept nothing incriminating at the clubhouse. This meant that the only firearms they had ready access to were legally held shotguns. The Lagos members were now scrambling for the gun cupboards, as they had practiced so many times before.
Felix was closest to the stairs and slammed shut the metal barred gate across the top of the stairs. Everyone else was moving their guests to safe areas behind the reinforced bar and fixed booths.
Sergeant at Arms Joao Alva was first to the gun cupboard; he took little time in emptying the cupboard. As each loaded shotgun left the cupboard Joao expertly threw it across the room to members he knew could best handle them.
First to receive a shotgun from Joao Alva was ex Royal Marine Steve Butler. Not being part of the Lagos chapter, Butler had not practiced the chapter's defensive drills, but

Between Stone & A Hard Place

the Sergeant at Arms instinctively knew Butler's military training would take over.

Immediately the gun was in Butler's hand he began unloading shot through the gate and into the stair well. To stay legal, the Watchers only had standard double barrel shotguns, but Butler's expert hands could reload faster than most people could rack a pump action mechanism.

It did not take much longer before Felix, Cai and Cuba all had shotguns in their hands too.

The repeated explosions from the Watcher's weapons stopped any of the raiders from making the climb up the stairs.

By the time Butler had made his third reload and the others had each discharged both barrels, the true nature of the raid became known. A loud hailer boomed out, "inside the building, your attention please", the phrase repeated in both Portuguese and English. Stone knew the voice was familiar, but could not place it, especially over the repeated shotgun blasts.

Once the next instructions were given, Stone realised he had heard the voice on the TV many times over the last few days. "Armed police, put down your weapons", shouted Chief Inspector Ricardo De SA.

Skull's attention quickly moved to the CCTV monitors and he saw the marked police vehicles which now surrounded his clubhouse.

"Cease fire" shouted Skull to his club members. The club could not afford a gun battle with the police and should have nothing in the clubhouse to hide from an official police raid. Although the Watchers were not always completely legal in their tactics and business practices, they were rarely too far over the line and always kept anything incriminating at safe houses, not their clubhouse.

But then Skull realised that this time they did have something the police wanted, a fugitive in a kidnap and murder investigation. "They're after Nev" he said more quietly to his club brothers. Then, rapidly processing their

options added, "Priest Hole, quickly while the gate holds them".
Skull was directing them to hide Stone in a compartment built into an artificially thick wall within the clubhouse.
The building was not old enough for the compartment to really have been a Priest Hole, as the term began during the reign of England's Queen Elizabeth the first in the 16th century, when the Protestant monarchy hunted down Catholic priests. The hiding place was most likely to have been made during the time of the dictator Salazar, but the Watchers had found it while renovating the clubhouse and kept it maintained for just such an occasion as this.

Chapter Vice President Miguel Cuba had now moved to the locked gate at the top of the stairs. He was politely talking to the police, but doing his best to delay unlocking the gate to give the others time to hide Stone. If he was found, then not only would his friend be taken into custody, but most likely the rest of his club for assisting a fugitive.
Although the Watchers had stopped firing, the police needed to risk assess before moving up the stairs. This gave them valuable minutes to properly seal the Priest Hole, hiding Stone away inside the bar wall.
As soon as Skull was happy with the seal, Cuba stopped procrastinating with the police and unlocked the gate. The Watchers were careful to keep their hands in sight and away from the shotguns. Shots had been fired and the police would be very edgy.
Once the Watchers were secured and the shotguns collected in, Chief Inspector De SA entered the bar.
"They can put the guns down", said Stone, "we're cooperating now that we know you're police".
"Until we've got some cuffs on you I'm happier with the guns", replied De Sa. His Agentes handcuffed the Watchers, but unexpectedly seated them all in the booths.
"Waiting for the van are we?" asked Skull. "Not necessary" replied De Sa. "We're just looking for Nev Stone, give him up and we're on our way."
"Take your time", said Skull, "Nev's not here. Oh and the

Between Stone & A Hard Place

shotguns are legal and you didn't exactly knock.
While the Agentes began a search of the clubhouse De Sa continued his conversation with Skull. They would take the shotguns for checking, but De Sa had done his research and knew there was little chance he would catch them at their own clubhouse with illegal guns.
"I don't suppose it's worth checking for the CCTV tapes is it?" asked De Sa. "Never", replied Skull, "it's just for our security, we don't need evidence, and we sort out our own problems".

As soon as the police handed Cuba their search warrant he put a call in to their lawyer. Luckily Tony Smart, the Watchers' International Secretary was still in Portugal. Smart, the MC's solicitor was based in their Derbyshire chapter, but had come to Portugal at Skull's request to help with Nev's problem. Smart needed a clean record, so tended to distance himself from the club's murkier practices and was staying on a rented yacht at Sagres Marina, not the clubhouse. But he was close at hand and was now scrutinising the warrant.
"I don't expect you will be inconveniencing my clients for too long Chief Inspector. Your warrant is only for Nev Stone, not for any property", said Smart. "My clients will assist you in any way they can, but Mr Stone is not here and there are not many man sized cupboards to check ". The solicitor was subtly pointing out that the police could only search in places it would be reasonable for a man to hide. The terms of their warrant did not allow them to search drawers or smaller cupboards and certainly did not permit a destructive search. The police were thorough, but they were finished within an hour. The Watchers' Priest Hole was well hidden and Stone remained safe.
As the police left Tony Smart called after them "is it Villa Do Bispo where I send our account for the shutter door? and I'll expect a receipt for the shotguns please".
De Sa said nothing in reply. He knew the bikers had tricked him somehow. His own surveillance team had seen Stone enter the clubhouse and not seen him leave. The Chief

Between Stone & A Hard Place

Inspector hung onto some hope that he would find a firearms offence, but knew that was unlikely. The bikers had certificates for everything seized, no shot had left the confines of the clubhouse and no one had been harmed.

"How many lives have you used up now Nev lad", asked Jonah as they helped Stone out of the Priest Hole.
They knew they had to move Stone out to a safe house, but could be sure that De Sa would be maintaining surveillance on the clubhouse. "Bike convoy" decided Skull. "If we use vans or cars there's a good chance we will be stopped and searched. But the bikes can starburst and they can't catch all of us."
The Watchers often rode out of their clubhouse in convoy, it is what being an MC is about, and so it would not raise any unusual suspicion. The Faro safe house was the obvious choice, as it was already part of their operation, so the bikers set about planning who would go and what route to take.
Skull called in as many prospects and hang arounds as he could find to make up the numbers.
His plan was a simple one, they would ride to Faro in a standard 1% biker convoy, just like they had used at Andre Felix's bare knuckle fight with Ferko Mordecai. Stone would be able to hide within the pack on his borrowed Yamaha, his face hidden by a dark visor.
Once they reached heavy traffic at the outskirts of Faro, the pack would separate, giving any surveillance team 20 different subjects to follow.
It always amused Stone seeing Skull put a bike convoy together. His friend was an extrovert showman, who always reminded Stone of a circus ringmaster. The spectacle of any public appearance the MC made always had to look right. The bikers always rode two abreast, with the most impressive of the customised motorcycles on show at the pavement side. They all enjoyed the attention and Skull rewarded those who had worked hardest on their bikes with prime positions in the convoy.

Once Skull was happy with his formation, his convoy roared

Between Stone & A Hard Place

noisily out of the clubhouse garage, with Stone's Yamaha tucked into the centre of the pack.

All MC clubs are expert in keeping a pack of motorcycles together. Years of practice enable them to ride in close formation at high speed. The whole pack moves as one, with no opportunity for anyone to cut into the convoy.

Skull led his club along the coast road from Lagos to Faro. This took longer than the motorway, but fitted better with his cover of them just being out for a club ride. The attention they received riding through each town was always the same; children would wave, old men would gaze at them, enjoying memories of their own youth and those in between ranged between fear and admiration.

As the convoy rolled into Faro, Skull's plan moved to its next stage where the pack of 20 motorcycles became 10 pairs, all heading in different directions.

Stone peeled off from the convoy with Cai on his customised Ducati cafe racer. Skull had put the two together as Cai's racer was one of the few bikes in the pack which would keep with Stone's FJR 1300 if the riding got serious. Then suddenly, it did get serious. When the convoy split, the police realised something was afoot and needed to stop someone. They could not follow all 10 pairs, so took a gamble, which today was right on the money. The marked police car, which until now had been hanging back shadowing the surveillance, moved up behind Stone and Rui.

The police driver had no illusion of catching Rui, even to none bikers, Ducati are renowned for speed and handling. But they had underestimated Stone. They saw only a touring bike with faring and luggage, not the sports tourer chosen by many of the world's police forces as fast dependable motorcycles.

Stone had spent most of his 20 years in the police as an advanced motorcyclist. Now all of that experience was in play as he split from Cai and forced all the performance he could out of the bike. With a lead opening up, Stone turned into more narrow streets, where he could lose the police car

in a succession of turns and double backs.
It was a tired man who pulled the Yamaha into the safe house garage. But rest would have to wait until Stone was certain he had lost any surveillance. Two of the Watchers technicians were still at the safe house monitoring cameras close to Georgi Dimov's brothel, so Stone had help in checking the safe house's local security cameras. Only when they were sure he was clear, did Stone text a single word to his friend Skull, "safe".

Collapsing onto the settee, adrenalin was slowly subsiding in Stone and his thoughts rewound to events before the police raid.
Morocco still seemed the next logical step, but he had to be patient while their local members and Barbara's NGO contacts made their enquiries. So his thoughts turned to what had gone wrong leading up to the raid.
A leak was the most dangerous possibility, and outsiders were never completely trusted in the world of 1% MCs. There were only three significant outsiders; Barbara Cuba, Jonah and Muppet Henson.
Stone quickly ruled Barbara out, she was less an outsider than he was, with a history going back to her brother Miguel helping found the MC and becoming Vice President.
Jonah had immersed himself completely in the operation, but he was still a very recent ex cop. The suspicious Watchers had bugged Jonah's phone when he first arrived and he had made no calls which could have endangered Stone.
That just left Muppet, a serving Chief Inspector, who was part of the investigation against him. Stone searched his memory for anything he could have told Muppet, which could have led to the raid. Other than Stone's link to the MC, there was nothing and his ties to the Watchers were not a secret.
All Stone could do is be very careful in meeting the MC, as continued surveillance of them seemed a certainty while the police continued to hunt him.

Between Stone & A Hard Place

Chapter 16

Much needed sleep overtook Stone before he could check in with anything more than his earlier "safe" message to Skull. But this gave time for Skull to gather in the information he and Barbara had tasked to their contacts in Morocco.

The two Watchers based in Morocco were both body guards for British businessmen in Marrakech. Many European manufacturers had been relocating their factories to Morocco to take advantage of the low wages this very poor country demanded.
The mix of nationalities arriving in Morocco had created a very cosmopolitan environment for those at the top of the food chain. But a culture of petty crime in urban Morocco's poorest sectors created a dangerous undercurrent for the investors and their staff.
It was risky to be seen openly with money or jewellery and women in particular were wary of going far alone.
It was this ever present danger which kept the bikers in demand as body guards.

John Prince and Kenton Simms were both members of the Derbyshire chapter, although they had lived in Marrakech for more than a year. The two had become friends in the British Parachute Regiment, seeing action in Northern Ireland and the first Gulf War. Both had barely escaped with their lives in too many Iraqi ambushes, so when deployment to Afghanistan looked likely, they left to sell their skills in the private sector. Both were lifelong motorcycle enthusiasts and former Royal Marine Steve Butler had brought them into the MC.

Often people hold information which is of great interest to friends or colleagues; they just don't know it at the time. So it was with the two ex paras, whose daily lives involved just what Stone was looking for.
"The adjacent factory to theirs is Portuguese," said Skull over the phone to Stone. "The guys thought they made Jack

Between Stone & A Hard Place

Wolfskin gear, but now they are sure it's actually O Lobo's symbol on their sign".
"Is that enough for us to head for Morocco?" asked Stone.
Skull's reply confirmed that they would soon be travelling.
"No, but the guys always thought it odd there were white faces among the machinists. Moroccan labour is cheep, that's the point of relocating. You don't import Europeans for the menial work, unless you're not paying them European wages".

Barbara Cuba had also got results from members of her Good Shepherd Sisters order working against the sex trade in Morocco.
"Barbara's nuns know of Eastern European girls working in brothels at tourist areas, particularly Casablanca and Fez.
"Then we are going", said Stone.
"Oh it gets better", came Skull's reply. "There are unconfirmed rumours about selling guaranteed virgin brides. Young girls taken pre-puberty are used as servants until they can be married off".
Stone's relief was obvious in his reply. "So Lucy could be unharmed?"

Even though Barbara's information was sketchy and unconfirmed, it was the first news he had heard to suggest Lucy might still be alive. Until now he and the Watchers had been running on pure hope.
Stone could not keep this good news from Trudy Varley and prepared for the ride back to Pedralva.
He knew that he would need to be particularly careful with the police increasing their operations towards finding him.
He had worn fairly nondescript black riding kit during the chase, so he still had his khaki coloured Ewan McGregor kit which the police had not seen. His borrowed Yamaha looked like many other similar bikes, so a change of number plate would suffice in disguising the generic looking Japanese bike.

After closely checking the CCTV monitors with the

technicians, Stone carefully rolled his bike out of the safe house garage and away from Faro.

The road network in the Algarve is sparse and there are few options for the journey between Faro and Pedralva. Stone chose to randomly swap between coast road and motorway. The toll sections of the motorway activate electronic sensors fitted to Portuguese vehicles, but Stone had a sensor bought with a credit card in a false identity. By swapping route randomly he could confuse any surveillance team.

His final tactic for spotting a tail was to avoid the Tarmac road into Pedralva. The long dirt road from Budens would provide a dust cloud to hide him, but also ensure he could see any dust cloud following him from the coast road.

Most of the police presence at Pedralva had been scaled down. Dog teams were still methodically searching the surrounding farms and forest, but the ever increasing search area was now some distance from the village.

The forensic teams had long since left the village, with detective work being coordinated from the Villa do Bispo incident room.

With the police cordons gone, Stone was much less nervous about riding into Pedralva to meet Trudy. The secluded well had now become her spot and Stone quickly found her propped against it, reading another paperback novel. When not engaged in some form of publicity for the police, or helping locals with the searches, Trudy often came to the well for solitude. Watching the Algarve's migratory birds or reading was the only release Trudy had from the reality of her missing daughter.

"Fancy finding you here", said Stone.

"Thanks for coming", replied Trudy. "I still can't convince Chief Inspector De Sa that you're innocent. He seems more certain than ever that you have Lucy, so I know it's a risk coming here. Have you got any news?"

Stone took his time bringing Trudy up to date with everything the Watchers had achieved so far.

She was attentive and intelligent, often suggesting

connections before Stone had time to explain them. He was always amazed how controlled Trudy appeared, she often shed tears, but usually managed to avoid completely falling apart.

"Is Lucy alive Nev?" asked Trudy. "The Family Liaison Officers are always upbeat, but I keep reading that anything beyond 72 hours without a ransom demand is unlikely. Especially as our family have nothing to pay a ransom with". Stone had saved his best news and decided that now was the time to give Trudy a little hope. "We don't have a firm lead", said Stone as he explained Barbara's virgin bride theory. "But all the pieces seem to fit and it's the best chance we have".

Trudy seized on the new theory and immediately became more positive. "You must tell your friend Muppet, so he can get the police searching in Morocco".

"No, please don't tell any of them", asked Stone. "They are all so sure I'm involved that I don't think Muppet could keep them from interfering. I'm not convinced the Moroccan police would be too cooperative either from what I've heard. "Let us go and see what we can find, and then I'll tell Muppet Henson everything I know".

Trudy was desperate for this new information to lead them to her daughter. If the police were not going to Morocco, then Trudy wanted to be there.

"It's too dangerous" replied Stone "and its Skull Murphy's show. As President he calls the shots and the MC doesn't like involving outsiders ".

But Trudy was relentless; she had spent too long waiting for good news from De Sa. Now Stone and his biker friends seemed to be onto something. The police would never involve her in anything more than a press conference. But with Stone, she had chance to really feel she was doing something positive towards finding her daughter.

Reluctantly, Stone agreed to find a way of including her. It was the happiest he had seen Trudy in the short time since they had met, he did not want to endanger her, but liked this cheerful Trudy and did not want to bring her back down.

Between Stone & A Hard Place

"You agreed what?" yelled Skull when Stone told him about the meeting with Trudy.
"It would mean a lot to her to feel involved", replied Stone. "She feels pretty helpless as a mum; with a missing daughter she can't do anything to find. Besides, if we don't take her, I'm worried she might tell De Sa anyway".
Skull was not happy at the prospect of having someone on an operation that he did not know and who had not earned his trust. But having the Portuguese police follow them to Morocco was not an option either.
"We'll have to vote it", said Skull. "But if she does come, she stays with Jonah in the support van".

While Stone had been out meeting Trudy, O Lobo's gang had acted on the bracelet planted by Stone at the big house at Ingrina. The Watchers' reprogramming of the security system's computer had put in the delay planned by Stone, so the gangsters were more than half an hour behind them.
The Roma, Ferko Mordecai and his wife Chavali had been picked up from their camp by four of O Lobo's men. The bare knuckle boxer did not know he could be in any trouble, but even if he had wanted to resist, the automatic weapons would have dissuaded him.
Once they arrived at a remote farm house used by the former PIDE gangsters, Ferko realised how serious his situation was. Chavali had been taken to another part of the house and Ferko now found himself naked and tied to a broken chair.
Ferko Mordecai, like many who worked for the Wolf, had never met O Lobo. But somehow he instantly recognised the old man walking into the room. Despite his 80 years, Carlos Lobo was still an imposing figure. He was tall and still powerfully built for a man his age. Most frightening though were his eyes; there was something about his gaze that projected pure evil.

"Why have your clan broken into my house?" asked O Lobo. His soft tones added to the malevolence of his stare.

Between Stone & A Hard Place

Ferko could not answer as he had no idea of what he was accused.

"Do you like James Bond?" asked O Lobo. "My men do. They watched Casino Royale and liked it very much"

Ferko too had watched the remake of the 007 film and now realised the significance of his chair's broken seat and his nakedness. The gangsters were going to re-enact the torture scene where Bond is beaten about the genitals from underneath his chair.

Carlos Lobo was swinging a South American bola weapon. Portugal's historic links with Brazil meant that someone with Lobo's violent nature had many such weapons in his collection.

The first blow was the most painful, but those that followed added to his agony and soon he was screaming at the Wolf. "What house? What break in? We have done nothing!"

Slowly, swing by swing O Lobo told Ferko what his men had found.

"My Ingrina house", swing. "Through the back window", swing. "Merchandise room door disturbed", swing. "Your bracelet", swing. "With your clan crest ", swing.

When the swings of the bola stopped, Ferko could barely speak, but he sobbed out "not broken into house" "Been before with Georgi, might have dropped bracelet".

This just enraged the Wolf further, but as always, the rage showed only in his eyes. Slowly and calmly the bola began to swing up through Ferko's broken chair.

"Ferko", swing. "Georgi was there hours earlier", swing. "He knows I like a tidy house", swing. "The bracelet was not on the floor", swing.

The Roma was now in agony, but worse was his fear for Chavali. If O Lobo could do this to him, what would they do to his wife?

Chavali Mordecai was as yet unharmed. Carlos Lobo learned his trade in the Secret Service of one of the world's most ruthless dictatorships. When torturing for Salazar's PIDE, the Wolf learned that psychological torture could be as effective as physical pain.

Between Stone & A Hard Place

Chavali too had been stripped naked. She was tied to an old bed and gagged, but was otherwise untouched by the gangsters and left alone in the room.
Her room was next to the one in which Ferko was going through his agony. Chavali lived every scream with her husband and heard every word from the Wolf. This was the psychology of O Lobo's method, her fear would grow, but without the pain she would have time to think.
By now Ferko Mordecai could do little more than weakly sob his replies to O Lobo. "Not us". "Done nothing". "Serve you well".
"Ok", said O Lobo. "Time to see what your wife can tell me".

Somehow, through the fear of what she might suffer next, Chavali fitted together what her husband was accused of. Then, with a flood of relief, realised it could not have been her husband, or any of their close family.
Chavali was in floods of tears, but through them she was desperately trying to give her story to O Lobo. Before her tormentor could ask a single question she was pouring out information through her tears.
"Wedding, a wedding". "Ferko couldn't be at your house".
"All family here from Bulgaria for our son's wedding".
Now O Lobo's icy gaze turned towards his men. If they had failed to check such an obvious alibi, they would soon be facing their boss's displeasure.
Tuning his attention back to Chavali, O Lobo's soft voice asked, "tell me about this wedding".
Struggling through her tears, Chavali told how her son and the rest of their family had travelled from their Bulgarian homeland for his wedding. Their regular travels had led to their son meeting the daughter of an Algarve gypsy chief. Their wedding was held at a church in Aljezur, close to their camp. The reception at a nearby hotel had lasted all evening and well into the next morning. Ferko, his sons, brothers and cousins were all there and too drunk for house breaking.

Turning again to his men, O Lobo said "make them comfortable and check. Someone here is wasting my time".

Between Stone & A Hard Place

The Wolf's soft tones carried much greater menace than if he had shouted at them. All of the gangsters prayed that the woman was lying; their boss would take his anger out on them if Chavali's story could be easily verified.

The gangsters talked to the hotel staff, the taxi drivers who plied their trade outside the hotel and neighbouring bar owners. Across the length of the Algarve fear of O Lobo meant that everyone went the extra mile when a request came from him. No one had left the wedding and the self proclaimed King of the Gypsies had drawn attention to himself all night with his extrovert behaviour.

Reluctantly, the four men made their way back to O Lobo. They knew their boss would be angry. Carlos Lobo rarely got his hands dirty with his business, but something about this break-in had enraged the old man. Because of them, not only had O Lobo dirtied his hands, but he had tortured a trusted lieutenant who it seemed, was innocent.

Carlos Lobo seemed unexpectedly calm when his men passed on their news. They expected rage and doubted they would escape with their lives, but he was quiet and controlled. It was Carlos Lobo's eyes that gave him away. O Lobo proved that the eyes are the window to the soul and the wolf's soul was a very dark place indeed.

When his soft voice spoke, it was not to berate his men. "Bikers. It can only be the bikers". "Bring me Nev Stone and I might let you live". "Fail me and I will let Ferko have his revenge".

Between Stone & A Hard Place

Chapter 17

The Lagos clubhouse was no longer a safe place for Stone after Chief Inspector De Sa's men raided it, so Skull Murphy had moved his team to their Faro safe house.
While the Watchers planned their trip to Morocco, they had no idea that in addition to the police, they now had former Secret Service gangsters hunting for Nev Stone.

To keep their presence in Morocco low profile, Skull Murphy only wanted a small team making the trip to Africa. Choosing the team members almost worked itself out.
Barbara Cuba was essential for her Good Shepherd Sisters network. When Barbara went into any danger, her brother Miguel would never be far from her side.
Jonah had become indispensable; the retired DI's forensic mind had already taken Stone's case in directions no one else had considered.
With a small team, Skull needed a big hitter to even the odds in any fight. His chapter's Sergeant at Arms was the obvious choice. The giant Joao Alva had emptied many Algarve bars without assistance in his years as a night club bouncer.
Stone had convinced Skull to take along Trudy Varley, but he did not consider her part of the team. Skull's trust was hard won and Trudy would have to prove herself to Skull before he would accept her.
The final team member became obvious when they worked out the best way for Stone to avoid customs and immigration. The former Royal Marines Commando had some very special skills from the Corp's Special Boat Squadron that the Watchers could put to use.

Hollywood always forgets that with any mission there is plenty of fairly mundane admin needed to make it happen. International Secretary Tony Smart and the Lagos chapter's De Costa twins were busy organising documents, travel bookings, vehicles, cash and everything else the Watchers would need in Morocco.

Between Stone & A Hard Place

With MC members already working in Morocco, Skull's small team could legitimately travel on business under their real identities. This was not the case for Stone, who as a fugitive would need false papers acceptable in Morocco. Paulo and Pedro De Costa visited their godfather, Hugo Franco, to provide papers. The old forger extended the identity package he had created for Stone's Nev Shaw identity. Stone was not going on the ferry and through immigration, but his papers would have to satisfy the local police that he had entered the country legally.
John Prince and Kenton Simms, the Watchers in Morocco, had assured Skull that junior ranks of the Royal Moroccan Police could be bribed cheaply. With cash inside the documents, they would not be thoroughly checked.
Obtaining local cash was a pre departure task given to Treasurer Paulo De Costa.
Moroccan currency could not be legally imported or exported. But the Watchers needed access to bribe money from the moment they arrived, so could not wait to exchange their money in Morocco.
The MC did not worry themselves with what they saw as minor regulations, so felt no guilt in finding ways around the currency rules.

"What about bikes?" asked Pedro De Costa. He knew Moroccan roads would not suit their choppers and custom bikes. They would need much more rugged motorcycles for the trip ahead.
"Ask Costa Del Sol for help", replied Skull.
Like most other chapters of the Watchers, their Spanish south coast chapter owned a large Triumph motorcycle dealership. As well as earning money for the MC, the bike dealerships enabled chapters to assist visiting members with bikes.
Spain's Costa Del Sol is one of Europe's busiest tourist areas, so the Watcher's motorcycle dealership ran a sizeable hire fleet. Most of their hire bikes were 900cc Triumph Bonneville Scramblers, ideal for the rough North African terrain they were about to encounter. Skull of course would

Between Stone & A Hard Place

always be a showman and was not satisfied with an identical bike to the others, he asked for Triumph's impressive 1200cc Tiger Explorer.

Skull's team would have to wait for their Scramblers. The Costa Del Sol chapter had promised to deliver the bikes to the Spanish ferry port, but the Lagos members would still need to cross the Portuguese border and ride down to meet them near the port at Algeciras.

The port was close to Spain's border with Gibraltar, so meant a long ride for the Lagos members.

"Hiding in plain sight still seems our best option", said Skull. "De Sa is watching too closely to sneak about".

Skull knew that Chief Inspector De Sa had arranged for the uniformed branch of the National Guard of The Republic (GNR) to run checkpoints at the border between Portugal and Spain.

The most direct route crossed the Guadiana Bridge, where Skull knew there was a major checkpoint. There were ways around, but using them would instantly make De Sa suspicious.

"We'll cross the bridge in full dress, just like we travelled to the Gypsy fight. It needs to look like business as usual", said Skull.

The Watchers' President was making the ride to the south of Spain a compulsory run for his chapter. All members, prospects and hang arounds would ride to meet the Costa Del Sol chapter together. His smaller team would then break away on their borrowed bikes to head for the ferry port.

Next morning the Watchers were ready to roll out of Lagos. Jonah had left early in one of the MC's vans to collect Trudy from Pedralva.

"I can see why Nev is so taken with her, she's lovely", thought Jonah as they drove back to Lagos.

Trudy was as friendly and engaging as Stone had described. But Jonah was also impressed by how sharp and enquiring she was about their investigation. "Must be one heck of a nurse" thought Jonah. "There's not much would escape her

on a ward".
By the time they reached the Lagos clubhouse Jonah had brought Trudy up to date on their search for her daughter. But the old detective had also learned a lot about Trudy and her family. "Make a good catch for you Nev lad", thought Jonah. He hoped that when all this was over, his younger protégé might hit it off with the beautiful and engaging nurse.

This time Stone was not present to be amused by Skull Murphy going into ringmaster mode. Every time his friend started to showboat and organise a public appearance, Stone could not help comparing it with a circus.
When the Watchers' circus left town, Stone and Steve Butler were in Sagres organising their own departure.
Stone hated missing the big compulsory runs; in all his time with the MC he never tired of being part of the spectacular convoys of motorcycles.
Today's departure was as impressive as ever, the long column of customised motorcycles left the old walled town of Lagos in a cacophony of loud exhausts and gleaming chrome.
As always, the rear-most position of the convoy was taken up by the Watchers' van loaded with the bikers' kit bags. Usually the chapters' prospects drove the sweep van as full members hated being without their motorcycles. But today it was Jonah's job to drive the van, as the old DI did not have a bike licence. With Trudy for company, Jonah had no complaints at being relegated to the sweep van.

Just as they expected, the GNR were still stopping everyone trying to cross the Guadiana Bridge into Spain.
A few of the Watchers, like Skull Murphy and Miguel Cuba had been to prison for crimes of violence. But compared to most 1% motorcycle clubs, their members were not hardened criminals. This never stopped the police treating them in the same way as the drug dealing outlaw MCs, so, they were well practiced in getting through police road blocks.
The bikes pulled in tightly to the road side and the club

officers called members forward as police Agentes became available.
The bikers documents were always close to hand in their jackets, because they were asked to present them so often.
"Where are you going?", the Agente asked Skull.
"Just to party with our brothers on the Costa", came his reply.
Skull danced verbally with the Agente for a while, always polite, but never quite answering his questions.
Eventually the Agente tired of the dance and started to wave the bikes through.
The Watchers practiced routine involved regrouping at the first suitable parking area; in this case it was a viewpoint car park where they could watch progress on the bridge.
Despite Skull toying with the Agente, the other Watchers progressed smoothly through the checkpoint and their convoy was soon on its way towards Algeciras.

Spain is a sparsely populated country and the Watchers had no difficulty finding secluded meeting points a short distance from the major highways. It was in one of these agricultural areas that the Costa Del Sol members were waiting for Skull's chapter.
They had brought a hired box van with a tail lift to transport the hire bikes Skull's team would need in Morocco. The MC members would never go far without bikes, so the van came complete with outriders.
MC bikers consider themselves brothers and every meeting involves hugs and back slapping. The Lagos and Costa Del Sol chapters had not met up in several months, so their greetings were more animated than ever and took some time to complete.
It was the first time Trudy had seen men behave this way, so she asked Jonah, "are they always like this?"
"All the time Trudy luv, it took me a while getting used to them", came his reply.
"There's a lot to get used to", said Trudy. "We are taught to fear outlaw bikers, but here they are helping me find my daughter. Then there's so many huge men hugging. Add to

that a motorbike riding nun and I keep wondering when I'm going to wake up".

Eventually the bikers finished their greetings and switched into business mode. Even from different chapters, the Watchers seemed to work effortlessly together. Rarely did anyone need to give instructions when a job needed doing, everyone just found a task and got on with it.
Today's task was unloading bikes for the Morocco team. Bikers gathered around the van as the tail lift whirred into action. Six times the tail lift dropped to the ground, each time with a Watcher riding to keep the Triumph upright. Then, once the Scramblers were unloaded, the lift worked four more times to load the bikes that were staying with the Costa Del Sol chapter for safe keeping.
Barbara Cuba's Harley Davidson Sportster went first, then her brother's Norton Commando.
Next was Joao Alva's Moto Guzzi California.
"You still riding a cop bike Joao?" shouted one of the Spanish bikers, referring to Alva's police styled bike.
"Who said we Portuguese can't be ironic?" replied the huge biker. Despite his fearsome size Joao Alva could always be counted on to retain a sense of humour.
Last to be loaded was Skull Murphy's customised Triumph Rocket III. Many more of the Watchers joined in as Skull's bike started its journey up the tail lift. This was in part due to the huge bike's 360 kg weight, but also for fear of damaging their President's pride and joy.
"Watch the boss' baby", shouted Miguel Cuba. He knew how attached his old friend was to his expensively customised motorcycle.
Six bikes came off the van, but only four went back on, because two of the Scramblers were for Nev Stone and Steve Butler when they arrived in Morocco.
The bikers' final task was to load the last two Scramblers onto Jonah's van. The van and its cargo would have to survive the ferry crossing to Tangier, so plenty of straps and padding went around the bikes.

Between Stone & A Hard Place

Once they were happy with the way the bikes were secured on both vans, it was time for a repeat of the arrival formalities. Except it was not an exact repeat, as very different things were happening as the bikers parted.
Most of the members were leaving together as Costa Del Sol were hosting some of the Lagos members for a party at their clubhouse.
But some of the key Lagos members did need to return to the Algarve and continue the search for Lucy. So they were leaving for the long ride home.
It was Skull's Morocco team which attracted the most emotional goodbyes, as everyone knew that this would be one of the most dangerous adventures their club had undertaken.
The police were still hunting for Stone and the shoot out at the clubhouse was still fresh in their minds. Violent crime was common enough in Morocco, without the added problem of O Lobo and his gangsters. The factories and brothels they needed to explore in Morocco would almost certainly interfere with the Wolf's business. Carlos Lobo never took such interference lightly and they still had no idea that the gangster had put a contract on Stone.
It was all these unspoken fears which caused tighter than usual hugs between the departing bikers.
Even Jonah and Trudy attracted heartfelt and emotional goodbyes from the departing bikers. "I could get used to this, they seem really genuine", said Trudy. "They are Trudy luv", replied Jonah. "So long as you don't cross them, then they turn genuinely frightening".

After the document checks at the Spanish border on the Guadiana Bridge, the Watchers expected more thorough checks at the ferry port. They were not disappointed, as the convoy of four motorcycles and a van were directed into the customs search building.
The customs officers did not have enough information to warrant an extensive search, but they were as thorough as they could be. The only contraband they had was Moroccan currency and that was well hidden. They carried electronic

Between Stone & A Hard Place

surveillance equipment, but they were the tools of their legitimate security business. So although they attracted customs attention, there was nothing unlawful about them. Any weapons they might need would be supplied in Morocco by John Prince and Kenton Simms. The Watchers were always too careful to be caught for something they could so easily avoid.
"Why the extra bikes?" one of the customs officers asked.
"Just spares", replied Skull. "We've heard how bad Moroccan roads can be".
More questions came about the nature of their trip, but Tony Smart had managed to secure legitimate business visas. They were passing off their trip as a promotion to build on the body guarding opportunities for their security company. They eventually cleared customs, with the search team visibly disappointed that they were unable to catch the bikers at anything.

As Skull led his team towards the ferry, he knew without doubt that someone would now be on the phone to Ricardo De Sa, He wondered what the Chief Inspector would make of Trudy Varley's presence on a Watchers business trip. "Should keep him guessing for a while" thought Skull.

Between Stone & A Hard Place

Chapter 18

While the rest of the Watchers were riding to southern Spain, Tony Smart was driving Stone and Steve Butler to Sagres. With them were two of the Watchers' staff who Smart had crewed with before and trusted.
The MC's International Secretary was a keen ocean going yachtsman, who raced on the worlds big oceans with a crew from the MC.
Smart's own boat was usually kept at Cowes on the Isle of White. With more notice of a trip to Spain or Portugal he would have got a crew sail the boat ahead of him.
But the search for Lucy had come about so quickly that Smart's boat still sat in its birth off England's south coast. To protect his solicitor status, Smart needed to keep his distance from some of the Watchers excesses and never slept at their clubhouses. He preferred a boat to a hotel, so had rented a yacht soon after arriving in Portugal.
Smart would spend the next few nights in a hotel, as his rented boat was now needed for the Watchers' mission.

The hardest part of planning their trip to Morocco had been working out how to get Stone, a wanted fugitive, through the three sets of border controls in Portugal, Spain and Morocco. The forger Hugo Franco advised against forged documents. With the level of police interest in Stone, computer checks would be a certainty leaving Europe. Given time, Hugo could create false identities with a checkable history, but his god sons had given him only a day's notice of their needs.

The Watchers were working out how to build a secret compartment into their van, when Steve Butler came up with the solution.
Butler had spent many years in Britain's Royal Marines Commandos before joining the Watchers. The Marines are part of the Royal Navy, so Butler, like most other Commandos, was a proficient sailor.
"Do you think Tony would lend us his boat", asked Butler.
"With a bit of help I can get it to Morocco. If the dope

smugglers can make the crossing, I'm sure we can pull it off".
"It's only a rental", replied Skull "and if I know Tony it will be rented through a shell company".
Soon the plan was agreed and that was how Stone and Butler came to be in Sagres with Tony Smart's ocean racing crew.

The crew members had arrived early to prepare the yacht for the sea. As well as checking over the sails, engines and navigation equipment, they had provisioned the boat for their crossing.
Stone and Butler waited a little later into the morning. They wanted the marina bustling with sailors and tourists to cover their arrival.

Their yacht was being rented out while it was up for sale; Stone was shocked by the £100,000 asking price for the 15 year old boat.
The 12 meter yacht had a high specification with, three sleeping cabins, two bathrooms, a galley and a saloon. There was also a bewildering array of electronic communication and navigation equipment. But it still seemed to Stone a lot of money for an old boat.

Stone had with him a small overnight bag. His larger kit bag for use in Morocco was making its way in the back of Jonah's van.
So it was a surprise to see Steve Butler hoisting two huge black holdalls out of his car. "Didn't you get your bags to Jonah in time?" asked Stone.
Butler smiled and replied, "oh yes, my Morocco kit is on the van. This is the surprise I mentioned. Ever fancied learning scuba?"
The former Special Boat Squadron Commando was an expert diver. But Stone had never done more than snorkelling, he suspected he was about to become a very fast learner.
"It's too obvious to make port with you on board", said Butler.

Between Stone & A Hard Place

"The crew will get us in as close as they can. Then we'll find a secluded beach to swim ashore. We can then direct Skull in by gps",
"You've got a day or so to run me through it then", replied Stone.

The direct crossing across the Straights of Gibraltar is about 14km, but their much longer sailing from the Algarve would take a little over 24 hours. Most leisure sailors hugged the Portuguese and Spanish coasts, but the Watchers planned to get further out into the ocean.

Stone stayed below deck while Butler and the two crewmen negotiated their way out of the marina. They left the town's seafront using the boat's inboard engine, but as soon as they reached open water the small crew hoisted the sails to see how the boat performed under sail.
The racing crew were eager to try out their new boat, but they also knew that using the sails would make them look much more like the leisure crew they pretended to be. Technically, they were smugglers and smugglers rarely travelled by sail.
Modern sailing boats are rigged so that they can, when necessary, be crewed by a single person. The ropes, or sheets, as sailors call them, are run through pulleys to easily operated winches. These quickly run the sails either up the mast to catch the wind, or down to a position they can be easily stowed. But with two racing yachtsmen and a Royal Navy trained sailor, the boat proved easy to handle.

Once the crew had the measure of the boat and could manage without him, Butler left his post and called Stone up on deck.
He unpacked one of the huge bags to begin coaching Stone with the diving kit.
Butler had asked Stone if he fancied learning scuba. The acronym scuba stands for Self Contained Underwater Breathing Apparatus and described the standard kit used by leisure divers the world over. The divers carry a tank of

compressed air, which they breathe in, then exhale through a valve into the water around them. The scuba system creates a stream of bubbles each time the diver exhales. This is no problem for a sport diver, but could have been fatal in one of Butler's military missions with the SBS.
What Butler had brought was more correctly called CCUBA, or Closed Circuit Underwater Breathing Apparatus. This military grade equipment is commonly known as a re-breather. Chemicals within the equipment, usually Soda Lime, absorb the carbon dioxide in the diver's exhaled breath, then recycles the unused oxygen in the breath, by adding a small amount of pure oxygen. By using the CCUBA system, Stone and Butler would be much less conspicuous from the surface, as they would leave no tell tale bubbles.
"It looks very space age", said Stone." Actually it's not that modern a concept", answered Butler. "The French built the first portable kit in the 1800s, but the technology has been around since the first English submarine in 1620".
"It's not that complicated either", added Butler. "I'll set it running, you wait three minutes for the chemical reaction to start, then jump in. Just watch your depth gauge, as the pressurised oxygen can get toxic below six meters".
"Toxic oxygen!" exclaimed Stone. "Any more cheery information for me?"

The wind faded with the daylight and the crew packed away the sails and switched to the inboard Diesel engine.
Stone sat on deck watching reflections from the bright full moon dancing on the water surface ahead of their boat.
The crew members were old hands at night time sailing and knew what to look out for in this part of the ocean. "Hey Nev, come and look over the side".
The steady hum of the engine was stirring up the plankton, activating it and making it shimmer with a silver light.
"Quite a show isn't it Nev?" added the crewman".
Stone replied, "I don't think I've ever seen anything quite so special, as he gazed intently at the light show. The beauty was added to by the stars shining brightly in the cloudless sky.

Between Stone & A Hard Place

The ocean's display of lights continued after they had passed over the plankton field. This time it was the lights of other boats. Most often it was the two or three lights on other small yachts crossing the distant Bay of Cadiz. But occasionally their horizon was lit up by what looked like a floating Christmas tree. Cruise ships passing from the Mediterranean to the Atlantic glowed with thousands of lamps lighting up their multiple decks.
"Time for some kip", said Butler. "The crew can handle it in turns through the night. We need to be rested for the swim ashore".
With that, Stone and Butler headed down to two of the boat's three cabins. Neither of them knew exactly what would face them in the morning and both knew the sense in grabbing sleep when they could.

The crew had been resting in the third cabin, taking two hour shifts each at the helm. It was almost dawn when one of them burst into Butler's cabin.
"You'd better check this out Steve. I spotted lights behind us when I took on my watch two hours ago. It looked like it was following, so I changed direction a couple of times and it stayed with us".
Butler looked off the back of their boat with binoculars, but could only make out the silhouette of the distant boat. He then ran to the saloon to start up the boat's navigational radar.
With the aid of the radar, Butler could make a reasonable estimate of position, size and speed of the following boat.
"It looks about the same size as us, but I can't make out the type", said Butler. "Crank up what you can from the engine, let's see if they stay with us as our speed increases".
They managed to coax a few extra knots from the Diesel engine and Butler carefully watched the radar screen for any increase in their shadow's speed. With their own faster speed, the distance between the two boats should have widened, but there remained a constant gap between them.

Now Butler was worried. It could just be another leisure boat, with an inexperienced crew wanting the security of another boat nearby. But coastguard seemed more likely, or worse, something connected to O Lobo.

Butler slipped effortlessly into his former role as a military sergeant and began to issue orders to his crew. "Rouse Nev and put him on the stern with the binoculars. One of you take the helm, the other on the radar. I want positions every five minutes".

As soon as Stone and the crew were at their tasks, Butler began to ready his kit. Butler did not know enough about the threat, so fight or flight could both prove to be appropriate options.

For flight, Butler laid out the CCUBA sets, together with masks and flippers. If need be, he and Stone could slip over the side.

If fight was needed, they had a small supply of weapons. Each diving kit came with a spear gun and several spears, which would provide a close quarter option.

They had a single shotgun on board. The gun was legally held, but licenced to the chapter's Sergeant at Arms, Joao Alva, who of course was not present as he was travelling to Morocco with Skull Murphy's team. Piracy in this part of the ocean was rare, but not unheard of. They could justify the single shotgun if boarded by coastguard, but not a wider armoury. Just in case, Butler bagged the shotgun in a waterproof dry bag. Close to hand if needed, but safe to go over the side with them if necessary.

Then, as dawn brightened into early day light, Stone and the radar operator shouted up almost simultaneously. "She's closing in, and coming fast".

The approaching boat was still some distance off, but as the distance closed Stone could see it more clearly through his powerful binoculars.

"It's UCC", shouted Stone.

Portugal's police differed from the system in Stone's native England. All of Britain's policing is done by police officers with no connection to the military.

In Portugal, cities and large conurbations follow this model, but rural areas and motorways are policed by the National Guard of the Republic (GNR). The GNR, like the French gendarmerie and Italian Caribinari are branches of the military. This was bad news for Stone as it meant that his nemesis, Chief Inspector Ricardo De Sa had influence over the coastguard, which was another part of his own organisation.

The GNR's Coastal Control Unit (Unidade de Controlo Costeiro,or UCC) is responsible for surveillance and interception at sea and along the Portuguese coast. Their particular area of responsibility is combating the smuggling of drugs and refugees from North Africa to Portugal.
As well as patrol boats of various sizes, the UCC has use if the Integrated Surveillance, Command and Control System (SIVICC), distributed along the Portuguese coast.
Stone realised that they could have been tracked from the marina if De Sa had picked him up with a surveillance team. But if their route away from the coast was picked up on radar, it may also have aroused the UCC's suspicion.

The Watchers' hired yacht would be no match for the UCC's patrol boat. Their 12 meter boat's 50 horsepower diesel engine would be lucky to make 15 knots.
The UCC's Rigid Inflatable Boat, or RIB, was a similar size to them at 12.5 meters. But its twin 450 horsepower engines were capable of pushing it along at 41 knots.

"Gear up Nev ", shouted Butler as he rushed towards the CCUBA sets."We're going over the side".
Then he shouted to the crewman at the helm, "hard to port, give me a blind side to work from".
The crewman did as asked and turned the yacht 90 degrees to the left, showing its port side to the oncoming patrol boat.
Hurriedly Butler began to strap the futuristic back pack onto Stone and started the rebreather system working.
Most modern boats have their rudder rear and centre, but historically the right hand side had a large oar, or steering board fitted to steer the boat. The name starboard stuck for

the right hand side, but there was no such oar to block Stone and Butler going over the side as they slipped silently into the ocean.

Hidden from the patrol boat's view by the hull of their yacht gave them the precious three minutes they needed for the chemical reaction to begin removing carbon dioxide from their breath.

Guided by expert diver Butler, Stone swam under the hull, where they took up positions either side of the yacht's keel. They knew the CCU patrol boat was fitted with both radar and echo sounder, so if they strayed far from the yacht's bulk they would be quickly spotted by the sonar operator.

Between Stone & A Hard Place

Chapter 19

Stop your engines and prepare to be boarded", came the amplified voice from the patrol boat.

With no hope of outrunning the RIB, the crew had no option than to do as they were told. But they were confident that their solicitor Tony Smart would have left them with impeccable paperwork for the yacht. They were carrying no contraband, with Stone and the shotgun both over the side. Butler had assured them that the CCUBA sets would last more than long enough for them to comfortably sit out a CCU search.

The racing crew had been hired for their sailing ability. Their only role in the Watchers' businesses was to gain the advertising publicity which came from winning races. But like all employees of the MC, they had to have displayed discretion and a willingness to follow instructions. They had been briefed on how to handle being boarded by the authorities and went through the motions of appearing cooperative, while keeping the Agente's attention away from anything that could give away their mission.

The CCU were thorough in their search, but found nothing, because there was nothing to find. As soon as the patrol boat was out of sight the crew tapped out a prearranged rhythm on the side of the yacht. This brought Stone and Butler back to the surface, where the crew helped them back aboard.

"Great work guys", said Stone to the crew.

Butler added "you did pretty well yourself Nev. it's not the easiest kit for an inexperienced diver".

Adrenalin was still coursing through all four of their systems, but they knew they had to get underway to begin making up the time they had lost dealing with the CCU.

The wind had returned with the daylight, so while Stone tidied away their diving kit, Butler helped the crew get the yacht back under sail and heading towards North Africa.

Between Stone & A Hard Place

Before long they saw the African coast looming ahead in the coastal mist, which stayed as an indistinct landmass for quite some time.
Then Tangier finally appeared. Stone had read lots of novels and seen lots of movies about the famous Moroccan port. The rocks and hills were higher than Stone expected. It looked a quiet little town, nestling between the hills, with a big harbour.
They would not use the harbour, as their rendezvous was further around the coast. But having attracted coastguard attention by sailing far from the coast, they now planned to behave like tourists and sail close enough to view the Moroccan coastline.
They saw fifty or more old fishing boats, tied to each other. It looked like a carpark without an inch of space wasted. When the boats leave, they would have to go in exactly the order they lay there. The boats looked both colourful and shabby, painted blue and red with brown and black patches.
Stone took in all of this colour in through his binoculars, but he was also watching for any undue attention from the Moroccan authorities. He saw nothing to worry him as they sailed east around the small peninsula on which the port of Tangier is built.
Their destination was a quiet beach close to Findeq on the opposite side of the headland.

Together with the matching headland on which Gibraltar is built, the spit of land they were sailing around formed what the ancients called "the pillars of Hercules". Today they are more often called the Straights of Gibraltar and form the entrance to the Mediterranean Sea.
As they left the Atlantic Ocean, Stone knew the water would become calmer and warmer.
"Should be in for a nice swim Steve", observed Stone.
"Let's hope so Nev", came the reply. "It's got to be better than 40 minutes under a boat in the murk of the Atlantic".
But things were not destined to run as smoothly as they hoped.
The crew had used the yacht's modern navigation equipment

Between Stone & A Hard Place

to locate the isolated cove on which Butler and Stone planned to go ashore, positioning themselves about 200 meters from the shore. Then using the same tactic they used with the patrol boat, turned one side to shore, giving a blind side from which the divers could enter.
This time they were under much less pressure to get into the water, there was no approaching patrol boat and Butler was confident that Stone now had some experience with the CCUBA equipment.

They slipped smoothly over the side and began to fin steadily towards the beach.
Stone had watched documentaries about diving in the Mediterranean and the reality of it was living up to his expectations. The calm beauty of the swim took his thoughts away from his status as a fugitive and the desperate need to find young Lucy Varley.
In his thoughts Stone described the underwater scene as breathtaking. But gradually, despite the calming effect of the swim, he began to breathe more heavily.
"Perhaps it's just the swimming I'm not used to", thought Stone, who could usually run for miles.
The more he tried to work through it and control his breathing, the harder it became. Stone was breathing harder and faster, then faster still. He was sucking in air, but still became more and more desperate for breath.
Now Stone was so consumed with trying to breathe that he had stopped swimming.
"What's happening", thought Stone. "I haven't run out of air, but I can't breathe". His mind, desperate for air, could not work out the logic. Air was still flowing through his mouthpiece, but the more air he sucked in, the worse he felt.

Suddenly Butler realised what was happening to Stone. The CCUBA sets had been prepared for the swim to shore. He had not taken account of the 40 minutes hiding under the yacht's hull while the CCU searched their boat.
The rebreather system depends on a steady trickle of pure oxygen to top up the exhaled breath. But far more important

Between Stone & A Hard Place

is the chemical "scrubber" which removes the exhaled carbon dioxide.
CCUBA is unlike a conventional compressed air scuba set, which simply runs out of air. The rebreather never runs out, as it continuously recycles your own exhaled breath. What does happen is that once the chemical is depleted, the carbon dioxide content increases with each breath.
Butler knew that continued use of a rebreather with an ineffective scrubber is not possible for very long, as the levels will become toxic. Stone was already experiencing extreme respiratory distress. This would very quickly be followed by loss of consciousness and death.

Butler had to act fast, so finned rapidly over to him. The usual remedy for a scuba diver without air is to buddy breathe from a single mouthpiece. Butler tried to remove Stone's mouthpiece so they could share his.
The more experienced diver had been breathing more efficiently and his CCUBA set was still working.
But one of the effects of carbon dioxide toxicity, or hypercarbia, is that the desperate urge to breathe often prevents removal of the mouthpiece because the diver is sucking so hard.
Butler tugged desperately at Stone's mouthpiece, trying to dislodge it. He screamed at Stone, although through his mouthpiece it only came out as a stream of bubbles.
Just in time Butler prized the rubber mouthpiece from Stone's mouth and quickly inserted his own. He knew that his own scrubber pack would not last much longer, so needed to plan his next move. Despite the stress of the situation, the former Royal Marine was working through the options, just as he had done in the many war zones he had served in.

Stay under, return to the boat, or surface and swim ashore? All had pros and cons.
Staying submerged risked both of them
suffering hypercarbia when Butler's pack eventually failed.
Surfacing and returning to the boat risked blowing the boat's

Between Stone & A Hard Place

cover and he already knew they could not outrun the coastguard.
The shore seemed his only option. Butler hoped their dark wetsuits would keep them hidden if they used snorkels to remain submerged.
Together they finned steadily towards the beach.
Butler had chosen well from the maps and satellite photographs. The cove was difficult to access and was deserted. All they needed to do now was hide among the rocks until they could call in Jonah to meet them.

Stone was back on dry land and breathing air; he was back in his comfort zone and started to work with Butler as an equal again. Butler was apologetic for not calculating Stone's dive time correctly. But Stone was a professional, and accepted these things happen on an operation.
He retrieved his gps unit from his dry bag and checked their position. The many coves looked the same and they had come ashore in a less than calm situation. But they had been spot on for the RV point with Jonah and Trudy.
Next from the dry bag was one of several untraceable pre pay phones that Stone had packed for Morocco.
"On target" was Stone's brief message to Jonah.
"20 minutes" came Jonah's equally brief reply.
Stone and Butler now needed to hide close to the road and await the black van. Jonah would not risk stopping for more than a few seconds so close to the coast. As soon as the side door opened, they would need to throw themselves inside.

Stone spent the next 20 minutes scrutinising the surrounding area with his binoculars. He was watching for the van approaching, but more importantly, looking for signs of surveillance.
The van cruised slowly along the coast road. Then, as Jonah's gps registered the correct 100 meter grid square, he slowed to a crawl.
Two very fit men sprinted from the shadows towards the van. The second they reached the van, the side door slid open

Between Stone & A Hard Place

and they threw their dry bags inside.
Stone was surprised to see Trudy had come to help with the pick up. She crouched inside the van with Miguel Cuba and offered her hand to Stone, pulling him though the side opening.
"Great to see you Nev". "We were worried", she said, hugging Stone and planting a quick peck on his lips"
"Get a room Nev lad", shouted Jonah, catching a glimpse of them through the rear view mirror. But he could not continue his banter as he concentrated on powering the van away along the poor road surface.

Cuba took over briefing his friends, but not before he had observed biker tradition by hugging the new arrivals.
"We've found a quiet diner a bit further down the coast. The guys are busy checking your bikes over. Once you've eaten we're heading south towards Fez.
As they drove, Stone and Butler told the others about being boarded by the CCU and of Stone's near death experience with the CCUBA set.
Stone could not help but notice Trudy's expression. As a nurse she saw things many people were pleased never to encounter. But the few days she had spent with the MC was starting to feel like she was a character in an action movie.

"We'd better not get out of the van wearing wetsuits", said Butler. "I think the locals might wonder what we're up to ". He and Stone started to peel of their wetsuits and change into more suitable motorcycling clothes.
"Hope you're not offended Trudy", he added. "You can shut your eyes if you like ".
But Trudy had no intention of shutting her eyes. She tried not to make it obvious, but was taking in every inch of the two athletic bikers.
Despite Trudy's efforts at not being obvious, Stone had spent too many years as a cop to miss her checking him out. Too much was riding on them finding Lucy for him to distract himself with a woman, no matter how attractive he found her.

Between Stone & A Hard Place

Stone had little time for any more thoughts as they very soon reached the roadside cafe where Skull and the other Watchers were waiting.
"Bit scruffy isn't it?" said Stone, looking at the dilapidated cafe.
"Don't be fooled", replied Trudy. "It looks rough, but the drinks are cold and the food is good".
"Try the Berber omelette Nev lad", added Jonah.

Within seconds of pulling up, the bikers were into their almost ritual hugs and back slapping. Stone had never met John Prince and Kenton Simms, the Morocco based Watchers, and so introductions were in order.
The former paratroopers filled Stone in about life in Morocco and some of the pitfalls.
Stone knew about the constant threat of crime, as this was what kept Prince and Simms in work. What he hadn't been warned about is the traffic chaos.
"There are no rules of the road", said Simms. "If you think someone is driving at you, they probably are", added Prince. "Give way at junctions or roundabouts? Yes, no, sometimes, possibly".
They went on to explain the ratty old Honda Transalps they both rode. Outside of cities and major routes, the road surfaces are terrible, making the adventure bikes a good choice. But with every archaic car forcing you aside, wanting your piece of road, a nice bike would not stay looking nice for long.

"Talking of bikes, let's see these Scramblers", said Butler. So Skull led them around the side of the cafe where they had parked the spare bikes. Being part of the Costa Del Sol chapter's hire fleet, all five Triumph Bonneville Scramblers were identical. The only different bike among them was the Triumph Tiger Explorer which Skull had brought.
"Oh go on rub it in", said Stone. "My Explorer has been in storage since this all began". The 1200cc adventure bike was what Stone routinely rode in the Algarve. But with the police looking for him, his own bike had been hidden away.

Between Stone & A Hard Place

"Hey, Costa Del Sol only had one on the fleet and I'm President", replied Skull.
Stone knew the constant showman would always want to stand out from the crowd. For Stone, blending with the crowd was exactly what he wanted, so the identikit Scrambler suited him well.

"What are you pair drinking?" shouted Miguel Cuba to Stone and Butler. "Suppose a beer's out of the question", replied Butler.
"Moroccan whiskey for you Steve lad", shouted Jonah. Trudy quickly jumped in, explaining what the bikers had renamed the local mint tea. With the exception of a few big hotels, the Muslim country was almost completely dry. But despite the heat, they had found the hot mint tea refreshing.
So, over fresh cups of Moroccan whiskey, the bikers studied maps and planned their route to check all the leads the Moroccan members and the Good Shepherd Sisters had found.

"First stop Fez", said Skull. "The Sisters know of a brothel using East European girls. It's 200 miles, so we should get it done by nightfall".
Once the tea and omelettes were finished, the eight bikers prepared to hit the road. Rather than their usual leathers, they had all brought armoured mesh suits to keep them cool. So, looking much less of a circus than usual, the small convoy headed south, followed by Jonah and a Trudy in their van.

Between Stone & A Hard Place

Chapter 20.

They were a few miles into the ride south before Stone realised he was actually having fun. Their reason for being in Morocco could not be more serious, but the bikers were enjoying getting used to the unfamiliar bikes.
Apart from Stone who usually rode an adventure bike, most of the Watchers' riding was on customised bikes, along Tarmac roads.
Riding the small framed Scramblers on poor quality roads was a rare experience for them. They constantly overtook each other and often showed off by sliding into corners speedway style.
A casual observer would say the bikers were playing, but they were learning to handle the bikes and preparing themselves for whatever Morocco could throw at them. None of them could know exactly what was in store for them as they followed up the leads into O Lobo's sex trafficking network.

The Watchers had already experienced one cultural experience at the cafe, getting to grips with unfamiliar menus and the strange concept of mint tea instead of beer. So they were surprised to see that most of the road signs were written in both Arabic and English, making navigation far easier than they expected. But relief at being able to understand the signs just made them less prepared for the next culture shock.
Eight motorcycles and a van pulled into the petrol forecourt. Prince and Simms had warned them that filling stations, like most things in Morocco, could be chaos.
The drivers of dilapidated cars were jostling for position, with no concept of queuing. If you saw a space near a pump, you needed to be in it before someone else was.
Eventually Stone got his bike alongside a pump and the others slotted in around him.
As the attendant started to fill his tank, Stone thought that with an attendant in charge fuelling should be painless. How wrong could he be, as soon as Stone's bike was full, the

attendant was off to the next pump while Stone refitted his fuel cap.

Stone checked the amount and followed the attendant to pay. He handed over a note of the local Dirum currency, which he thought was more than enough to cover the cost. "No change", said the attendant as he moved onto the next pump. "Note to self", thought Stone, "have the right money next time".

The giant Sergeant at Arms, Joao Alva started to give chase shouting "oi, shithead, come here". But Skull intervened, holding back his chapter enforcer. "Leave it Joao", said Skull. "We're supposed to be keeping a low profile and its pennies anyway".

Back home the bikers would not have stood for being short changed. But here, with the forecourt chaos and the small amount of money involved, they let it go and continued their eight hour ride towards Fez.

The twisting and interesting roads continued as they rode further south, but so did the appalling standard of driving. The bikers' convoy would be looking for an opportunity to safely overtake the many overloaded lorries, when a car would come tearing past on the crest of a hill or a blind bend. The driver of one precariously loaded lorry was waving frantically out of his window for the bikes to overtake.

Usually wary of following such a direction when he could not see past, Skull yielded to the drivers insistent waving and led the convoy out.

"Bloody hell!" shouted Skull as a car hurtled towards them, "he's only after a look at the bikes".

They all managed to tuck their small manoeuvrable bikes back in, and then eventually overtook with a serenade of horns and gestures to the offending truck driver.

Their route through the Riff Mountains took them to the town of Chefchaouen, where they stopped for more mint tea.

"Hey", said Trudy, those mountains look like goat horns", pointing at the twin mountains overlooking the town.

"That's where the town's name comes from", replied Kenton

Between Stone & A Hard Place

Simms.
After washing the dust from their throats with tea, the Watchers went off to stretch their legs around the narrow streets of blue rinsed houses.
Trudy and Barbara wandered through the narrow streets, checking out the street markets selling woollen and woven goods.
Miguel Cuba walked with them; he would not leave his sister Barbara alone for long in this country. But in Chefchaouen, Miguel had another reason to worry about his sister and Trudy.

"The whole region is awash with cannabis", said Skull, as he walked through the town with the other Watchers.
"Yes", replied Kenton Simms" "you can buy hashish pretty much anywhere around town. But it's also the start of one of the export routes that end in your Algarve clubs".
All of the Watchers were vehemently anti drugs. The bars and clubs on the Algarve which hired them for security were usually kept drug free by the bikers' hard line. But criminal gangs, including O Lobo's were constantly trying to breach their security to sell their drugs.
"We haven't got time to mount any sort of drugs operation", said Skull. "But it can't hurt to get a feel for the place".
Kenton Simms continued to brief Skull and the Portuguese Watchers. "We've spent a bit of time out here, riding through the Riff Mountains. We've not heard any foreign accents. It all seems to be a local industry".
"But its big business", added John Prince. "For a collection of family cottage industries, they shift some major weight. Most of it seems to head into Europe in your direction, on fishing boats and in through the Algarve".

As Skull walked with Prince and Simms, he was amazed at how openly the local farmers were moving their cannabis crops. A truck load of the plants was unloaded into one of the larger blue rinsed buildings.
Then the same truck was loaded with sacks. "That's got to be the processed hashish on its way to our clubs", said

Between Stone & A Hard Place

Skull. "Can we do anything about it?" he asked the two ex paratroopers.
"I've got something I've wanted to try for a while. But I'll need the toolbox from the van and about ten uninterrupted minutes with the truck", said John Prince.
After he explained to Skull what he had in mind, the MC president called his team together out of sight of the hashish factory and briefed them on Prince's plan.

All the time the truck was being loaded, its driver sat in the sun, leaning against the front tyre and looked to be smoking some of his own merchandise. Skull had just the distraction in mind for him.
White women were rare in the rural parts of Morocco. Prince and Simms had warned Barbara and Trudy that they could be certain of receiving unwanted harassment from Moroccan men.
Barbara Cuba would have looked stunning wearing almost anything, but her tight fitting motorcycle suit emphasised every curve of her shapely figure. She could not fail to get the truck driver's attention.
Skull had put a kink into the fuel pipe of Barbara's Triumph and run the engine until it cut out. "Just straighten this out and the bike will start", he briefed Barbara, before sending her to ask for the truck driver's help.
As they expected the driver was falling over himself to help Barbara, but he was obviously no bike mechanic and could not find Skull's simple trick.
The driver looked into the tank, shook the bike, then hunted for a petrol tap which was not there.
The more simple motorcycles available in rural Africa have a tap to turn the flow of petrol on, off or onto reserve. Modern bikes such as Barbara's Scrambler have a vacuum tap which turns itself on and off. This concept was beyond the simple farmer, who alternately looked puzzled at the bike and longingly at Barbara.

While Barbara kept the driver occupied, Prince and Simms went to work on the truck. Much of their army careers had

been spent fighting terrorist methods in Northern Ireland and Iraq. Since leaving the army they maintained their interest and kept abreast of some of the methods in use by terrorist groups.
What Prince wanted to try was a way to turn a vehicle's air bag into a bomb.
Using the tools Jonah had brought up from their van, Prince expertly stripped the truck's dash board, removing the cylinder which fired the passenger side system and inflated the bag.
He cut off one end of a cylinder and took out the discs containing the chemical component sodium azide. He carefully crushed the discs into powder, massively increasing the explosive and incendiary properties of the chemical. Then, with even more care than he removed them, he packed the chemical compound back into the cylinder before taping the opened end. Finally, Prince re assembled the airbag assembly.
"All we need now is a little accident", thought Prince.
When triggered by the impact of a crash, the sodium azide burns fast to create a gas that inflates the airbags. With Prince's modification, he hoped it would burn fierce enough to ignite the truck's cargo of hashish. The best part of the plan was that it would look like an accident rather than sabotage.
With Prince's work done, a low whistle told Barbara she could draw her subterfuge to an end. A quick twist of the petrol pipe miraculously fixed her bike and she rode off waving to the puzzled driver.

There was only one road out of town, so the Watchers knew which way the loaded truck would have to go.
While Prince and Simms worked on the airbag, Skull, Stone, Joao Alva, Steve Butler, Trudy and Jonah headed out onto the mountain road to prepare an ambush.
They chose a steep section of the mountain road, with a tight bend and a strong looking wall to stop the truck going over the edge.
Stone waited on his Scrambler.

Between Stone & A Hard Place

Unusually for an MC biker, Butler rode pillion with Skull. While Alva parked up his bike and rode in the van with Jonah and Trudy.
As the heavily loaded truck passed their parking spot, the Watchers put their plan into action.
Stone went first, executing a risky overtake, which caused the truck driver to break heavily, destabilising his truck.
Close behind Stone came Skull and Butler on the Triumph Explorer. Across his lap Butler held one of the spear guns he had brought with his diving kit. Skull followed Stone's risky line, overtaking the truck on the entry to the bend. As they passed, Butler let loose a gas powered spear into the truck's front tyre.
The overloaded truck was already unstable after avoiding Stone's motorcycle; the rapidly deflated tyre was enough for the driver to completely lose control.
The truck lurched first one side into the barrier wall, then back across both lanes, crashing into the cliff face.

Both airbags fired instantly, with John Prince's airbag adaptation going off like the incendiary bomb it now was. Flames shot out through the shattered windscreen and started to spread back towards the trucks load of hashish.
This was Jonah's cue to bring their van down from its parking position.
Joao Alva prepared himself at the vans side door for a quick exit.
Trudy Varley had not been told of their plan and was now screaming at Jonah, "what have you done? I can't be a part of this".
As they reached the burning truck, Alva jumped out of the side door to meet Steve Butler who had jumped off the back of Skull's bike and run back up the hill. After retrieving the spear, Alva and Butler pulled open the truck's door and roughly dragged out the driver. Without pausing, they pulled the driver around the corner into the shelter of the cliff.
"Go, go go", shouted Butler as they dived through the side door of the van. As soon as they were in, Jonah sped away, gaining as much distance as he could before their

improvised incendiary device did its worst.
Trudy was by now becoming inconsolable. "Have you killed him, is he dead?" "We came out here to clear Nev of a murder, now you've all committed another one".
Jonah was as always the calm elder statesman. "Trudy lass, the Watchers aren't killers and I wouldn't be party to a murder".
Jonah went on to explain that Prince and Simms had rigged the passenger side airbag, leaving the steering wheel airbag to protect the driver. Alva and Butler's quick action was part of the plan; and the driver would have little more than superficial burns.
The cargo of narcotics was a different matter though, as they could see the glow from the flames.
"That's one load of dope that won't be heading for our clubs", said Alva.

The Watchers now needed to regroup and get out of Chefchaouen before anyone suspected their involvement. The driver would remember nothing more than two crazy bikers overtaking him. The modified airbag cylinder would have burned up with the truck and the Watchers would be long gone.
A fortune in drugs gone and no one to blame but the truck driver's poor driving.

The little convoy was soon back together and everyone back on their own bikes. They quickly fell back into enjoying the twisting mountain roads as they descended out of the Riff Mountains on their way to Fez.
"Do you think I'll find a fez in Fez, Trudy lass?" asked Jonah. "Not like that. Just like that", he added, mimicking the English comedian Tommy Cooper, whose trademark was a fez hat.
"I hope not", replied Trudy, "not if you're going to keep on with the awful impressions".
With the joking in the van and the bikers enjoying the fantastic riding, they soon reached the outskirts of Fez. The fun stopped there as Moroccan traffic chaos returned with a

vengeance.

Cars changed lanes without warning. Traffic jams built up at every junction, requiring them to force their bikes down through the stationary lines of vehicles.

One offending driver cut Skull up so closely that it clipped the indicator of his bike. Skull was, as always, quick to react. His huge boot had put several dents into the car door. The driver raced off, presumably to find the nearest body shop.

Reaching their hotel was a relief, as it meant an escape from the bedlam and chaos of Moroccan drivers.

Fez was touristy enough to have a few hotels from big international chains. The Watchers took advantage of this for more comfortable standards and something rare in Muslim Morocco, a cold beer at the bar.

Once they all had a beer in their hands, Skull threw out the room keys. "Everyone's paired for safety. Girls, you're next door to Miguel and me, so bang on the wall if you need us. Stone and Jonah, Joao and Steve, then Prince and Kenton". Then he added "showers then back down, we've a lot to plan".

Between Stone & A Hard Place

Chapter 21

The bikers' very presence ensured they had a quiet corner of the bar, with other customers gravitating to tables well away from them. That suited the Watchers well, as they had to decide what to do next with the Good Shepherd Sisters' information.
Barbara started the briefing, "the Sisters have been working in Fez for a few months. Anywhere with a tourist trade is attracting the traffickers"
"Is it O Lobo?" asked Stone.
"We don't know", replied Barbara. "The women used to be sub Saharan, but recently we are seeing more from East Europe."
Stone badly wanted the Eastern Europe connection to be a positive lead, so jumped in with, "it must be O Lobo and Georgi Dimov then".
Barbara's Good Shepherd Nuns had been chasing the ghost like traffickers around the world for years, so she knew not to rush to conclusions. "We can't be sure. With what we've learned recently it's a possibility. But we've not seen any Portuguese in Fez".

"What about the young girls?" asked Trudy. "Could Lucy be here?"
"The youngsters are just rumour at the moment ", replied Barbara."But we're hearing the stories more often recently".
Barbara suggested the market was a good place to start. The medina in Fez was Morocco's largest car free market, which was the city's biggest draw for visitors. In common with many similar places, the market attracted beggars, many of them children, pressed into begging by adults. Barbara wanted to start by trying to speak with some of the children.

"The bikes can stay safe in the hotel car park", said Skull. "Prince and Simms have found us some taxis.
Outside the hotel were three ancient Mercedes taxis. The bikers tried to guess how close to a million miles each car

had driven. But they also wondered how the cars had survived so long with the frightening driving their owners displayed.
"I thought it was scary enough on the bike", said Stone. "But at least I'm in control of my bike. This feels like a theme park ride ". With that, Barbara and Miguel started to wave their arms in the air, mimicking their childhood roller coaster rides. Somehow the clapped out taxis with their homicidal drivers, managed to deliver the Watchers safely to the medina.
Barbara and Trudy set off together to look for children to talk to. The women would seem much less threatening alone, but they were shadowed at a distance by Miguel and Stone.
The others fanned out with no particular brief. As well as child beggars, there was a good chance of finding street prostitutes, so they kept a radio link with Barbara.
They were also on the lookout for anything that could be connected with the former PIDE Portuguese mafia.

The market was publicised as being car free. But it was not: moped, donkey, barrow or bicycle free. All of which displayed as little road sense as the Moroccan drivers.
"Blooming heck Skull lad", said Jonah as he moved one way to dodge a donkey cart, but stepped straight in the path of two bicycles. "You need eyes in the back of your head lad".
"You certainly do Jonah", said Skull as he stepped over a pile of donkey dung. "Extra eyes would be useful, but I could manage without an extra nose, it prongs a bit".

The bustling medina was the busiest place many of the Watchers had ever been. Almost anything could be bought at the hundreds of stalls, from traditional Moroccan items to modern electrical goods.
Between the rows of stalls darted a multitude of touts and guides trying to sell their services to the Europeans. The Watchers politely engaged most of them in conversation, before dismissing them. If they were handing over money, they wanted to be sure of a return.
Eventually, Skull and Jonah were happy with a would-be guide who approached them. First they tested him out with

leading them to various items of food. Then they slipped in a request for beer, which they knew would not be sold openly in the market.

When the guide came through with providing a case of imported bottled beer, they knew they could turn the conversation to girls.

Skull and Jonah felt like stereotypical street drunks, drinking beer from inside paper bags and nibbling on the nuts and dried fruits they had bought. They did not need the beer, but wanted to play a role with their guide of footloose British tourists.

Their rouse was working, as the guide spoke freely, proud of his knowledge of Fez's black market and underworld. He claimed to be able to get almost anything: hashish, opium, girls, or boys. But very little was suggesting a connection to O Lobo, his contacts all seemed to be home grown. Eventually they had convinced him that they were not interested in local girls and would only pay for Europeans. The guide led them outside the market to a pizza restaurant. "There are white girls here" said the guide, but it does not open until evening. "They are not good people though. They do not tip the guides and they often hurt the girls".

Jonah tried to get more from the guide, but he seemed terrified of even being near the pizza place. The moment Skull had tipped him; the guide disappeared back into the throng of the medina.

Barbara and Trudy were having very little success finding English speakers amongst the many child beggars. Every turn was met with another child holding out their hand. But all were Moroccan and none spoke English, or admitted to doing so.

Just like with Skull's search for a guide, Barbara was starting to think her quest was hopeless, when an unlikely candidate appeared. A boy of about ten or eleven appeared from nowhere. He looked a particularly scruffy and almost malnourished Moroccan boy, but unlike any of the others, he spoke passable English. The boy was obviously at the point

that he was aspiring to progress from beggar to guide, so was desperate to demonstrate his language skills to the women.
Barbara let the boy lead them around the medina's points of interest. All the time keeping him talking about his family and life in Fez. Eventually she was able to steer the conversation to other children, asking if he had learned his English from playing with British children.
The boy, like many Moroccan's, had learned to speak English from watching television. This was obvious to Barbara from the American twang to his speech, but it gave her a hook with which to lead the conversation.
Their young guide was now quite high on their flattery and steady stream of small coins and was eager to continue pleasing the two western women.
There were sometimes young white girls in Fez. But they were never allowed out to play; the boy only saw them moving from big cars into hotels.

Barbara was starting to wonder if he was just talking about families visiting on holiday, but then the boy mentioned pizza. All the Watchers were wearing hidden ear pieces and Skull had already told her of being led outside the medina to the pizza restaurant.
Eagerly the young boy led Barbara and Trudy through the medina's entrance and to the same restaurant that Skull and Jonah had visited.
"Sometimes I see white girls on the roof terrace, hanging washing", he said. "Not often, but they always look sad. I try to wave, but they go back inside".
"Are there any there now?", asked Trudy, desperate for a lead to Lucy.
But the boy said it had been many weeks since he had last waved to a white girl, too early to have been Lucy, who was happily with her family in Pedralva then.

With two leads taking them to the pizza restaurant Skull called the team back together to plan.
Trudy was eager to see what their next move would be, but

Between Stone & A Hard Place

as she and Barbara headed for the meeting, something caught her eye.

"They said you could buy anything here", she said to Barbara. "Look, there's even a helmet and leather jacket. If they fit, it would be nice to ride with Nev instead of in the van".

It was Trudy's lucky day and the bike kit did fit, but Barbara added a note of caution. "Don't take the guys for granted, they won't like it if they feel railroaded. Skull especially will need to feel like it's his decision ".

Keen for more European tipping, the three Mercedes taxis were waiting outside the medina for them. The Watchers had decided to return to the hotel and prepare for the pizza restaurant to open later in the evening.

The journey back was every bit as hair raising as their ride to the medina. But somehow it seemed to go quicker, as each of them ran possible scenarios through their heads.

Despite Skull Murphy's extrovert style as club president, the Watchers did operate as a democracy and all the members' opinions were considered. So steadily during the afternoon, their plan came together. Everyone's skills fitted somewhere; surveillance skills, soldiering, Barbara's NGO work and the plain upfront bravado of the MC members.

The big surprise came as Skull was allocating roles and turned to Trudy. She was expecting to be left at the hotel, but Skull asked "Trudy, it could be dangerous, but will you ride in the van for this one? I'm worried we might have need of a nurse". It was the first sign that Skull was starting to accept her and she readily agreed. Trudy was pleased that she had a useful part to play, but hoped her skills would not be needed in treating any of her friends.

Shortly after opening time, Skull, Stone and John Prince walked into the
pizza restaurant. They played heavily on the stereotype of English males abroad; loud, extrovert and drunk, flashing money around. Although in reality they were far from drunk and ready to go into action.

Between Stone & A Hard Place

The three were seated on cushions at a typically Moroccan low table and ordered pizza.
They made a loud fuss about not being able to order beer, as was the case in most restaurants in the Muslim country. Although in their heads they laughed at the irony of being able to buy sex, but not alcohol. By the time their pizzas arrived the establishment's secondary function had become obvious, as several men had been met on the stairs by attractive young women.

Playing his part like an actor, Stone convinced the proprietor that he too wanted a woman to celebrate his birthday. The plan was for Stone to learn the layout upstairs and anything he could from the girl, and then if they could not get Barbara in, change his mind, pay her and leave.
He had asked for a white girl and had been promised a very special one. "Very new, just come from Europe", the tough looking proprietor had told him. This sounded promising to Stone, as it potentially confirmed the East European connection.
To whoops and cheers from Skull and Prince, Stone was led up the stairs by an attractive looking girl with blond hair and Slavic features.
Feigning unsteadiness, Stone was able to plant two tiny cameras in the upstairs corridor. Then, suddenly needing the toilet, he was able to radio Jonah in the van to describe the layout. Most importantly, on the way back to their room, he managed to unlatch a window overlooking an adjacent flat roof.

Steve Butler and Kenton Simms were next to play their parts. The former Royal Marine and Paratrooper slipped up the alleyway alongside the restaurant and swiftly climbed a lamppost onto the flat roof. Once there they uncoiled two wire caving ladders, letting them drop, almost silently into the alley.
With a tiny monitor picking up the feed from Stone's cameras, they opened the window and slipped inside.
Using a tiny fibre optic camera, they checked through each

keyhole of the six doors along the corridor. Stone was in one with his girl. Three others were in use by the men who were led up before Stone. The other rooms were empty and there was no sign of the children they hoped to find.
"Ok, bring her up", said Butler into his radio. Miguel and Barbara Cuba ran to the wire ladders and quickly climbed to the roof.
Drawing on their military experience, Butler and Simms took up protective positions in the corridor while Miguel Cuba brought Barbara in through the window and into the room with Stone and the girl.
Barbara was wearing clothes suitable for the climb, but she had put on her nun's head dress as she entered the building. Despite Barbara's obvious religious regalia, the girl still looked terrified, covering her underwear with a towel and backing into a corner.
"Please don't be afraid", said Stone. "None of us are going to hurt you, you'll be paid and we'll be gone before my hour is up. This is Sister Barbara; she just wants to talk to you".

Barbara's years as a nun helped her calm the girl's fears and get her talking. Like many other women, she had travelled from Bulgaria on the promise of a job, but ended up selling sex to pay off the traffickers.
She also told Barbara about the younger girls. "Sometimes they are kept here to clean. We look after them because the men cannot come near them. They are promised to others and must be pure. I feel so sad for them".
Where would they take the young girls?', asked Barbara.
"Maybe Marrakech", replied the girl. I came first to a factory there. Those who are not so pretty, or are not healthy, work their debt in the factory".

They got no more from the girl as their ear pieces came alive with a single word, "evacuate".
This was the cue from Jonah that someone was heading for the stairs and they had to be out of the window quickly.
Skull helped delay trouble by drunkenly starting up the stairs looking for a toilet. So the proprietors had to deal with him

before themselves heading upstairs.
This gave Butler, Simms and Miguel time to get Barbara through the window and back down the wire ladders.

"Thank you", said Stone to the girl as he kissed her on the forehead and handed her the fee. "Don't worry, I'll tell them you were fantastic", he said as he headed for the stairs, stripping out the cameras as he walked.
Stone continued to play his role as he left with Skull and Prince. The three men playing the obnoxious tourists, slapping each other's backs and shouting lewd comments. As soon as they were clear, they ran for Jonah's van which would speed them away to safety.
"I'm glad I wasn't needed to nurse", said Trudy.
"Me too", replied Skull, "but thanks for being here".

Between Stone & A Hard Place

Chapter 22

Next morning the Watchers checked out of their hotel for what would be the longest day's ride of the trip.
They knew it would be a long ride, but would pass through some spectacular scenery and were looking forward to the ride.
Their 350 mile route skirted the edge of the Atlas Mountains, running along twisting roads into the foothills, before dropping towards Marrakech.
Marrakech was Prince and Simms adopted home town, where they provided protection for a rich English factory owner. They knew the route well and had spent the previous evening telling the others what they could look forward to. Although they did not know quite how many surprises they had in store as the day went on.

Prince and Simms thought they had seen the wolf's paw logo on a factory near the one at which they provided security. But the information from the pizza house brothel was making a link to O lobo's people trafficking operation much more likely. It made Marrakech an essential next stop in their hunt for Lucy.

Trudy had been worried about how to convince Skull to let her use the new bike kit and ride with them. But after the way she had involved herself in the last few day's operations, Skull was warming to her and beginning to respect her. He quite easily conceded to her riding pillion with Stone.
Trudy sat behind Stone, holding him tightly as she had not been on a motorcycle since a teenage date many years ago. Stone was a much more skilled rider than Trudy's teenage boyfriend, but it would still take her a little time to relax and enjoy the ride.

Stone was enjoying having Trudy holding him so tightly. Jonah was also secretly enjoying being alone in the van. Trudy was good company, but he did not share her modern

Between Stone & A Hard Place

taste in music and the old detective was now singing along loudly to his easy listening crooners.
"Can't beat a bit of Sinatra lad", he said to no one in particular, as he was alone in the van.

"This is fun", shouted Trudy, as they sped through the unearthly red landscape. It was fun; all the Watchers were enjoying the twisting roads and almost surreal landscape. The Triumph Bonneville Scrambler has a small saddle, but Trudy's slim frame fitted well behind Stone, who was actually quite pleased about Trudy's enforced closeness to him. Morocco's towns and cities were absolute chaos, but out here in the twisting mountain roads the traffic was much thinner. Despite the desperate need for Stone and Trudy to find Lucy, they were both managing to relax and enjoy sharing the exhilarating ride through a stunning landscape.

Everywhere the bikers went they attracted attention. Lorry drivers still tried to wave them past to look at their bikes, but after what happened before, they became much more cautious about drivers waving them through.
In every village they rode through the sound of the bikes brought out crowds of locals to see what was making the loud noise. Some of the villagers just stood and stared at a sight they had never seen before. Often they would wave to the bikers, with their children running well beyond the village limits to keep sight of the bikes for as long as they could. Then as they entered one remote mountain village, something very unexpected happened. A group of teenage boys were playing at the edge of the village, which had been the case for most of the villages they had passed through. The bikers were getting ready to wave at the boys, when suddenly a barrage of small stones began to fly at them from the group of boys. None of the stones were big enough to hurt, but they came as a surprise and were irritating the riders to the point of anger.
The helmet radios came to life with comments such as "I'm going to kill them" and bloody hell, what's this all about".
Before anyone could jump into any independent action

against the youngsters, Skull cut in with a voice of reason, "we can't beat up kids and they're not really hurting us. Just speed up and get the hell out of here".

So the Watchers gunned their bikes and sped out the other end of the small village. As they rode away, the gaggle of teenagers chased after them jeering and waving as they went.

"What happened there?" asked Stone. It was the local member Kenton Simms who provided the answer, "it's a game they play to round up goats. They just won't have seen a big group of bikes before; we're a long way from town out here".

The Watchers rode on chuckling from their encounter with the teenagers. "Let's hope that's the worst that Morocco can throw at us", said Stone, to a still grinning Trudy.

Their long ride continued in much the same way all day. Long periods of enjoyable riding through red mountain scenery, were interspersed with incidents which ranged from the unusual to outright bizarre.

Despite the light traffic, accidents were common due to the decrepit vehicles and appalling driving standards. The worst places were the remote cross roads, where the routes from valleys on either side of the mountains crossed without any form of traffic control. Tired drivers would have driven without seeing a junction for miles on end, then continued to cruise through the cross roads. It was a lottery as to whether another driver was doing the same thing on the joining road. If luck was against them, a crash occurred and the only route through the mountains was blocked for everyone else.

With many years of motorcycling experience between them, the Watchers had encountered most road hazards, but they were about to experience a new one as they tried to pass another lorry crash.

The two lorries had hit each other trying to cross the junction at the same time. Cars would have difficulty getting by, but there was plenty of space for their bikes. As well as avoiding the lorries, they also had to avoid the obstacles of dozens of plastic barrels rolling across the junction.

Between Stone & A Hard Place

Then suddenly, as they picked their way through the barrels, they found themselves riding on ice, but there was no way it could be ice in the searing Moroccan heat. The English Watchers had encountered black ice back home and were reacting accordingly. But the Portuguese had rarely seen snow, let alone ridden on ice, so their legs were flailing out as outriggers, trying to stabilise the bikes.

Somehow everyone stayed upright and the group pulled over to recompose themselves. It did not take long to work out what had happened. One of the crashed lorries had been carrying a cargo of vegetable oil, which was in the plastic barrels thrown loose across the junction and was now flowing across the road.

Very few of the health conscious Watchers were smokers, but those that did smoke soon lit up. Most of the others briefly wished that they did. Oddly, Trudy, who was new to motorcycling had taken it in her stride as part of the adventure and was still buzzing from the experience. Stone had expected the experience to put her off, but she seemed more eager than ever to climb back on behind him.

Once they had calmed their nerves and then stopped laughing at the ridiculous situation, the Watchers helped clear the junction to bring Jonah's van through.

They were soon back on their bikes and riding through the mountains towards the next adventure on this, the most interesting ride of their trip so far.

"What can happen next?" asked Stone, to no one in particular. It was Trudy who answered him, "whatever it is, bring it on. This is great".

Eventually they dropped out of the mountains and onto the main road towards Marrakech and the traffic rapidly became busier. Crashes became more frequent and the bikers had to concentrate hard on staying safe.

Entering the 60 kilometre per hour speed limit at the edge of town gave the Royal Moroccan Gendarmerie an opportunity to boost their meagre salaries.

Prince and Simms had warned them of the random police

Between Stone & A Hard Place

road blocks, but this was the first time they had encountered one.
Police corruption was rife in Morocco. Road blocks like this, on the run in to cities were common. Unlike most countries, where you pay your speeding fine to the court, Moroccan police were able to impose on the spot fines, payable to them in cash,
The amount of the fine seemed to depend on the driver's attitude and weather or not you wanted a receipt.
All the Watchers had already loaded their driving licence wallets with cash in readiness for such road blocks.
The official fine seemed to be 300 Dirum. But no one paid that much, as their licences were pre loaded with 200 Dirum. It seemed a small price to pay for no red tape, as Stone could not afford too close scrutiny on his Nev Shaw identity. Pedro and Paulo De Costa's godfather was a talented forger, but Stone saw no sense in pushing his luck with the local police.

The Royal Moroccan Gendarmerie is a relatively young police force, formed in 1957 to replace the French Gendarmerie which previously looked after law and order in the former French colony.
Like its predecessor and the Portuguese GNR, the Royal Moroccan Gendarmerie is a branch of the military. As well as having investigative, public order and traffic divisions,
the Gendarmerie can also call on air and marine branches to support their operations.
Stone was pleased to see that it was a two man motorcycle unit which was staffing the road block. The Gendarmes stood proudly beside their gleaming 1200cc BMWs, which Stone knew neither officer earned enough to own anything similar in their off duty lives.
The usual bond between bikers would no doubt help the Watchers. They could be sure that the bike cops would be interested in other bikes, just like bike cops the world over. Stone knew the Gendarmes were usually friendly and chatty at their road blocks, as long as there was a bribe involved. Prince and Simms had told him of many occasions chatting

with the police about their bikes.
But Stone knew there could also be another side to the Royal Moroccan Gendarmerie. The Gendarmes came under the direct control of the Moroccan King, who, as a descendent of the Prophet Mohamed retained a significant amount of power in this Muslim country. Stone had seen news film of the Gendarmes putting down a demonstration against the King's spending plans with much more force than the British police would be allowed. They seemed not to worry about the news cameras as they set about the demonstrators with their batons.
Knowing all this, the Watchers rode carefully into the checkpoint and were falling over themselves to be polite and friendly.

With their licences checked and the 200 Dirum donations removed, the Watchers spent time admiring the Gendarmes' BMWs and flattering the officers on their shiny motorcycles. Everything was organised to keep attention away from Stone and Butler, neither of whom had legitimately entered the country.
The check went just as Prince and Simms had predicted. With a polite attitude and a small bribe there was rarely any problem from the Moroccan police and the Watchers were free to seek out their Marrakech hotel.

In Fez, their hotel had a secure fenced car park where they could safely leave their bikes. Here in Marrakech, the only available parking was on the street in front of the hotel. With the epidemic levels of petty crime in Morocco, the Watchers were very nervous about leaving their motorcycles unattended over night.
Morocco's black economy had an answer to this problem with security "associated" with the hotel. The Watchers had become split into several small groups by heavy traffic and arrived at the hotel a few minutes apart. As the first few bikes arrived at the hotel, several men dressed in blue overalls appeared, introducing themselves as the hotel's security.

Between Stone & A Hard Place

The security men were offering to make sure that nothing happened to the bikes, on payment of a fee. The men represented both daytime and night time security and both sets of men were asking for their own fee. Or rather, they were not asking. The message was delivered in such a way that you could expect something to happen to your motorcycle if no payment was made.

"This is just a protection racket", thought Stone. "We'll see how long they keep it up when the guys arrive".

Their sales pitch began in a very intimidating tone, as their numbers were larger than the small group of Watchers who initially arrived. But as more bikes steadily pulled up, the security men began to become much more polite.

Barbara and Trudy were among the first to arrive, along with Stone and Butler, who while being fit men, were not physically large. The security seemed much braver with the women and smaller men, but the bikers who followed became progressively bigger. Skull Murphy was a big imposing body builder whose appearance frightened most men. Former paratroopers Prince and Simms were both tall heftily built men.

The security men's courage finally evaporated when the last of the bikes pulled up. The Lagos Watchers' Sergeant at Arms, Jaoa Alva, was a giant of a man. All heads turned towards him as he approached the apparent leader of the security men.

Alva put his huge arm around the shoulder of the much smaller Moroccan and said, "tell you what. We'll pay you, in the morning, with a bonus, if the bikes are undamaged". The Moroccan seemed to relax a little, until Alva continued, "I'm making you personally responsible for our bikes. Anything happens to them and I'll find you and rip you apart". "How's that for a deal?" he asked as the security guard began nodding so fiercely they thought his head might fall off.

Between Stone & A Hard Place

Chapter 23

The Watchers' Marrakech hotel was a good one, with comfortable rooms, a nice bar and a swimming pool. So the group all spent a fairly relaxed evening recovering from their long ride and planning the next stage in the search for Lucy. All were agreed that the factory identified by Prince and Simms was the best lead they had and that little could be done until their local members had made their initial enquiries.
Most of the bikers were planning to use the morning checking over their bikes and exercising around the pool. But Trudy and Barbara were keen to explore everything the UNESCO listed city had to offer, so Stone and Miguel Cuba agreed to ride out with them into the old parts of the city. Marrakech is Morocco's third largest city, but is arguably the most interesting. Its fortified Jemaa el Fnaa square is possibly Africa's most famous historic square and is the main reason for UNESCO listing the area as a World Heritage. The whole area is surrounded by well kept mosques, palaces, parade grounds and a vast array of shops and markets. Despite letting Trudy and Barbara think they were doing the girls a favour, Stone and Miguel were actually looking forward to a few hours of sight seeing.

They headed out to the street where their bikes were parked and found Joao Alva's new best friend still personally guarding their motorcycles. The giant Sergeant at Arms had so frightened the Moroccan, that he had clearly not slept for fear that anything should happen to the bikes.
The payment the security man had initially demanded was small by European standards. He had wanted two Dirum per bike, or less than two pounds. The Watchers had always been prepared to pay more to protect their bikes, but would not yield to intimidation. Now their point had been made and the bikes looked after well, Stone handed over five Dirum for each of the eight bikes the Moroccan had been watching over.
The man instantly became the most grateful person Stone

Between Stone & A Hard Place

had ever seen and his services were guaranteed for the remainder of the Watchers stay in Marrakech.

After paying the security guard and paying suitable attention to his extended gratitude, the four of them stood by their bikes discussing which of the historic sites they should visit first.
Stone was vaguely aware of a noisy scooter approaching from his left, but badly ridden mopeds had become so common in Morocco that he paid it very little attention.
But the approaching scooter should have warranted the attention that it was not getting from the bikers. The scruffy scooter with its two young riders was not following the main flow of traffic, it was veering off towards them.
The first they knew that something was amiss was when the scooter drew alongside them and the passenger's arm shot out towards Barbara.
"My chain", shouted Barbara. "He's got my chain".
Being a nun, Barbara wore very little jewellery, but she did have a chain and crucifix that her brother Miguel had bought her many years ago.
The scooter shot off along the pavement, avoiding the heavy traffic on the road past the hotel. Stone tried to give chase on foot but was not quick enough.
Miguel had gone straight for his bike though and was soon tearing off after the scooter.
Stone had very quickly back tracked to his motorcycle and was pushing it hard to catch up with Miguel.
Their Triumph Bonneville Scramblers had 900cc engines, so were infinitely more powerful than the small scooter. But the scooter's lighter weight and the rider's local knowledge were giving the thieves an early advantage.
Also to their advantage was a lack of concern for anyone or anything that got in the way of their escape. Miguel and Stone were being much more careful about the pedestrians they were riding through, as they forced their way along the footpath.

Soon the density of pedestrians became too great even for

Between Stone & A Hard Place

the scooter riding thieves and they shot out into the traffic, to a cacophony of car horns and screeching brakes.

Miguel and Stone were now much more comfortable. Forcing their way through traffic was something they had both done regularly in cities across Europe. They were also much less worried about damaging one of Morocco's decrepit cars than they were about injuring a pedestrian, so gradually, meter by meter they began to gain on the scooter. Soon it became clear the scooter riding thieves were heading towards the old part of Marrakech, the streets were getting narrower and more congested and the buildings older and more interesting. Not that they had much opportunity to look at the buildings as they skilfully pushed their Triumphs through the crowded streets after the scooter.

Riding deeper into the old town, it became even more difficult to make any progress. Neither the scooter nor the Triumphs had any real advantage in the crowded streets as they weaved their way through the slow moving traffic. Car horns around them sounded constantly as the bikes cut close to the cars, or on many occasions scraped alongside them in the narrow streets.

Before long, they reached the part of Marrakech with a high density of mosques. This just increased the number of pedestrians milling around the cars, trying to cross from one side or the other. Initially the scooter riding thieves were showing little concern for the pedestrians and continued to push recklessly through them. Stone and Miguel were by now also using their horns constantly, along with lots of shouting to clear a route through the crowds.

Eventually the chase came within sight of the historic Jemaa el Fnaa Square and the narrow crowded streets became too much even for the thieves. They abandoned the scooter and ran for the square, hoping to lose themselves in the hubbub of tourists, merchants and street entertainers.

Like most of the Watchers, Stone and Miguel ran and worked out regularly to stay in shape for the security aspects of the MC's businesses. Although the fully patched members were all company directors, most remained hands on with

Between Stone & A Hard Place

the work they enjoyed.

The bad news for the thieves was that, despite the age difference, their only advantage over the older men was in local knowledge.

The two young thieves darted in and out of the stall holders and the multitude of other entertainers and street hawkers. They came close to failure as one of them tried to hurdle a basket, only to find its resident snake charmer's pet unhappy at the interruption. The snake lunged towards the passing leg, missing him by millimetres.

Stone and Miguel had enough warning to dodge around the snake charmers pitch, but lost valuable distance in doing so.

They saw the young men dart into an alleyway off the main Street. Stone had studied the tourist guide book and knew they could easily lose them in the maze of intrinsically linked alleys full of stalls and street sellers. So they pushed hard to pick up their pace and close the gap.

"Where are they now?", shouted Miguel as they momentarily lost sight of the thieves in the crowd. After catching his breath and studying the crowd, Stone replied "there, going into that shop". He had seen the two young men dart out of the crowd and into one of the many scruffy shop fronts along the broad alley.

"Doesn't look too big a shop to find them in", said Miguel, heading for the shop doorway.

Once inside, what appeared to be a tiny, scruffy shop, morphed into an Aladdin's cave. The shop seemed to go back for miles and was packed to bursting with rugs, baskets and all manner of Moroccan craft work.

Stone and Miguel worked methodically through the overstocked shop searching for the two thieves. There was plenty for them to hide behind, but it was a narrow shop which did not appear to have another exit, so the bikers were confident of finding them.

Then Miguel saw movement towards the rear of the shop. "There", he shouted, pointing towards a barely visible door in the back wall. The two thieves were trying to move stealthily from behind a display of rugs towards the door. But Miguel

Between Stone & A Hard Place

Cuba's sharp eyes had caught them.
Alerted by Miguel's shout, the thieves gave up stealth and darted for the door. Stone and Miguel quickly went back into chase mode and ran after them into another alleyway crowded with entertainers. The four men chased through the maze of alleys, dodging the acrobats, monkey trainers and magicians as they ran. After their last brush with a snake, they were careful to give the snake charmers a particularly wide berth.

The young thieves were fit and should have had no difficulty outrunning the bikers. But Miguel had something else driving him on.
Throughout their years of boarding at the English monastery school, far away from their native Portugal, Miguel and Barbara had become very close. Then, after losing his faith, all that Miguel had left, was his sister and the siblings grew closer still.
Now, these young Moroccans had attacked his sister and worse, stolen a gift from him which he knew Barbara held dear.
With temper and hate driving his adrenalin surge, Miguel charged down the alley like an out of control bull. He was soon on the two men and went straight for the passenger who had taken Barbara's crucifix.
The man cried out, momentarily distracting his partner in crime. This gave Stone just enough advantage to catch him too.
Stone had taken his man to the ground and was trying to decide exactly what to do with him, when he heard screams of agony and what he assumed to be pleas for mercy behind him. Miguel had completely lost control and looked to be in the process of beating the young man to death.
Stone knew that they could not have a death on their hands, so hitting his own man hard to incapacitate him; Stone turned his attention to Miguel.
"That's enough Miguel! Get the chain and let's go. We can't be caught here".
It took Stone some effort to pull his friend away from the

thief, but eventually he managed to calm Miguel down.
The man was hurt badly, but would survive and eventually heal. "Let's find the scooter and make sure they never use it again", added Stone.
So they retraced their route to where they had left their own Triumphs and the scooter abandoned.
"That's poetry", said Miguel. He saw the scooter was no longer there and realised that what must have been the thieves' most valuable possession had been stolen.

Before the Gendarmes could arrive and ask too many questions, Stone and Miguel mounted up and rode back towards their hotel. This time, as they rode past the historic buildings and beautifully kept mosques, they were able to enjoy the ride and take in the scenery.

Back at the hotel, Barbara Cuba was beside herself with worry for her brother. It took all of Trudy Varley and Joao Alva's persuasion to stop her joining in the chase. Eventually she accepted they had too big a head start and she would have risked too much in giving chase. But the waiting just gave Barbara time to worry for Miguel's safety.
Trudy too was worried, but for Stone more than Miguel. She was becoming close to Nev Stone, but had to work hard in concealing it from the other bikers. It had been difficult gaining their confidence and they were risking everything to find her daughter. She did not want to do anything which would damage their commitment to finding Lucy.

Barbara and Trudy were overjoyed to see Stone and Miguel pull their motorcycles up outside the hotel. Barbara's relief at seeing her brother unharmed, multiplied when Miguel returned the crucifix and chain that she had worn for over 20 years.
"I thought I would never see it again and you saved so hard to buy it for me when I took my holy orders." "Thank you my brother", she said burying herself in her brother's arms.

The security men who Stone had earlier paid were still falling

Between Stone & A Hard Place

over themselves to be helpful to the bikers. They had been paid well for their services by local standards. But they were also relieved that the giant Joao Alva was not going to harm them.

They were now offering to clean the bikes while they watched over them. Stone found it difficult to explain through the language barrier that no one should touch their bikes, even to clean them. All the Watchers took great pride in their motorcycles. The Triumph Scramblers may have only been loan bikes, but they did belong to another Watchers chapter and the Lagos chapter were responsible for their care. The bikers planned to use some of the morning cleaning their bikes and attending to routine maintenance anyway.

John Prince and Kenton Simms were still away checking out the factory outside Marrakech, which they suspected was owned by Carlos Lobo. This was by far their best lead and they needed much more information about the layout, security and routine of the factory and its staff.

Until Prince and Simms returned, there was little the other members of the team could do, so once they had attended to their motorcycles, all took advantage of the hotel pool to work out and top up their tans.

With the theft incident so easily dealt with, the rest of the morning became something of a relaxing idyll within a serious mission. But the bikers' peaceful morning was soon to be disturbed.

Between Stone & A Hard Place

Chapter 24

O Lobo's henchmen, who had got it so terribly wrong with Ferko Mordecai, had not been idle. Their lives depended on them bringing Nev Stone to their boss as penance for causing him to torture the Roma.
Carlos Lobo's organised crime network was based on the former PIDE Portuguese spy network, so it remained an efficient intelligence gathering organisation.
His men were using all their contacts to track down Stone and although he had himself dropped off the radar, Skull and the others were legitimately in Morocco and so could be traced.
Stone had completely dropped out of sight of the gangsters' informants in Portugal. That meant he was either under effective house arrest, or had somehow left the country. The gangsters were beginning to lose hope of finding Stone before O Lobo's patience with them ran out, when a border guard at Spain's Algeciras Port reported the group of Watchers boarding the Morocco ferry.
This had to be the answer to Stone's disappearance. Somehow Stone must have avoided immigration formalities and must be in Morocco with the other bikers.
O Lobo did not have as extensive a network in Morocco, but his organisation was gaining a foot hold with their factories, brothels and hashish dealing.
His men had also been passing out bribes in their search for Stone. They usually found that most people had a price and in Morocco that price was cheep.

The hotel's security guard came hurriedly to the Watchers, gathered around the pool. "They offered money to know about you", said the guard. "More money than you paid, but you have been good to us and we must please Mr Alva", he said, obviously still in awe of the giant Sergeant at Arms. Stone eventually got out of the guard that men from the big factory had been asking questions at all the hotels about the bikers. His men had said very little, but the motorcycles could not be more obvious parked on the road outside their

Between Stone & A Hard Place

hotel.
"Ok", said Skull, briefing his group. "Joao and Butler on watch. Everyone else pack, and quickly, we're on the move!"

When the gangsters did arrive, they were few in numbers, but they carried pistols, and guns will often make cowardly men brave. They also took courage from knowing the Watchers had come through customs and the border guards' search found no weapons.
The two men who had messed up with Ferko Mordecai arrived with three Bulgarian thugs from O Lobo's factory. All five carried Russian made pistols under their shirts. Even with the easily bribed Royal Moroccan Gendarmerie the gangsters could not risk openly carrying larger weapons.

Alva and Butler had both taken up discrete positions to watch the hotel's two entrances. The gangsters were trying to enter discreetly by using the pool entrance, but had failed in their efforts at stealth by walking in together as a group. It was their unusual grouping of two Portuguese and three Slavic men together that made them look out of place.
Butler was the first to spot them and his years of counter terrorism work in Northern Ireland gave him a keen eye for trouble. An eye which spotted without difficulty the tell tale bulge at each man's waistband.
"Five men, pool entrance", said Butler into his throat mic. "Two Iberian, three East European. Look to have side arms in waistbands, covered by shirt tails".
Joao Alva added his observations "front entrance clear. The hotel guys still have our bikes secure".

On hearing the radio messages, Skull started to calculate the odds. Prince and Simms were too far away to get back to the hotel quickly. With himself, Stone, Alva, Butler and Miguel, Skull had five fighters. Barbara, Trudy and Jonah were not fighters, but they all had other skills which helped tip the odds in the Watchers' favour.
Skull instantly moved into tactical mode and started to issue instructions through his radio and the team were now so

Between Stone & A Hard Place

used to working together that they went seamlessly into action.

"Cameras down lad", reported Jonah as he pulled the power cable from the CCTV recorder. The last thing the Watchers wanted was evidence of their involvement in a gunfight. Shooting seemed inevitable in a confrontation with O Lobo's men.

"Portuguese registered Merc won't be going far ", said Barbara as she pulled her pocket knife from the last of the Mercedes' tyres. Causing such damage did not sit comfortably for the catholic nun, but she knew that stopping the gangsters following could save their lives.

Trudy had pulled the van around to their rooms and Jonah was hurriedly throwing kit bags through bedroom windows towards the van. When they had dealt with the gangsters, Skull wanted to get well away from the hotel. Jonah's van would move more slowly than the bikes so he needed to be ready to roll.

All that was left was for the rest of the team to incapacitate the gangsters.

Stone, Skull, Butler, Alva and Miguel had all hidden themselves around the hotel lobby and bar. Their plan was to catch the gangsters unawares. It was a safe bet that through bribes the gangsters knew the Watchers were in the hotel, but that did not mean they had to behave like sitting ducks.

The five gangsters moved across the hotel lobby with their pistols now in their hands. Hotel customers scattered to get clear of the obvious trouble that was about to start.

Steve Butler was chuckling to himself as he watched the gangsters' clumsy approach. "No real soldiers amongst this lot then", he thought to himself.

Apart from Stone's experience as an armed police officer, the former Royal Marine was the only Watcher present with military service. But he knew his fellow bikers would acquit themselves far better than their pursuers.

As the gangsters fanned out to search for the bikers, the Watchers went into action. The giant Joao Alva was the first to break cover, as one of the East Europeans passed him, Alva smashed a stool across his back, taking him out of the fight.

The noise of Alva's attack alerted the other gangsters, but they still could not see the hidden Watchers. All they could do was rush towards Alva's position, which took them all past Stone and Skull's positions.

Two more of the gangsters were dispatched by Stone and Skull, using the same bar stool technique Alva had used so successfully.

"The odds are looking better now" said Skull as he checked the two men they had just knocked out.

The odds were better, but the two men left were the Portuguese gangsters who had the most to lose. They were effectively under a death sentence from O Lobo if they failed to bring in Nev Stone. They knew Carlos Lobo would make sure it was a painful death, so they were prepared to risk everything for success.

The men ran towards Stone and Skull's position, firing their pistols indiscriminately as they ran, hitting several innocent customers in their desperation to kill the bikers.

Stone, Skull and Alva were now all pinned down and vulnerable as they had no guns. This was the situation the gangsters had envisaged, believing the Watchers were unprepared and had no weapons. But the gangsters had not taken account of Butler and Miguel, who had yet to show themselves. Neither had they taken account of Butler's illegal entry to Morocco.

They were counting on the Watchers being unable to sneak weapons through immigration, but Butler and Stone had swum ashore with two spear guns and a shotgun. Miguel and Butler were now making their way towards the gangsters, with these weapons in their hands.

Miguel Cuba sent a meter long metal spear flying towards the gangsters, propelled by its compressed air charge. But these are not the most accurate of weapons and his spear embedded itself in an indoor palm tree. It did fly close enough to the gangster to spook him and send him diving to

the floor.
Miguel quickly followed up with a shot from the last of his two spear guns, which this time pierced the man's thigh, starting him screaming in agony.

It had been a long time since Stone had been in this type of situation. But that had all been with the police, on the right side of the law. The atmosphere was much more tense in the hotel lobby. Morocco's heat was bad enough to bear, but add in the panic of hotel staff and guests, and this was all very new to Stone,

The remaining man was handling himself much better, shooting accurately and reloading his pistol efficiently. The shots kept Miguel pinned down as the gangster approached his speared colleague. Soon the two men were back together and although one of them was in pain, there were now two pistols firing towards the Watchers' positions.

The bikers had no idea if the gangsters had any reinforcements close by, or how quickly the police could respond, so they needed to get away from the hotel.
It was now Butler's turn to go into action. He would have been more accurate than Miguel with the spear guns, but he was also the most proficient with a shotgun. When Ricardo De Sa's men raided their Lagos clubhouse, Butler had proven that he could load and discharge a double barrelled shotgun faster than most people could use a pump action. Butler was again displaying his commando expertise by sending a constant hail of shot over the Portuguese gangsters' heads.
The covering fire allowed the other four bikers to sprint for their bikes. By the time Butler joined them, firing and reloading as he walked, Stone had Butler's bike running for him and ready for the off.
As the five Triumphs turned the corner at the end of the street, their convoy was joined by Barbara Cuba on her Scrambler and Jonah and Trudy in the van.

Between Stone & A Hard Place

"Where to Skull lad?", asked Jonah through their radios.
In the same way he automatically did for most eventualities, Skull had run all the available options through his mind and come up with a plan.
"Prince and Simms have a place this side of the Tizi n Test Pass. They showed it me on the map last night and it should be remote enough to be safe", replied Skull as he described the local members' house.
Barbara's work on the gangsters' tyres had given the Watchers enough of a head start to hide their direction of travel, although there were limited options they could have used.

The six Triumphs and the van changed to lower gears as they started their steep and twisting climb towards the Tizi n Test Pass.
As they climbed towards the pass the road became steeper and more twisty, with the road surface deteriorating the higher they climbed.
Hairpin bends always carried the risk of a Moroccan driver speeding round the corner on your side of the road. The poor diving would force motorcycles towards the broken edge of the road and into further danger from the steep drop. On most occasions the Watchers would have reacted by leaving a boot sized dent in the car door, but here, faced with vertical rock walls and sheer drops, the bikers concentrated on staying safe.
Occasionally Stone had chance to look back on the winding ribbon of road they had just ridden. "Beautiful", he thought to himself. "No wonder Prince and Simms have settled up here".
Confident that they were not being pursued into the mountains, the Watchers stopped at one of the many viewpoints they passed on their way up the mountain. Skull wanted a chance to take in the view, but also more importantly to check the area around them through powerful binoculars. Marrakech had now become a much more dangerous place for the MC and Skull was taking no chances.

Between Stone & A Hard Place

Trudy took advantage of the stop for her own purposes. She could not get out of the van fast enough, putting on her helmet and leather jacket as she went. Trudy was no longer sure which was the greater attraction, the motorcycle or Nev Stone. She was fast becoming very attracted to both and wasted no opportunity in climbing onto Stone's pillion seat and wrapping her arms around him.

It was not just the beauty of this mountain road which had attracted Prince and Simms, as Stone would quickly appreciate when they reached the house.
The Moroccan based Watchers were constantly aware of the danger in the protection work they had chosen. Crime rates were high in parts of Morocco and life was often cheap. When they factored in the rising problem of former Soviet Union criminal money fuelling the black economy, they saw the value of a defensible bolt hole in the mountains. The former soldiers both appreciated the military significance of holding high ground.
Prince and Simms' home was perched on the apex of a particularly tight hairpin bend. This gave it the protection of vertical drops on three sides. The fourth side had a high wall, built to look like an ornamental castle wall, but Stone knew the castellation and slits in the wall had a defensive as well as ornamental purpose.
Stone looked back at the road in both directions. "Clever", he thought, "the high point of the bend gives a view in both directions". They would see anyone approaching from either side of the pass.
Stone was moving towards the large double gates when Skull shouted out, "hold it Nev! The guys have some pretty gruesome security". The former paratroopers, John Prince and Kenton Simms had rigged a series of trip wires and booby traps around their house and gardens in the same way that they protected their battle ground positions when in the army.

Right on cue as Skull finished telling Stone about the booby traps, Prince and Simms rode up on their battered Honda

Between Stone & A Hard Place

Transalp motorcycles. Slowly and carefully they demonstrated their improvised security measures to the other Watchers.

"We're only here body guarding, so haven't got the MC's technical back up", explained Prince. "But you can't beat a bit of British Army improvisation", added Simms.

They carefully unhooked the series of trip wires one by one. The first sets of wires were only attached to pyrotechnics and flash bangs, intended only to deter intruders.

Triggering one of their flash bangs would create a lot of flash, noise and smoke, but would not cause injury. But the further an intruder pushed into their property, the more dangerous the explosives and fragmentation devices became. Their rationale being that anyone coming through that amount of noise and smoke meant business and needed treating as a serious threat.

The most dangerous of the explosive mines were packed with shrapnel which would maim and probably kill any intruder triggering the device.

Prince and Simms took time over demonstrating their security measures, not just through pride, but to make sure his friends would not be harmed by any of the booby traps. Once their macabre tour was over, the Watchers settled around the large kitchen table to agree their next actions in the search for Lucy.

Between Stone & A Hard Place

Chapter 25

Prince and Simms had been keeping a careful watch on the factory next to theirs. They had also been making discrete enquiries through their own employers and a network of contacts they had cultivated since arriving in Morocco.
They were now as sure as they could be that the factory was part of Carlos Lobo's criminal empire. Everyone of any significant importance at the factory was Portuguese and O Lobo's wolf paw logo was discretely displayed on most of the buildings and vehicles.
The next group of any significance were Eastern European, this group seemed to comprise all of the security and enforcers.
Everything they had seen and heard was pointing towards it being a partnership between Carlos Lobo's former PIDE network and Georgi Dimov's former KGB gangsters. The Watchers had learned that this was a very dangerous partnership and they had to prepare carefully for any contact with them.

On the face of it, O Lobo's factory was a legitimate business. They produced a huge range of clothing for retail clients across Europe. The majority of the workers were legitimate employees, earning the bare minimum, but earning all the same. The employees were a mix of local Moroccans used to the low wages and young travelling Europeans, paying their way around the world
Prince and Simms' sources all agreed there was something not quite right with the factory, but no one could offer anything concrete.
There were rumours about prostitution and slavery, but rumours were all they could come up with.
"If Lobo is involved they will be more than rumour", said Skull.
"I agree", said Stone. "But what do we do about it? There is far too much security for any sort of attack".
As was becoming a bit of a pattern, Jonah, the old Detective Inspector came in with a voice of reason. "Softly softly

catchee monkey Nev lad! We do what we're good at, we watch, review, plan and then act".

Barbara Cuba suggested their next move. Throughout their search for Lucy, the nun had regularly displayed a streak of bravery every inch as wide as her biker brother and she was about to do it again.
"I'd like to get inside", said Barbara. If they are hiring European back packers as casual labour, I'm sure I could pass as one".
"No, it's too dangerous", said Miguel Cuba, always protective of his younger sister.
Barbara insisted that with their sophisticated radio and surveillance systems and the Watchers as back up, that she could pull it off. "Anyway, how else are we going to know what's happening inside?" she added.

Over the next day Prince and Simms worked with Barbara to find out how the factory hired their labour and secured Barbara an interview.
Stone and Jonah had easily dropped back into their old systems of work. They were conducting reconnaissance of the area around the factory looking for observation posts and stand by locations, should they need to extract Barbara in a hurry.
The rough, mountainous area was perfect for them to use the CROP techniques they learned as police surveillance operatives. Covert Rural Observation Post techniques involved moving invisibly through rural locations, using stealth and camouflage to observe a suspect.
The two former detectives had already planted several remote cameras around the factory compound. Each placement had taken an hour or more of crawling slowly around the factory, moving between bushes, rocks and other pieces of sparsely placed cover. But they were now satisfied they had the entire outside sufficiently covered.
With the cameras in place, Stone and Jonah were now exploring a hidden gully which seemed perfect to hide a small extraction team in case Barbara got into trouble. "Just

enough room for Prince's jeep and nicely out of sight from the road", said Stone.

"Aye Nev lad", replied Jonah. "We just need to come back at night to sabotage that fence. If we do it right they won't notice the work, but the jeep will crash through easily if needed".

Barbara started work in the factory the next day, packing finished garments into boxes for transport. The wages were a fraction of what similar work would pay in her native Portugal, but she earned a UN salary and would be unlikely to remain at the factory long enough to draw her wage.
To maintain her cover as an impoverished world traveller Barbara travelled to the factory by train. Miguel had dropped her off a few stops along the line so that she could arrive looking like any other worker.
Despite her cover story of being a traveller with limited resources, Barbara travelled first class on the train. Most Europeans did so, as it is cheep by European standards and second class was considered unpleasant and often dangerous.

The Eastern European thugs who ran most of the factory gave Barbara very little by way of a welcome; she was shown straight to a conveyor belt and told "pack, ten in a box!"
With that brief instruction the man moved off to a raised platform where Barbara could feel his eyes burning into the shape of her tight jeans.
As she packed, Barbara looked up and down the production line. A few people along she spotted a familiar face. "That's Tanja", thought Barbara.
She was too far away to speak to her, but Barbara was sure that it was one of the Bulgarian girls she had spoken to near Georgi Dimov's brothel in Faro.
Barbara had met Tanja and her friend Silvija outside a small cafe in Faro, waiting to start their evening selling their bodies in Dimov's club.
The girls were working off their trafficking debt to the former

Between Stone & A Hard Place

KGB gangsters, under threat to their families back home. So it made no sense at all to Barbara that Tanja should swap the lucrative sex trade for poorly paid factory work. She would be indebted to Dimov for much longer on the minimal factory wages.

Barbara got her opportunity of speaking to Tanja when her line broke for lunch. The two women found a patch outside in the sun where they could eat their sandwiches and talk without being over heard.
"I catch sickness from a man", said Tanja. She explained that she had caught an infection from having sex with a client at Dimov's club. While she was being treated she could not earn in the brothel, so had been moved to the factory in Marrakech.
Tanja knew that Barbara was a nun, so she would likely be at the factory to check it out. Barbara was confident she did not know about her links to the MC and their search for Lucy Varley.
"It is bad here", said Tanja. "Many girls come here first, before pretty ones are taken to work in clubs". She explained that the trafficked girls all slept at the factory in a dormitory block at the rear.
Before Tanja could tell Barbara much more, their short meal break was over and the women were back on the production line packing garments.
Over the next few days Barbara was moved around many of the factory's more menial jobs.
Like most nuns she had learned to sew, but not to the speed demanded by factory work. So she was limited to packing, moving items between processes and eventually onto cutting material from patterns.
Moving around jobs gave Barbara opportunity to learn the lay out of the factory and to plant some of the Watcher's cameras and bugs. But it also meant that opportunities for talking to Tanja were limited as they were often on different break times.

Each night Barbara caught the train away from the factory.

Between Stone & A Hard Place

The railway station was a horrible place, packed with young Moroccan men either paying unhealthy interest in the European girls, or intent on crime. Despite knowing the MC members were out of sight watching her, it was still an unpleasant experience and she hurried to catch the first train she could.
Three stops along the line Barbara would leave the train and be collected by her brother Miguel for the drive up the Tizi n Test Pass.
Back at Prince and Simm's house Barbara had opportunity to relax over a good meal before debriefing her day for the bikers.
Most of their trip had been spent in hotels, so this was the first time the Watchers had catered for themselves. Trudy defaulted to the kitchen as she did not have technical expertise, except of course her nursing skills, which she hoped not to need.
The surprise came in Steve Butler. You could expect a former Royal Marines Commando to be able to cook, but not to Butler's standard. He had grown into the hobby through long periods of standby on military bases. Bored with military catering he learned to make the best of the available local ingredients and produce something quite interesting for his squad.
Needless to say, the bikers were pleased to be served something tasty at the end of their long operational days.

Jonah as always defaulted to leading the briefing. He and Stone were both of the old school, preferring to display their investigation on the wall, rather than a computer screen. So Prince and Simm's dining room walls were now covered with photographs, diagrams and snippets of information.
Jonah turned to the plan of the factory, which had been growing daily as more information came from Barbara, her cameras and the surveillance teams.
"We're getting quite a picture Barbara lass. But what about this building here?" asked Jonah.
"I don't know", replied Barbara. "I've seen no one go in or out and it doesn't seem to feature in factory production".

Between Stone & A Hard Place

"It's always guarded", added Stone, who had been working surveillance on that side of the site. "There are always at least two guards on each side. I've checked the camera feeds and it's the same overnight. Whatever is there, they don't want visitors ".
"Anything from Tanja about it?" asked Skull.
The factory staff were worked so hard that Barbara had very little chance to get much information from Tanja.
"She either doesn't know, or won't say", replied Barbara. "The trafficked women all live in this block. Most of the guards live in this one. Pretty much everywhere else is involved in production, as I've worked in most of it. But no one seems to dare go near that side of the compound".

"Options?" asked Skull.
Stone had already been giving it some thought, as he knew they needed to fill such an obvious intelligence gap.
"I can't see us getting inside and the windows are high", said Stone. "But if I can get there, a vibration camera on the glass might work".
The Watchers always operated democratically, so this, like all suggestions was opened to the group.
"Thoughts?" asked Skull, "is it achievable to get through their security?"

Former paratrooper Kenton Simms provided the answer. "Prince and I can get him in at night. We know there are no sophisticated access denial devices outside the buildings. They rely on fences, guards and dogs. So it's nothing different to what we were doing in Iraq".
The former soldiers were suggesting a fairly standard Special Forces infiltration. The dogs would be drugged with prepared meat. Then, moving carefully to avoid search lights and guards, they would slip under the fence and across the compound.
"I'm game", said Stone. "These guys are experienced and I'm sure I can keep with their plan. We'd better vote it".
Any major decision for the MC had to have a majority agreement. With the confidence of those who were to put it

www.neilhallam.com

into practice and the lack of any viable alternative, Simms' plan got a unanimous vote".

The next few hours were a flurry of activity for the Watchers, preparing for their operation at the darkest point of the night. Stone, Prince and Simms had the greatest risk and needed to carefully prepare their equipment for entering the site and the stalk towards the building.

But it was the surveillance equipment which took the most preparation, as they were using some cutting edge technology for the first time.

Stone had first considered using the same laser equipment he used to eavesdrop on the footballer Sergio Silva at the Faro brothel. But examining the angles to the windows from outside the fence, he had to rule it out as impractical.

But in the weeks before Lucy was taken, Stone had been working with the Watchers technicians to replicate some cutting edge work by the Massachusetts Institute of Technology, or MIT.

The university's researchers had found a way of using high speed cameras to capture the vibration of objects inside a room, caused by speaking.

Our school day physics lessons taught us that sound is caused by vibration; a tuning fork is a good example. Normally those sound vibrations travel to our ears, where they are decoded into sound.

What the MIT researchers found was that by filming the movement of a vibrating object, a computer algorithm could be used to do the decoding and reproduce the sound which first caused the vibration.

The Watchers had pulled in a lot of favours in America to obtain a copy of the software program. The hardware they had to put together themselves. Tests in their workshop had been mostly successful, but this was the first time they would use the new technique in earnest.

Stone, Prince and Simms managed a few short hours sleep, or combat kip as they liked to call it. Then in the early hours,

Between Stone & A Hard Place

when the factory guards would be at their most tired, the Watchers set off to their individual tasks.
With the dogs out of action from meat laced with tranquillisers by Trudy and Butler, Stone and the two former paratroopers slipped through a gap they had cut in the fence.
High quality night vision goggles lit their way across the broken ground between fence and factory yard.
At regular intervals they had to lie motionless as searchlights and guards toured the grounds. But slowly and steadily they moved closer and closer to their target.
All the small building's windows were over six feet from the ground, so Stone used a short collapsible ladder to reach the window.

Prince and Simms stood watch while Stone positioned the small camera at the window. Stone needed something which would vibrate with sound waves from in the room. The MIT researchers used a potted plant; Stone spotted a Portuguese flag hanging on the wall which would do the same job.
With the tiny high speed camera in place, Stone started it transmitting and the three Watchers carefully retraced their steps to the fence.
"Clear", said Stone into his radio, indicating to Skull that their mission was a success.

Between Stone & A Hard Place

Chapter 26.

Even as Stone, Prince and Simms were making their way back to the house, Jonah was analysing the video feed from the camera.

Stone had been lucky with his choice of window. Of the dozen available to him, he had chosen one of the four windows overlooking the main living area of the unit. He had deliberately avoided the two frosted glass windows, which were useless to his camera. But that still left six windows which overlooked bedrooms and the kitchen where very little conversation would be captured.

But Stone had chosen well and as Jonah looked at the video, he knew that when daytime arrived there would be plenty of conversation to test their new equipment.

When daylight did arrive, Stone was asleep, recovering from the exertions of the night. But Skull and Trudy were with Jonah, eager for anything to appear on the video monitor. Their patience was rewarded as the first sunlight streamed through the high windows, lighting the inside of the room. Two women began to move about the room, tidying away books and magazines, straightening cushions and setting the table for breakfast.

"Four settings", said Jonah. "But I'm only seeing the two women so far. I hope we haven't just found two couple's living quarters".

Skull shared Jonah's concerns, but the MC President knew he had to stay positive for his team. "We'll soon know if two blokes turn up for breakfast", he replied. "Trudy, go and wake Nev would you. I'm sure he'll want to know what's happening".

Trudy was glad of the chance to wake Stone, because her feelings were growing ever stronger towards him as the mission went on. She knew what Stone had been through over night with Prince and Simms, so took care to wake him gently. Trudy took opportunity to place a kiss on Stone's cheek. Stone was barely awake and was not quite sure whether or not he had dreamed the kiss. But if it was a dream, he thought it was a pleasant one.

After quickly throwing on some clothes, Stone had joined the others around the video monitor before there was any more movement. The Watchers would very soon learn who the other two breakfast places were set for as the two women returned to the living area.
Following the women to the table were two young girls. Both appeared about ten years old. One looked Arab in appearance. But the other girl struck Stone with her similarity to Lucy Varley. Trudy's gasp made Stone turn towards her. From the look on Trudy's face Stone could tell that Lucy's mother had also seen the likeness in the young blond haired girl.
"Can it be coincidence that she looks like Lucy"? asked Trudy.
Stone moved closer to comfort Trudy, as she realised that it was not her daughter.
Jonah replied with his usual note of caution, "all part of the puzzle Trudy lass. Don't jump to conclusions; we need all the pieces before we see the picture lass".
Both Jonah and Stone did think it significant that the girls of Lucy's age, with one looking like her, were so well guarded. Throughout their search there had been rumours of kidnapped children and virgin brides. This was providing significant corroboration to that theory, but neither man was going to raise the mother's hopes until they had more to go on.

The events unfolding in the living unit seemed very much like normal family life. The two women seemed to be looking after the girls as they would their own children. After breakfast they left the living area, returning after having showered and dressed.
Then came a period of school work. Stone and Jonah had not yet worked with the sound recognition software, but the books, pens and note books needed no words for interpretation.
Skull was learning from Jonah's cautious approach to

theories and asked, "are they captive, or protected? We are seeing guards and security, but the girls seem well cared for".
"Either is possible Skull lad", replied Jonah. "We'll know more when Stone works his magic on the sound".
It took time for the MIT system to isolate speech from vibrations caught on the high speed video. While he was tidying up the images and running the software algorithm, he would not be able to watch the live feed. So Stone was delaying making a start until he had a better picture of what was happening inside the unit.
They watched the live images throughout the morning as the girls did their schoolwork and then started to help with chores around the living space and kitchen.

Stone tired of waiting for something to happen and went to work putting the MIT system into practice. He concentrated on snippets of footage throughout the morning's recording, to confirm what they thought they had watched.
The Portuguese flag on the wall was ideally placed to be vibrated by speech in the living area. The high speed footage from the camera worked perfectly, allowing the algorithm to reproduce clear speech from the film. But every snippet which Stone decoded, confirmed that the girls were simply doing lessons.
Stone selected a section where the women had moved into the kitchen to prepare lunch while the girls worked on their books. This would provide the best opportunity for some unguarded conversation between the women.
"I'm struggling with this", said Stone. "They're too far from the flag and facing away from it. All I'm getting is the girls counting".
Jonah sat with Stone as they replayed the video, trying to come up with a solution. "There Nev lad", said Jonah, pointing to an empty crisp packet on the work surface. "The MIT boffins used a crisp packet in one of their demonstrations. See if you can zoom in on that".
The empty packet was a long way from the camera and Stone knew that zooming in would reduce the image quality,

Between Stone & A Hard Place

so he took great care in manipulating the footage.
The MIT algorithm worked, interpreting the crisp packet's minute vibrations, which could be measured in fractions of millimetres. But it only worked in the sense that it reproduced sound, not understandable speech. Stone had more work to do with sophisticated audio software to try and recover what the women were saying to each other.

Eventually Stone's persistence paid off and fragments of conversation started to become clear.
"How can she want so much sugar?" asked one of the women.
"Sounds like the kid has a sweet tooth", observed Stone.
But then two women turned away from the work surface and the sound became too distorted to understand. Stone tried every audio technique he knew to clean up the speech, but could not make it understandable.
Then Trudy came up with something Stone and Jonah had missed. "Would that lamp shade work?" she asked, pointing at the ceiling lamp above the women's heads.
It was certainly worth a try and Stone again went through the process of isolating the right section of video and applying the algorithm. This time the shade was so close to the women that Stone had very little clean up to do of the resulting audio.
It was a very short snippet of conversation before the women again turned away, but it seemed significant. "Shame Carlos wanted the other girl for himself. This one looks like her, but has none of her personality. We'll get nowhere near as high price".
There was no audible reply as the women started to walk away from the kitchen, but what they had caught had excited everyone in the Watchers' team.
"They mean Lucy. They must do" exclaimed Trudy. No amount of caution from Jonah could curb Trudy's emotion at this being a concrete lead to her daughter. Here mind leapt between relief at a concrete lead, and terror at what O Lobo might be doing to Lucy.
"Trudy lass, even if they are talking about Lucy and Carlos

www.neilhallam.com

Between Stone & A Hard Place

Lobo does have her, all we know is that she isn't here. We've still got to find her" advised Jonah.
Despite seeing the logic in Jonah's advice, Trudy remained convinced they were on the way to finding Lucy.

While Stone and his team at the house were working on their project, Barbara had gone in for what would be her last shift in the factory. She was back where she had started, packing finished garments into boxes. But by chance she had been placed next to Tanja and was using the opportunity to learn about the traffickers' methods.
What Barbara did not realise was that O Lobo's guards kept a close eye on the trafficked women and were taking a keen interest in her friendship with Tanja.
The speed they were expected to work at made conversation difficult, but Barbara was convinced that Tanja knew nothing about the trafficked children.
She was able to learn that the women, like Tanja, who were travelling on legal documents, were moved by road through Tangier to Algeciras port in Spain. This was the reverse of the ferry route Skull and his team had used travelling to Morocco.
Tanja had overheard conversation that the illegally travelling women, including some who had been kidnapped, travelled to Portugal by sea. The traffickers had talked about using Essaouira, a small coastal town west of Marrakech, which was much quieter that the main ferry port at Tangier. But she could not add any more detail to what she had heard.
When the line stopped for their tea break, Tanja was moved to another task in the factory, away from Barbara. But the guards were now interested in Barbara as well

The now constant presence of the guards, along with Tanja's sudden removal was starting to make Barbara uncomfortable. They were doing nothing to confirm their interest in her, but Barbara was now worried she was under suspicion. All she could do for now was keep her head down, work hard and hope that she was wrong.
The end of Barbara's shift seemed to take an eternity

arriving and along with many of the factory workers she started walking towards the nearby train station.

As she walked, Barbara became increasingly aware of being followed. Her shadow was not being completely obvious, but what started as a feeling, was gradually reinforced by glimpses of reflections in windows as they passed and too quick reactions if she turned around.

Barbara considered using her hidden radio to call in her back up. But that would instantly blow her cover and ruin any chance of going back to the factory again. She was nearing the railway station, so decided to quicken her pace a little and hope for safety among the crowds there.

Although Barbara had been doing a great job maintaining her cover as a factory worker and placing bugs, she was a nun, not one of the Watchers' operatives. Now, with the pressure on and her stress levels rising, she was starting to behave too obviously. The initial quickening of her pace had been steadily increasing as her nervousness grew. Now, she was almost at a jog and her follower had to significantly quicken his pace to avoid losing her.

Now any doubts Barbara had about being followed had disappeared. As she turned the last corner into the station, Barbara broke into a run. There was a single train at a platform which looked ready to pull off. Barbara was sprinting hard to reach the distant platform, but knew she had several fights of stairs and bridges between her and the other side of the tracks. The conductor blew his whistle and Barbara knew she would never get to the platform in time to board the train. Barbara's pulse was racing as panic built within her and she tried to calculate her options.

Then fate took a turn in Barbara's favour. An ageing Moroccan man was trotting across the tracks towards the wrong side of the train, as a woman inside the carriage opened the door for him. Without the benefit of a platform it was a big step up to the door and the man needed a pull from inside to help him board.

Barbara acted instantly and sprinted towards the door in the hope of following him onto the train. But it was too late, as the man was pulled into the carriage the train started to pull away from the platform. Barbara was about to give up as she saw the man and woman waving her on and shouting encouragement. Spurred on by her new found supporters, Barbara put everything she had into one last sprint. From somewhere deep within her reserves came a powerful jump towards the door. The man and woman inside just managed to catch Barbara's wrists and pull her inside.

Fired up with adrenalin, struggling for breath and with her heart pounding Barbara fell to the carriage floor. She was absolutely spent, but safe.

Gradually Barbara's breathing and pulse rate began to steady and she started to take in her surroundings. As a European, Barbara could easily afford the Moroccan first class fares, so this was the first time she had found herself in second class. Becoming aware of her surroundings, she started to realise just how crowded the carriage was. The cramped surroundings did not smell very pleasant either, as the carriage was not just crowded with people, it was also packed with livestock of all varieties.

Pausing to thank the couple who had helped her, Barbara started to ease her way through the mass of Moroccans towards the end of the carriage. Barbara was still queasy from the exertion of running for the train. The heat from so many living things and the smell from animals and sweating human bodies only made her feel worse.

Just at the point that nausea was going to get the better of her, Barbara broke through the last of the bodies and reached the first class carriage. She instantly collapsed into one of the vacant chairs and called up her brother Miguel on the tiny radio set the Watchers had equipped her with. Barbara now felt safe, her follower could not have made it onto the train and she would soon be with Miguel. Her brother and Steve Butler would now be speeding towards the next station to collect her.

Miguel Cuba was on the platform when Barbara stepped off the train. Relief flooded through Barbara as she fell into her

Between Stone & A Hard Place

brother's arms with tears streaming down her face.
"It's over sis, you don't need to go back. We're all going home", said Miguel.
"What? Have you found her?" asked Barbara. "No, but we're pretty sure she's back in Portugal and alive".
While Steve Butler drove them back up the mountain road towards the house in the Tizi n Test Pass, Miguel brought Barbara up to date on what they had learned from Stone's surveillance of the two women.
If Carlos Lobo had kept Lucy for himself, there was almost a certainty that she would at least be physically unharmed.

Between Stone & A Hard Place

Chapter 27.

Steve Butler went straight to the kitchen, leaving Barbara to tell her story to Skull and Stone. Like all the former servicemen within the Watchers, Butler knew the importance of eating well when on assignment.
A detailed debrief and planning session would follow after dinner, but there really was only one viable option. In all their time in Morocco they had found masses of evidence pointing to Carlos Lobo's involvement in sex trafficking. But the Watchers already knew about O Lobo's crimes before they travelled to Morocco. What they desperately needed was evidence about Lucy Varley's kidnap and their only lead was back towards Portugal.
"Looks like we're going home, but we need to tread very carefully if we're going after The Wolf" said Skull.
Jonah, as always, had been analysing their information so far. "There's one thing we haven't followed up", he said. "If the girls are going out through Essaouira, we should see if Lobo has any organisation there".
Skull thought about Jonah's advice, then suggested "if the yacht picks up Nev and Steve there, they can check out the sea route. Then, after looking round the town, we can run the bikes north along the coast road."
The whole team quickly agreed and began to plan their next day.

Stone relaxed into his last Moroccan ride, with Trudy again holding tight on his pillion seat. Traffic away from Marrakech was much lighter and it was a relief to be free of the constant cacophony of car horns. The road towards the coast was a much nicer experience and Stone was enjoying the wide sweeping bends and cooling air blowing in from the sea.
As the road twisted and turned through the red, rocky landscape, Stone got the occasional view of the sea.

Essaouira was a pleasant surprise; the fishing port and old fortified town were very different to the urban sprawl they had left in Marrakech.

Between Stone & A Hard Place

Something familiar was nagging at Stone, who observed "I feel as if I've been here before, but I've never set foot in Morocco before".
Jonah had been reading up on the area, and provided the answer. "It's Saint-Malo, the same Frenchman designed this port and it's sister in Brittany".
Stone stood with Trudy taking in the similarities with the Breton town he had visited so often on motorcycling trips through Northern France.
The noise of the screeching seagulls overhead was softened by the sound of the steady wind that had cooled their ride from Marrakech. Again Jonah had some guidebook information, "they call the wind alizee. Most of the time it provides this cooling breeze, but it can be strong enough to clear the beaches with horizontal sand storms. Essaouira is often called the Wind City of Africa".
Stone then noticed the number of windsurfers and sailing boats enjoying the coastal water. "Our crew will be happy if there's some wind for their sails", he added.

The Watchers split up to investigate the town and uncover any links to O Lobo's criminal network. Couples would always raise less suspicion than the men alone, so Barbara and Trudy set out together with Stone and Miguel, through the historic walls and into the old town.
As always if Barbara was heading into possible danger, her brother Miguel was not far behind. Stone found himself volunteering to back up Miguel in support of the women. He was becoming ever more concerned for Trudy as, the longer their trip went on, the greater his feelings for her grew.

While the fishing port was very "Breton", once through the red city walls with their mid day shadows of Palm Trees, Stone felt very much in traditional Morocco. The narrow alleyways of the Medina were like the others they had visited in Fez and Marrakech, but on a smaller scale. The smells of fish guts and damp sea air from the port mixed with the aroma of spices and the Atlas Mountain's aromatic Thuya Wood.

Between Stone & A Hard Place

It was Miguel's turn to play tour guide, the English educated Watcher had heard of the rare wood through its use in Rolls Royce dashboards.
"The wood the furniture craftsmen are using, only grows in these mountains. Furniture made from it is a bit of a status symbol and Rolls picked it for its beautiful smell and exclusivity".

Working deeper into the Medina, they were reminded that this was a traditionally Muslim country. Women in white veils, or haiks listened to the sound of drums and Gnawa Singing reverberating from shops and houses.
This ancient blend of African Islamic rhythms and ritual poetry had been adding life to Morocco's markets for centuries. Barbara and Trudy could not help tapping their feet along to the drums.
Behaving like tourists was partially about keeping relaxed, but it was also about maintaining cover and not drawing attention to themselves. The Watchers were looking for signs that O Lobo was operating in Essaouira, but they also had to be wary that the gangster's men knew they were in Morocco and were on the hunt for them.

While Stone, Miguel and the girls were touring the old town, Steve Butler and Joao Alva were preparing for the yacht's arrival.
Butler was readying everything he and Stone would need for their voyage. He had recharged their CCUBA diving sets, prepared their spear guns and waterproofed his shotgun and personal kit.
Alva concentrated on the bikes. Stone and Butler would not need their Triumph Scramblers once the yacht set sail, so the giant biker was loading the motorcycles into the back of Jonah's van.

Jonah on the other hand was working with Prince and Simms on one of the few technical toys the Moroccan Watchers had available to them. Without the support of the Watchers' technicians, the full range of cameras and bugs were beyond Prince and Simms reach, but they had learned to use one very useful piece of kit.

The tiny remote control helicopter lifted smoothly from the harbour wall on its four rotors. Nestled in the centre of the rotors was a video camera which fed live pictures back to its controller.

Prince and Simms found the drone particularly useful in guarding their businessmen clients.

The former soldiers knew the benefits of good reconnaissance and would often use the drone's cameras to scout ahead before they brought their clients into a location.

This time they would use it to speed up their search of Essaouira. The Watchers needed to get back to the Algarve and hunt down leads to O Lobo. But they also knew that they had to be thorough at Essaouira, or the search was not worth doing at all.

Prince carefully flew the little drone up and down the streets outside the old town's walls. Jonah watched the remote monitor intently, looking for any signs of O Lobo's presence in the town.

"I'm not seeing anything Prince lad", said Jonah, getting disillusioned with their so far, fruitless search of the town.

"Make one more pass on the north", said Simms who had been matching street plans to the aerial footage. "There looks to have been some development there".

Prince flew the helicopter around the buildings to the north of the port. Two of them had been recently modernised and extended, but appeared to be holiday apartments with no obvious signs of O Lobo's gang.

Butler and Alva had now finished their preparations, so took two of the motorcycles to check out what the drone had found. But despite their efforts there was no evidence there, not even a wolf's paw logo to be seen anywhere on the buildings.

As Butler and Alva were exploring the buildings, Stone and his group were returning to the van. "Nothing in the old town", said Stone. "Barbara has spoken to lots of people and

found nothing. The constant wind keeps away the seedier side of tourism, so there's no sex trade as such".
Jonah added his thoughts "Steve just checked in too. We've no evidence anywhere of O Lobo having a presence here. Either it was bad information about using this port, or they just use public facilities".

While they were debriefing, the Watchers' leased yacht arrived in port to collect Stone and Butler. They had swum ashore to avoid detection, entering the country illegally. But everything they had seen of law enforcement since arriving, suggested they were unlikely to be discovered leaving. If they were unlucky enough to attract police attention, a small bribe would take care of things.
"Hope you've still got your sea legs Nev?" joked Butler.
"Salty sea-dog me", replied Stone as he started gathering his kit together for loading.

Barbara had wandered off to talk to some children fishing off the end of the dock. Despite the nun being unlikely to have children of her own, Barbara enjoyed being around them, and their simple level of fun.
As she chatted to the youngsters, she noticed a gated area at the end of the pontoon dock. "How could we have missed this, right under our noses", thought Barbara as she spotted the wolf's paw logo discretely worked into the pattern of the gate.
She waved Stone over to look at her find, but there was very little for him to see. Aside from the gated birth, there was no infrastructure there. It was just a reserved spot to guarantee being able to moor a boat.
"Looks like Steve and I have a diving job before we leave", said Stone. He was already plotting how he and Butler could secrete cameras on the dock by approaching from under water.

Stone and Butler said their goodbyes before boarding the yacht. As with all biker partings they exchanged their ritual hugs and back slaps, but it was his hug with Trudy that

Between Stone & A Hard Place

ignited something inside him. With all the bikers watching it looked nothing more than a goodbye hug, but both Stone and Trudy felt the same warm, tingly feeling down their spines.
Before Stone could dwell on his feelings too deeply, he and Butler threw their kit bags onto the yacht and jumped aboard. The bikers made a big show of taking their kit bags below deck and talking about stowing their gear.
Once into the cabin, far from stowing kit, they changed into their diving gear. Then, silently they slipped out to the seaward side of the yacht and into the water.
Like ghosts their bubble-less CCUBA sets let them swim undetected beneath O Lobo's private dock. There, the skilled technicians fitted the remote cameras that would capture any activity on the dock.
Stone had to think of a way to maximise the cameras' battery life. His solution was the type of infra red sensor, or PIR, used in household alarm systems. Set to a low sensitivity and facing out from the dock, the sensor would be triggered by a boat mooring and start all of his cameras transmitting.

Once they were safely back on board the yacht and confident they had not been detected, Stone gave his crew instruction to set sail.
Butler moved effortlessly into yachtsman mode. The former Royal Marine was as comfortable at sea as he was on land. Stone however was taking time to regain his sea legs. He knew from experience that he would soon adapt, but it always took him an hour or two adapting to the pitch and roll of a small boat at sea.
While Butler busied himself helping their two crew members sail the yacht, Stone took a seat on the upper deck and scoured the horizon with powerful binoculars. "Ship ahoy!" shouted Stone, taking the nautical theme a little light heartedly. He had spotted an expensive looking motor yacht sailing towards the harbour at Essaouira.
"I wouldn't have credited Carlos a Lobo with a sense of humour, but that's got to be his boat", said Stone, handing the binoculars to Butler.

Between Stone & A Hard Place

"Lon Chaney Jr", read Butler from the side of the luxury yacht. The boat was named after the 1940's actor who made his name playing the Wolf Man in Universal Studios horror films. "The Wolf Man has got to be him. Do you think he's aboard?"
"Only one way of finding out. I guess we're diving again", said Stone.

For the second time that day, Stone and Butler slipped off the blind side of their yacht. This time they had the assistance of Sea Scooters to pull them through the open ocean towards their target. The 500 Watt electric motors of the small torpedo shaped scooters, pulled the divers along at 5mph. Not a huge speed, but a great help in closing the gap before the boat pulled too far away from them.
The Sea Scooters were not the only piece of technical equipment Steve Butler had held in reserve. He was also carrying an underwater listening device which would allow them to hear conversations through the boat's hull.
The divers clung onto the underside of the Boat while Butler fixed his listening device to the hull. The gadget worked in a similar way to a stethoscope, allowing Butler to listen to activity inside the boat.
It took Butler time to separate out voices from the sound of the engine, propeller and waves breaking against the hull. But steadily he started to isolate, one, two, three, then four voices. "All male", thought Butler. "And Portuguese". Butler was disappointed there were no female voices among the crew, as that might connect to their sex trafficking investigation. "Possibly on a pick up", he thought. Then his imagination began to wander, considering whether Carlos Lobo himself could be aboard the appropriately named boat.

As Butler became better at separating the voices, he realised they all sounded too young to be the ageing gangster. Their conversation was that of hired thugs too, rather than wealthy and successful criminals. The men spoke of the money to come and their delight at getting hold of the boss' personal boat.

Between Stone & A Hard Place

Just before disengaging from the hull, Butler left one more device from his diving pouch. His device would provide a surprise to the crew at the right moment. He and Stone then activated their scooters and swam back to their own yacht. Back on board, Butler radioed Skull Murphy to explain what they had found. "Watch Nev's cameras and make sure there are no innocents", said Butler before signing off.

Working seamlessly again with his crew, Butler relaxed into sailing and pointed the boat towards Portugal.
Stone again had his binoculars out. Just as he expected, the Lon Chaney Jr docked at the berth with the wolf paw logo. Skull and the other Watchers had now hidden their motorcycles and were relying on feed from the cameras being transmitted back to their van.

Between Stone & A Hard Place

Chapter 28.

The infra red sensor worked perfectly, triggering the cameras Stone placed around the dock as soon as the boat touched the side.
Jonah and Skull were in the Watchers' van, monitoring the camera feed and physically watching the port's approach road through the mirrored windows.
Skull's senses started to tingle as a truck drove towards them. "That looks very similar to the hashish truck we blew up in the mountains", said Skull.
Jonah agreed, recognising the model and year. "It looks the same Skull lad. Seems too much of a coincidence, let's see if it heads towards the boat".
"We'd better give some thought to a rescue plan if there's kids in the truck", added Skull.
Jonah did not reply as he had gone back to studying the camera feed, where he could see the boat's crew were now busy connecting diesel and water pipes, in order to refill their boat.
Skull was right about the truck heading to the dock, as they saw it pull straight up to O Lobo's berth. But the rescue mission he hoped for was not to happen. Their hidden cameras showed a pair of Moroccan farmers ferrying bails of hashish down the pontoon and handing it to the boat's Portuguese crew.

Skull was quickly on the radio to Stone, comparing what he and Jonah were seeing with what Steve Butler had heard through the boat's hull.
"So are we sure there are just four Portuguese guys on the boat then?" asked Skull.
"Yes", replied Stone. "Steve listened for ages, no other voices and no talk of passengers.
"Ok", said Skull. "I'll send the signal as soon as they are out of the harbour".
Stone's yacht resumed its northerly course up the Moroccan coast, towards home. Skull and Jonah went back to watching O Lobo's men load their drugs onto the Lon

www.neilhallam.com

Between Stone & A Hard Place

Chaney Jr.
The gangsters were efficient in loading the boat and it was soon making its way out of the port towards the open sea. Skull was carefully watching the boat's progress, as he had an important decision to make. Then, as soon as the Lon Chaney Jr cleared the harbour gates, but before it travelled too far from shore, Skull pressed transmit. Skull's radio signal triggered the small underwater mine which Butler had placed under O Lobo's boat.

"Count them out Jonah", said Skull. The Watchers planned to make the hashish useless to the gangsters, but they would only kill in the most extreme circumstances. Jonah's task was to make sure that he saw all four gangsters safely out of the sinking boat.
"I'm only seeing three Skull lad", said Jonah as he watched the water through powerful binoculars.
Skull, Miguel, Prince and Simms were already sprinting along the harbour wall towards the wreck site. As they ran, they collected up life buoys, ropes and anything else that would help them with a rescue. Trudy had also switched quickly into her nursing role, heading to the van for her medical bag. The Watchers hated the thought of explaining their presence to the Royal Moroccan Gendarmerie, but they could not ride away and let a man drown.
Just as Skull was about to dive into the ocean, the spectre of police contact was removed. "There's number four Skull lad", shouted Jonah into his radio, as the fourth gangster broke surface.
The bikers quickly changed direction and returned to their bikes for a fast exit. They were quick enough to avoid the gendarmes, but O Lobo's men had spotted their distinctive motorcycles and would report back to their boss.
Carlos Lobo was already enraged by the Watchers involvement in his business, this would only add to his obsession with the bikers as they returned home to Portugal.

Prince and Simms rode with the Lagos chapter of their MC for the first hour. The coast road made a pleasant change

Between Stone & A Hard Place

from the mountain and desert they were used to. But they had business to return to in Marrakech and soon had to part company with their brothers.

A heartfelt round of hugs and back slapping preceded the bikers' emotional parting. They had all been through a lot in their short time together yet still had only the faintest of leads towards finding Lucy.

Riding back up the Tizi N Test Pass, Prince and Simms expected the next few days to be much more mundane as they settled back to their body guarding duties. But, the last few days' adrenalin would not have time to fully fade away.

Prince and Simms settled back into their house high on the road to the Pass. Phone calls to their employers came first, to organise the next day's protection. Then they sat down to enjoy a long overdue leisurely dinner.

But then their plans changed as the first set of flash bangs detonated. Someone was trying to get through their gates. The former Paratroopers reacted just as quickly as they had done in their many war zones. The two men leapt to where their shotguns and body armour were kept. Expertly pulling on the Kevlar vests and readying their weapons as they dived for cover.

It was O Lobo's men who had tracked the bikers to their mountain home. What looked like wooden gates had a reinforced metal core. The gangster's first attempt to breach them succeeded only in triggering the bikers' first line of countermeasures. But the gangsters had come prepared and a stolen digger began to roll forward towards the gates. Boom! The second line of countermeasures exploded. This time the explosives were powerful enough to take the wheel off the digger.

O Lobo's men moved around the digger, hopeful that it had taken the brunt of the paratrooper's countermeasures. But they hoped in vain as another military mine blew off one of the men's legs.

Prince and Simms were now sending volleys of shot towards the gangsters. The hail of lead shot briefly held back the gangsters. But they knew that they could not return with the Watchers still alive, such was Carlos Lobo's rage with the bikers. None of them wanted to imagine what the wolf would do to them, if they returned unsuccessful.

A hand grenade thrown towards the biker's position stopped the shot long enough for the gangsters to move forward. But their movement just caught another set of the Watcher's trip wires. This time the wires were linked to much more lethal fragmentation mines, which threw out shrapnel, killing one gangster, and seriously injuring two more.

But the Wolf had thrown all his available men at this assault and there were plenty more to keep moving towards the house.

More mines exploded, taking out two more of the gangsters before they reached the house door.

It had now become clear to Prince and Simms that the gangsters would stop at nothing to breach the security of their house. As O Lobo's men were setting explosives at the front door, the paratroopers were moving towards their rear terrace. The house builders had designed the terrace to enjoy stunning views out from the sheer cliffs, but they could never have imagined Prince and Simms adaptation to their design.

Tall Atlas Cedar trees at the edge of the terrace hid the infrastructure of Prince and Simms last line of defence. Strapping on harnesses, the bikers swiftly climbed one of the 30 foot conifer trees into its evergreen crown. From here began the biggest adrenalin rush Prince and Simms had experienced since leaving the Parachute Regiment. Their tree top perch marked the start of what was possibly North Africa's longest zip wire.

The bikers flew out of the Cedar canopy, sliding along the cable they had run across the deep ravine months earlier. With the smell of explosives and gunpowder in the air, both men were reliving their countless combat parachute drops. They were still airborne when O Lobo's men reached the terrace, but they were well beyond the gangsters' limited marksmanship skills.

Between Stone & A Hard Place

When the raiders started hacking at the cable, Prince and Simms were thankful they opted for a tough steel cable rather than rope. The strong cable allowed them just enough time to complete their flight and uncover the small trail bikes they kept hidden in the bush.

There was a long and winding road between the house and where Prince and Simms now were, so they had an ample head start on the gangsters to get out of the mountains. Expertly they rode the little motorcycles down the mountain, keeping to unmade farming tracks wherever they could.

The Watchers usually had some sort if contingency plan and today was no exception. Their escape route was backed up with a much smaller safe house in the old part of Marrakech. Safely inside they passed on what had happened to Stone and Skull, for them to be wary of the gangsters' increased level of aggression.

They were saddened by the loss of their beautiful house high in the mountains. But took some comfort in the knowledge that O Lobo's lieutenants would be made to suffer for their failure.

Once back in Spain, the Lagos Watchers again met up with the Costa Del Sol chapter to retrieve their own bikes. They had enjoyed riding the quirky Triumph Scramblers around Morocco, but back in Europe they were all pleased to have their own motorcycles back.

The two chapters meeting up should have heralded party time. But Skull was anxious to get his group back to the Algarve and continue their search for young Lucy Varley.

So after a brief meal, Skull formed up his convoy for the ride back to Portugal. Skull had back his huge 2.3 litre Triumph, Barbara had her Harley Davidson, Joao Alva rode his Moto Guzzi California, while Miguel Cuba was glad to be back on his expensive hand built Norton Commando.

All bikers are sentimental about their favourite motorcycles, so the MC members were revelling in the ride home after so

Between Stone & A Hard Place

long on borrowed bikes.
Jonah, as always, followed on with the van, accompanied by Trudy Varley, who would have much rather been sitting behind Nev.

Skull had expected some of the border security to have been relaxed since they last left Portugal. But as they approached the Guadiana Bridge, which forms the border between Spain and Portugal, they saw the checks were still in place.
Chief Inspector Ricardo De Sa was obviously still briefing his border force about the Watchers, as the guards recognised the MC members as soon as they pulled up.
"No quiet return home then", thought Skull as he produced his papers.
He knew that De Sa would be on their case as soon as they arrived back in Lagos, so decided to go straight to the MC's safe house in Faro instead.
With their motorcycles hidden away in the garage, the other members of the Lagos chapter started to arrive.

"Steve and Nev are about an hour from Sagres", said Skull, asking Pedro De Costa to collect them from the harbour.
"I'll come", shouted Trudy, desperate to see that Nev was safe.
The Watchers' yacht sailed into Sagres with much less ceremony than Prince Henry the Navigator's historic voyages. But for Trudy, seeing Nev again was every bit as important. She could not help throwing her arms around him the moment he stepped onto the dock. Stone allowed himself a few seconds intimate contact with Trudy, before reluctantly pulling away.
Stone had missed Trudy and his feelings for her were growing ever stronger. But he knew that his freedom depended on finding Lucy, so fought with himself to remain professional. He longed to spend time with her, but this was no the right time to pursue anything deeper.

In Faro the other MC members were bringing Skull and Jonah up to date with what had been happening in Portugal during their absence.

"We've been in virtual lock down", said Paulo De Costa. "Carlos Lobo's goons have been hassling our clients almost daily.

Andre has been covering for Jaoa as Sergeant and bumping a few heads". The MC role of Sergeant at Arms is essentially the club enforcer. In the absence of the giant Joao Alva , there could be no better candidate than cage fighter Andre Felix.

"After what Andre did to their bare knuckle champion, I'm surprised anyone wanted to take him on", replied Skull.

"That's not all", added Paulo. "De Sa has been keeping his cops on us day and night too. We can't move without a tail. Coming here needed two changes of car".

Skull thought for a moment, then said" we need a plan for that, but let's wait until the guys are back from Sagres".

Stone, Butler and Pedro had to take a circuitous route to Faro avoiding the police and the gangsters. So by the time they arrived at the safe house, Jonah had added most of the Moroccan information to his wall display.

"Ok, here's what we know", began Jonah. "Carlos Lobo is up to his paws in sex trafficking. Georgi Dimov's ex KGB network kidnaps the women, and then Lobo deals with Europe and Morocco. The women come into Marrakech, where they work at the factory before being sent out to brothels. Then crucially, there seems to be a very special market for the best of the young girls. The youngsters initially seem to be well treated, although who knows what their future holds. If we are right, Lobo has saved Lucy for himself. Which should mean she's somewhere close by on the Algarve".

Stone was examining the connections made on the walls and reworking all of Jonah's lines of logic. "All that makes sense Jonah. But the Algarve is a big area. We've already searched the only address we have for Lobo and come up blank".

"Aye Nev lad", replied Jonah. "But we're hardly going to give

Between Stone & A Hard Place

up are we?"
"Ferko Mordecai and his wife are our best link if Lucy is still on the Algarve", added Stone. "We know the boxer was involved in the kidnap somehow, because he was at the handover. We only pulled off him because we thought Lucy was in Morocco".
"So", said Skull. "We're back on Mordecai then".
"Good to me Skull lad", replied Jonah, knowing that they still had some of their surveillance cameras working around the gypsy camp. "But I think we should also push the wolf man's buttons. I'll see what I can give to Muppet".

Jonah planned to feed his former colleague, Chief Inspector Jim "Muppet" Henson enough information from their Morocco trip to start breathing down the neck of Carlos Lobo's network. "If it's difficult for him to conduct business, he might start to make mistakes".

Between Stone & A Hard Place

Chapter 29.

Unlike Stone who was on the run from the police, Jonah was able to meet openly with Muppet Henson. Jonah travelled over to Villa Do Bispo where the Portuguese police had their incident room. The two veteran police officers were enjoying coffee outside one of the village cafés, catching up on old times.

Despite their long friendship there was still a feeling of walking on eggshells. Muppet was a serving senior officer, involved in a kidnap investigation, while Jonah was in regular contact with the prime suspect.

"Nev should come in before De Sa catches up with him", advised Muppet. "He's convinced of Nev's guilt and the longer he's on his toes, the more guilty he looks".

Jonah was unequivocal in his reply, "Nev's intent on clearing his name Jim lad. He won't trust De Sa, and from what I've seen I can't blame him".

Muppet was treading a fine line between duty as a serving officer and loyalty to his former colleagues. He was no fan of Ricardo De Sa, but was too professional to say so. Instead he chose to praise Inspector Luis Enes, De Sa's deputy and a detective of similar maturity to Muppet and Jonah.

"Enes is a good guy. If you have anything, it will get more attention if I feed it through him", said Muppet.

Jonah had come with the intention of giving them something to use against the gangsters. He was especially interested in Muppet's connections to Interpol and therefore into Morocco. But the old campaigner let Muppet talk him into sharing his information.

The Watchers had more than enough information to damage Carlos Lobo's operations in Morocco, which they hoped would keep him too busy to bother them in Portugal. But Jonah was not sure the Moroccan police would be prepared to take them on. He therefore needed the help of Interpol to light the touch paper.

Many people think the 100 year old organisation is an

Between Stone & A Hard Place

international police force, when it is actually more of an intelligence sharing network. But Jonah new that pressure from within the international law enforcement community was his best chance of getting action taken against the gangsters.
As part of his long police career, Muppet had spent time on secondment to Interpol's headquarters in Lyon, France.
The organisation had used his extensive firearms and public order experience to spread good practice through their 190 member countries.
Since returning to his home force he spent short periods on loan to the small Interpol National Central Bureau in Manchester. Jonah knew he could rely on Muppet to feed his information into the Interpol intelligence machine, prompting, at minimum, a series of global alerts about O Lobo's activities.
But what Jonah really hoped for was for Interpol to instigate the Moroccans starting an anti trafficking operation as part of their Smuggling Training Operation Programme (STOP).

The file Jonah handed over had detail on Carlos Lobo's hashish farming operation in Chefchaouen and his clothing factory at Marrakech. Georgi Dimov's people trafficking route from Bulgaria through Morocco and into Portugal was also detailed in the file. What Jonah did leave out was the details of the mountain truck crash, hotel shoot out and ship wreck. Jonah also left out the information that Lobo could himself be holding Lucy close to home. The Watchers wanted to be sure that their best lead to Lucy was followed up promptly, so they themselves would take action.
"Thanks Jonah", said Muppet as they parted company. "I'll talk to Luis and make sure the intelligence is fed into the machine".
"Just do your best Jim lad", said Jonah, shaking his friend's hand and driving off, back into the world of the bikers.

Giving the police something more than Stone to focus on proved to be a good call by Jonah.
While Muppet Henson was going through Jonah's file and

Between Stone & A Hard Place

figuring out how best to use the intelligence, GNR officers were arriving back at Ingrina in the area around Stone's yurt. Chief Inspector De Sa had convinced the Public Ministry at Portimao to authorise the use of ground penetrating radar and sniffer dogs around Stone's camp, in expectation of finding Lucy's body. De Sa would not move from his belief in Stone's guilt.
His surveillance teams were also still active around Lagos. It was becoming increasingly difficult for the MC members to travel unobserved. This was hampering their efforts to track down Ferko Mordecai, as most of the members were confined to the safe house in Faro.
"We're spending hours watching the few cameras still working at the gypsy camp, with no sign of him", said Miguel Cuba. "I want to get Barbara back amongst the Roma with her missionary repertoire, but we can't get close to Lagos without picking up a tail".
One of the group could usually be expected to have a solution. This time it was Barbara who suggested, "since we are stuck in Faro, why don't I revisit Silvija before she starts her shift in Dimov's brothel? We should give her the news about Tanja, and she might know something about Ferko". The bikers quickly agreed her suggestion and Barbara set out with Miguel and Joao as her back up.

Silvija was a creature of habit. Just as Barbara had predicted, she cherished the brief period of normality provided by the pavement cafe. So even without her friend Tanja, she still drank coffee between leaving her accommodation and starting work in the club.
Dressed as before in her nun's habit, Barbara sat with Silvija at her table. Everyone notices a nun, but rarely does anyone actually take much notice. So the distinctive clothing was an ideal cover for Barbara in catholic Portugal.
Silvija was delighted to hear from Barbara that her friend was at least still alive, even if her conditions at the factory were far from ideal. It took Barbara some time to bring Silvija's thoughts off her friend Tanja and get her to focus on Ferko.

Between Stone & A Hard Place

"Ah yes, the boxer", said Silvija. "We see him sometimes, but more the in the last weeks. He seems more important now".

When one of O Lobo's lieutenants failed him, it was his style to have another of his men deal with the failure, and then take his job.

In recognition of unnecessarily torturing Ferko, Lobo allowed him to kill the man responsible. This left a vacancy much higher in Carlos Lobo's network and the gypsy boxer went from strong arm enforcer and kidnapper to having greater involvement with the women.

But Ferko and his wife Chavali had been given another task which Silvija did not know about and would have much more significance to the MC.

Barbara did not have long before Silvija had to leave for an evening of servicing Georgi Dimov's clients. But it was long enough for her to be sure that the Faro brothel was their best place to begin surveillance on Ferko Mordecai.

Miguel and Joao were waiting for Barbara inside one of the Watchers' vans. Barbara however, had no intention of travelling in the van on such a warm Algarve evening. In the back of the van she slipped out of her nun's habit, revealing underneath, her skin tight black leather suit.

"You don't see that every day", said Joao Alva, looking at the unusual transformation from nun to biker. Before long, Barbara was speeding away on her beloved Harley Davidson Sportster towards the safe house, to check in with Stone and Skull.

Skull had to dispatch a team of their company technicians to the cameras around the brothel. They had been running the longest of those currently in place, which were put into service before Stone got his compromising photographs of the footballer Sergio Silva. The batteries had therefore long ago run down. In the guise of maintenance men for the local businesses, the technicians serviced the tiny cameras and replaced their batteries.

"We're up and running Skull lad", said Jonah as the first

www.neilhallam.com

images of the brothel entrance flickered onto his screen. Stone started to rota their small team into shifts to watch for Ferko. Skull then started to work the phones, putting together a team of their employees who would not be known to De Sa. That team would take over the surveillance of Ferko once it went mobile.

As Jonah watched the screens, something odd began to happen. Gradually the police presence started to increase in Faro. At first they only noticed it around Dimov's brothel and assumed Chief Inspector De Sa had somehow learned of their interest in Ferko.
But over a period of hours they saw patrols increase around many of the businesses attributed to Carlos Lobo and Georgi Dimov.
Then reports started to come in from Lagos that there had been a corresponding drop in police activity around the Watchers' interests in the historic port town.
"Looks like Luis Enes has come through for us lad", said Jonah to Stone. "Muppet said that Inspector Enes was a good bloke. It looks like he has used our file and Muppet's Interpol connections to refocus their investigation."
Ricardo De Sa's obsession with the bikers was too great for him to be completely diverted away from Stone and the MC. But his Deputy had put up too convincing a case about Carlos Lobo for him to focus solely on the bikers.
"Let's hope it gives us the breathing space we need to chase down Ferko Mordecai then Jonah". "Looks like you did a good job convincing Muppet" replied Stone.
Jonah, as ever needed the last word. "Actually Nev lad, Muppet thinks he convinced me to hand over the intel. He's none to enamoured with De Sa's methods, he seems much more comfortable with Luis Enes. I think we have Luis to thank for the change of tactics"

As the day rolled on, none of the Watchers' cameras or surveillance teams had picked up Ferko. They were watching his tent at the gypsy camp near Lagos and the club at Faro, where Silvija had told Barbara he was now a regular

feature. It seemed odd that Ferko had dropped off the radar if he was now a bigger player in O Lobo's organisation. But it was precisely the promotion of Ferko and his wife Chavali that had taken them away from the Algarve. The Roma couple had negotiated a day away from their duties together and were driving north to Madrid in Spain.
The Mordecai's new found affluence was allowing them to replace the motor home seized by the police for its use in Lucy's kidnap. There were plenty of camper vans available on the Algarve, but the ornate versions which suited the Roma tastes needed a big city dealership to provide.

The drive north gave Ferko and Chavali an opportunity to talk, something which had become rare in the frenzy following the kidnap.
"I don't like it Ferko, the girl has Romanipen, she should not be caged".
The two women Stone had bugged in Marrakech seemed to have a high opinion of Lucy Varley. Now Chavali Mordecai was also acknowledging that there was something very special about her.
"I see Romanipen in her too Chavali," replied Ferko. "But we must do our duty to O Lobo. We have seen his anger and would die painfully if we cross him".

The Romanipen of which Chavali and Ferko spoke, is a complicated piece of Romani philosophy that means Romani spirit. Occasionally an ethnic Romani can be cast out of Romani society if they have no Romanipen. But sometimes and more rarely, a non-Romani may be considered Romani if they do have Romanipen. Usually this is an adopted child, but Ferko and Chavali had seen the spirit in young Lucy. Roma society is very male dominated. The head of a clan is always the elder male and women usually begin to gain influence only after having children. But it took a strong woman to become the wife of the gypsy's bare knuckle champion. Although Chavali respected her husband, she would not meekly follow his instructions.
Throughout the journey, Chavali tried to wear her husband

down to help Lucy. But Ferko was so afraid of Carlos Lobo after being tortured at the farm, that he concentrated hard on shutting out his wife's protests.

A few hours later, Jonah shouted "Got them Nev lad", as he watched his camera monitors. "Ferko and his wife are back at the camp. Looks like they've bought themselves a new home too".
Stone and Skull joined Jonah at the monitors and saw the elegant new motor home that the Mordecai's had driven back from Madrid.
"We're in business again", replied Skull, reaching for the phone to set a surveillance team travelling towards the camp.
Barbara and Miguel Cuba had been waiting for an opportunity to go back to the gypsy camp. On the day of Andre Felix's fight, they had gone into the camp as missionaries. Many of the Roma based in Portugal followed the catholic faith and readily accepted the nun and her missionary brother. With Ferko back on site, they had an opportunity to get back into role.
"'Once the team is in place, we'll see if there are any souls to save", said Miguel. He was still sceptical of his sister's faith, but realised its importance to a great many people, so trod a fine line between scepticism and admiration for the work of his sister's order.

Barbara's beauty was difficult to forget and she was quickly recognised by the gypsy families she had met at the fight. She and Miguel were again welcomed around the family table and offered tea.
Although they were really there for Ferko, Barbara's cover story was actually her genuine calling in life. She and Miguel slipped easily into offering pastoral conversation and support to the family, while keeping one eye keenly on Ferko.
Miguel's hidden earpiece clicked twice. This was the agreed signal to let him know the surveillance teams had moved into position. This brought Miguel great comfort as, while he took many risks himself, he still wanted back up for his sister.

Between Stone & A Hard Place

As they talked, Miguel and Barbara watched the Mordecai's moving to and fro between their tent and the new motor home.
"House move day looks easy when you own so little", thought Miguel. "Maybe Nev has the right idea living in his yurt".

Then Ferko and Chavali seemed to finish stocking their motor home and began to pack provisions into the 4x4 truck parked next to their tent.
This perked Miguel's attention, noticing that it was predominantly groceries and cleaning materials they were loading into the truck.
As they started to drive off, Miguel needed to tell the surveillance teams, but could not openly use his radio. So, talking to the gypsy family, Miguel opened his microphone.
"Looks like your boxer is on the move", said Miguel. "That's a nice red truck, did he win that boxing"?
Barbara soon cut in to move the conversation back to less controversial topics, but the surveillance teams were now alerted to look for Ferko's red truck.

Between Stone & A Hard Place

Chapter 30.

While Ferko and Chavali were organising their new home, the police officers digging at Ingrina made a grizzly find. A few hundred meters from Stone's yurt, the ground penetrating radar had led the officers to start digging. Human remains had been found and Chief Inspector De Sa had travelled to the scene awaiting arrival of the experts who would tell him more about the remains.
But De Sa did not need any experts, as his almost pathological belief in Stone's guilt told him this must be Lucy Varley.

Television cameras rolled against a backdrop of screens the police had erected around the dig site and De Sa spoke straight to camera. "Officers of the GNR have located human remains in the clearing behind me. The remains have yet to be identified and specialists are on the way to assist with forensic recovery and identification. But we are treating the death as suspicious. We are a short distance from the last known sighting of Lucy Varley. We are also close to the tent used by our prime suspect Nev Stone, a man we know to have killed at least twice before".
De Sa ended his speech with a further appeal for information leading to the arrest of Stone.

"Will this moron ever see the truth here?" asked Skull. "How much more evidence does he need to turn his attention towards the Secret Service gangsters?"
Stone was much more concerned for Lucy. "We have to trust Luis Enes and Interpol to make De Sa see sense. For now let's hope this isn't Lucy they have found".
He had started the search for Lucy to provide a witness who could clear him from suspicion of Blagoy Cvetkov's murder. But Stone had grown closer to Trudy Varley during their time in Morocco and reuniting mother and daughter was now more important than his own situation.
"I can't bear having to tell Trudy that we have failed and Lucy is dead", added Stone.

Between Stone & A Hard Place

Jonah could always be counted on to provide a level headed response and said, "Nev lad, that's out of our hands. Let's assume she's alive and keep on Ferko until we know different".

Which is exactly what the Watchers did continue to do. A Prospect was tasked with monitoring the news for updates about the human remains, while a surveillance team from their security company followed Ferko and Chavali away from their camp.

The Roma couple drove west from Lagos, into the wilder part of the Algarve National Park, with the Watchers' team keeping their distance and regularly swapping around the following vehicles.

"Raposeira left left, towards Ingrena", said the lead driver into his radio.

"Must be heading for Lobo's house", said Stone. "Can we get someone onto the high ground? We need to know what he's up to".

Skull was ahead of him and was already calling up the surveillance team leader to dispatch one of his off road bikers.

Using powerful binoculars from his hilltop vantage point, the surveillance biker began giving Stone and Skull commentary on the two Roma.

"We were right about them going to Lobo's place", said Stone. "But it sounds like they are just unloading shopping".

"What do you think?" asked Skull. "Moving in, or getting ready for Carlos Lobo to make an appearance?"

"Who knows!" commented Stone. "But whichever it is could be important to us. Can we get an obs van in there? The biker will get too conspicuous after a while".

Skull had no sooner passed his instructions to the team, than their situation was to take a dramatic turn.

The front door of the safe house crashed in behind the weight of a police battering ram. Chief Inspector De Sa and a GNR Special Operations Team burst through the door.

Between Stone & A Hard Place

Someone had been careless in returning to the house and had been followed. But the Watchers had no time to think about blame as they desperately thought of how they could hide Stone.
Security at the safe house was a fraction of that provided at their Lagos clubhouse. There was no downstairs garage to contain the officers, no gate to barrier the stairs, no priest hole to hide Stone and certainly no room to fire a shotgun. So reluctantly, the bikers had no choice than to surrender quietly to De Sa.

The whole team were left with feelings of failure and loss as they watched Stone walk away in handcuffs.
De Sa had arrested him for the murders of Blagoy Cvetkov and Lucy Varley, all Stone could do now was hope with every fibre of his being that the body was not Lucy's.

Chief Inspector De Sa was hoping for the opposite of Stone when he next stood in front of the cameras. "Agentes of the GNR have today arrested our prime suspect Neville Stone for two murders. Stone is accused of murdering Bulgarian businessman Blagoy Cvetkov in the area behind me. We are still awaiting forensic identification of the human remains found in the same area, but believe them to be of missing schoolgirl Lucy Varley".

Trudy heard the news of Stone's arrest at the police incident room. She had refused De Sa's request for her to join his press briefing. Trudy did not share the Chief Inspector's belief in Stone's guilt, and she had to believe the body was not her daughter. So, while his boss was playing to the cameras, Inspector Luis Enes did his best to comfort the distraught mother.
"Don't worry Trudy", said Enes. "Our investigation is bigger than Ricardo. Interpol are driving action against Carlos Lobo and the scientists will tell us whether or not we've found Lucy".
But Trudy did worry. She had to believe her daughter was still alive and far from believing Stone responsible, she

Between Stone & A Hard Place

thought him more likely than the police to find Lucy.

The investigation was proving to be bigger than Chief Inspector De Sa. Across the Algarve, police teams led by Interpol National Bureau officers were raiding Carlos Lobo's businesses.
Jonah's file of the Watchers' Moroccan adventures had piqued the interest of Interpol's General Secretariat in France. Or rather, the involvement of Barbara Cuba and her Good Shepherd Sisters had interested them. The Sisters' record on fighting sex traffickers added weight to evidence gathered by a bunch of bikers.
All along Portugal's south coast O Lobo's bars, massage parlours and brothels were being searched and the girls' immigration status checked. This was causing difficulty to the Wolf's day to day business, but despite the police activity close by, they were yet to go near Ferko Mordecai and the house at Ingrena.

"The child is a treasure Ferko", said Chavali Mordecai. "One so blond cannot have Roma blood, but she shines out Romanipen". Ferko's wife was still convinced the child they were guarding had true Romany spirit and was finding it hard to calmly do Carlos Lobo's bidding.
"If you value our lives Chavali, we will take good care of the girl and keep her safe for O Lobo", replied Ferko, remembering their own captivity at the farm.
His wife's reluctance to hold the child captive worried Ferko, but he now had another worry.
Carlos Lobo was taking a close interest in the girl's welfare and had been in contact several times a day. But now, with the police working so close, Ferko wanted the Wolf's guidance but could not reach him.

Carlos Lobo had spent a lifetime working in the shadows, always able to disappear when the opposition was getting too close. Of course, that always left someone else to take the fall, but the ruthless spymaster turned gangster cared little for others.

Between Stone & A Hard Place

Now was one of those times when Lobo wanted his lieutenants to feel the heat, rather than face it himself. Interpol staff officers were leading teams of Royal Moroccan Gendarmes and Portuguese Republican National Guard against O Lobo's assets on both continents.
The gangster would lose money as drug sales in his bars dried up and his girls were sent home. But Carlos Lobo had reserves of cash. What he could not afford was to be arrested himself.

The Wolf was still on the Algarve but his most trusted lieutenants had spirited him away to a safe location which had no audit trail leading back to Lobo or his companies. He was desperate to get his prize out of Ingrena, but of all his men, he trusted the council of these two the most.
"Carlos, she is too hot at the moment. We must rely on Ferko to keep her safe. There are too many police around the house, if we try to move her, we will surely be caught. The room is secure even if the house is searched and Ferko has seen what happens to those who displease you".

Chavali looked after the girl while Ferko put on the television news. Interpol's continuous raids against Lobo's assets was the biggest police operation the Algarve had ever seen, so the story was leading on every bulletin.
"Another Algarve sex club has fallen victim to a police battering ram, as trafficked East European girls are rescued and sent home", began the newscaster. "GNR teams, supported by Interpol have been raiding premises along the Algarve coast for the past two days. An Interpol spokesman told us the raids are all connected to organised crime groups across Portugal and the former Soviet Union. But sources close to this news channel suggest the raids are linked to the almost mythical crime boss O Lobo".

While Ferko worried about his boss, the Watchers were still plotting how best to find Lucy and clear Stone.
Ferko remained their best link to Carlos Lobo, but their surveillance confirmed neither he nor Chavali had left the

Between Stone & A Hard Place

house. All they could do was plan their continued surveillance and place their operatives, ready for him to move again.

"Movement ", came the voice over the Watchers' radio. "The truck is reversing closer to the house."

By moving his truck, Ferko had inadvertently blocked the Watchers' view of the door.

The constant news of raids against O Lobo and inability to contact his boss was now worrying Ferko. He wanted to get the girl away from the police presence at Ingrena,

Chavali just wanted her out of the small hidden room. They had talked about little else since returning from Madrid and Chavali was starting to wear her husband down.

"Off off off", went the Watchers' radio as the red truck pulled out of the electric gates and headed inland.

The Watchers and their operatives were close behind Ferko as he drove north along the wild, west coast road.

Despite the number of police working at the dig site, none of them noted the significance of the red truck leaving the walled house. So it was only the Watchers who saw Ferko turn away from the coast and start to climb the winding mountain road.

"Only leads one place Skull lad", said Jonah as he followed the progress of their surveillance vehicles through the hairpin bends towards Pedralva.

Ferko's destination confused Jonah. There was still a heavy police presence in the holiday village from which Lucy was taken and it seemed a big risk for the Roma to be going back.

Jonah would usually put one of his vehicles ahead of their subject, but it was impossible on the mountain road. He had to manage with one of the dirt bikes reaching high ground with binoculars.

It was the dirt biker who spotted Ferko's truck pause briefly in the village.

"He's stopped, but I don't have a clear view", said the biker as the red truck stopped behind a row of pretty cottages.

Between Stone & A Hard Place

Then, no sooner had he passed his message, the truck moved off again.
"Off, off. At speed towards Budens", reported the biker as Ferko's 4x4 truck shot along the valley's dirt road in a cloud of dust.
When the police eventually recovered CCTV, they would see a red truck pass the supermarket at Budens. But much more importantly, they would see a pretty blonde girl walk the short distance to the restaurant she had so often visited with her family.

The couple who ran the restaurant thought they were imagining things. "Lucy!" they exclaimed together. Despite a police search covering Portugal and Spain, Lucy Varley had walked calmly through their door.
Once inside, she lost her calm facade and ran in tears to the restaurateurs. The couple at first thought they were dreaming, but quickly moved to comfort the crying child.
Then they made the phone call to the police which would have a massive impact on the lives of both Nev Stone and Trudy Varley.
Trudy had only a short trip from the incident room at Villa do Bispo to meet her daughter in Pedralva. But it seemed the longest journey she had taken in her life.
Muppet Henson, a skilled police driver, was covering the distance quickly, but it could never be fast enough for a mother wanting to hold the daughter she missed so badly.

Muppet later recalled Trudy meeting the daughter she feared was lost, as "the nicest thing he had witnessed in all his years of policing".
"There are some things", he sad, "that make all the hard parts of the job worthwhile".

It took a little longer for the MC's lawyer Tony Smart to free Stone. Over several days of video recorded interviews, Lucy told of her kidnap by the Roma and Stone's attempt to rescue her.
She also told what she could remember about the boat trip

Between Stone & A Hard Place

to a very hot country, where she stayed in a house with other girls. Then, after a visit from an old wolf like man, she was brought back to Portugal.
Crucially, Lucy had not been harmed. The old man had been very clear that she should be well looked after.

Once free, the Watchers threw the inevitable biker party at their clubhouse.
But it was the next day that Stone really began to unwind. In a way typical of bikers the world over, he rode his motorcycle. Now reunited with his own Triumph Explorer, he rode the powerful adventure bike deep into the mountains.
Riding alone, Stone was lost in thought as he negotiated the mountain bends and took in the breathtaking scenery.
Stone wondered if he could make a life with Trudy, but he had heard little from the loving mother since getting her daughter back. He realised that she could never live his biker lifestyle and thought about whether he would be out of place returning to England.

As he rode, Stone's thoughts also strayed to his adventures in Morocco.
Despite all that he and the Watchers had done searching for Lucy across two continents; it was the conscience of a gypsy mother that saved Lucy and gave Stone his freedom.

Between Stone & A Hard Place

Epilogue

Months later, Stone sat in a deck chair, in Coventry's, suburbs, tapping away on his iPad. He smiled as he watched Trudy playing with her daughter.
With their mission over, Stone had allowed his feelings for Trudy to show and the two had enthusiastically begun a long distance relationship. Stone was dividing his time between Trudy's English home, and his own Algarve Yurt. Stone's press agent had already predicted a large advance for the book he was writing about the Moroccan adventure.

Young Lucy seemed miraculously unscarred by her ordeal and her unconditional love for her mum shone through.
As Trudy pushed her daughter on her swing, she looked over at the man who had risked so much to save her daughter. The strength of her smile gave away her happiness at having both her daughter back, and such a good man in her life.
Stone loved to see the mother and daughter so happy together.
Trudy would not let Lucy out of her sight, which was making a traditional romance difficult. Despite his happiness with Trudy, Stone was increasingly disappearing into his work and dreaming of another adventure.

Spending time in England gave Stone more opportunities to see Jonah. He had missed his old boss while living and working in Portugal.
Jonah's investigation agency was growing in strength, and he was often able to offer Stone surveillance work.
Stone was pleased of the work. But Jonah's secrecy over some of his clients intrigued Stone.

Muppet Henson had fared well from his part in the adventure.
Some, more political bosses might have argued that he had got too close to Stone and Jonah. But his part in the investigation had borne fruit for Interpol.

Between Stone & A Hard Place

Muppet had expertly managed the intelligence about O Lobo's criminal network, allowing both Portugal and Morocco to dismantle huge parts of his drug and sex business.
The Chief Inspector had been promoted to Superintendent, and given a senior role within Interpol.

O Lobo was far from happy. Now in his 80s, the gangster had hoped his partnership with Georgi Dimov would fund his retirement.
But now, with his income disrupted, and his reputation damaged, the wolf would need to be ruthless if he wanted to rebuild his empire.
Despite his advancing years, Carlos Lobo excelled at being ruthless. No one involved in the Watchers' Moroccan adventure believed they had heard the last of the wolf.

The Watchers had tried to resume business as usual after the media attention had died down.
The publicity had benefited their security business. But it somehow did not seem enough for Skull and his brother bikers.
No one jumps on a motorcycle without some level of adrenalin addiction, and the Watchers were no exception.
The thrill of the chase across Morocco was still buzzing through them, and they longed for another adventure.

Time was going to show, they should be careful what they wished for.

If you have enjoyed Between Stone & A Hard Place, don't miss the Watchers second adventure:

Stone, Paper, Bomb

Between Stone & A Hard Place

Stone, Paper, Bomb

A Nev Stone & The Watchers MC Adventure

Nev Stone's second adventure takes him and the Watchers to the Americas, where a fanatical sect plans to detonate an improvised nuclear device in the United States, blaming Islamic terrorists.

The action moves between England, Portugal, Cuba and New Orleans as the bikers track the players and the nuclear components. Time is against them as they race to prevent a bigger catastrophe than 9/11.

Between Stone & A Hard Place

Breath Becomes Stone

A Nev Stone & The Watchers MC Adventure

Nev Stone & the Watchers third adventure takes them to New Zealand.

Disgraced ex cop, Nev Stone now works with the Watchers MC and their global security business. Contracting for MI6, they are sent undercover to New Zealand, where smuggling of rare animals has caught the attention of Britain's Royal Family.
The action moves through Hong Kong, China and New Zealand, as the Watchers fight environmental disaster.

Between Stone & A Hard Place

Loxley: A dish served cold

A modern day Robin Hood tale.

Major Robin Loxley returns from the Middle East to attend his father's funeral and take on his duties as Duke of Loxley. Estranged from the old Duke for many years, this is Robin's first return to Sherwood since the death of his mother.

Robin learns that the old duke has mortgaged Loxley Hall to fund a lifestyle of drink, drugs, gambling and women. With the death of the Duke, the holder of his debt calls in the mortgage. This pits Robin and his Special Forces team against Nottingham's shadowy drug lord known as the Tax Collector.

Vowing never to use guns on the streets of their city, Robin's Outlaws use historic weapons to tear down the Tax Collector's empire.

Between Stone & A Hard Place

The Tricycle Spy

A biographical novel, based on my father's lifetime fight against communism.

Gordon Hallam first worked with Special Branch as a young soldier in the Malayan Emergency. On leaving the Army, Gordon joined the police, serving in Traffic and CID, before again working with Special Branch in England.

A crippling stroke ended Gordon's police career, but it did not end his involvement with Special Branch. Now disabled and riding a tricycle, Gordon's former colleagues put him back to work as an undercover agent. This time Gordon was spying on left wing subversives, trying to make a toe hold for communism in Britain.

Between Stone & A Hard Place

A non-fiction title

Rocking The Streets

Neil Hallam spent much of his youth in the Rock n Roll and Biker subcultures. Then, though working as a Night Club Bouncer and almost 25 years in the Police, Neil observed several decades of youth culture.

This book grew directly from my non fiction project; Mofos; a history of English biker culture. Through researching the various two wheeled sub cultures, I saw that alongside most of them ran an accompaniment of contemporary music.
The Rockers first had Rock and Roll and Rockabilly, moving later towards Heavy Rock. The Mods began with Modern Jazz, moving through Ska to eventually become Skinheads. The 1980's saw some very weird and wonderful fashions in both dress and music. The Hillbilly looking Hipsters of the early 21st century are said to have drawn their inspiration from the early Beatnik culture, which in turn was part of the American music scene.
The current street gang and drug dealing culture has its own accompaniment of Rap.
But the youth cultures went back even further than my biker research. In this book, I will lead you through what I learned of the Scuttlers of the 1800s and the Bright Young Things of the 1920s, before reaching the more contemporary cultures.

Between Stone & A Hard Place

The Robin Hood 500 Route

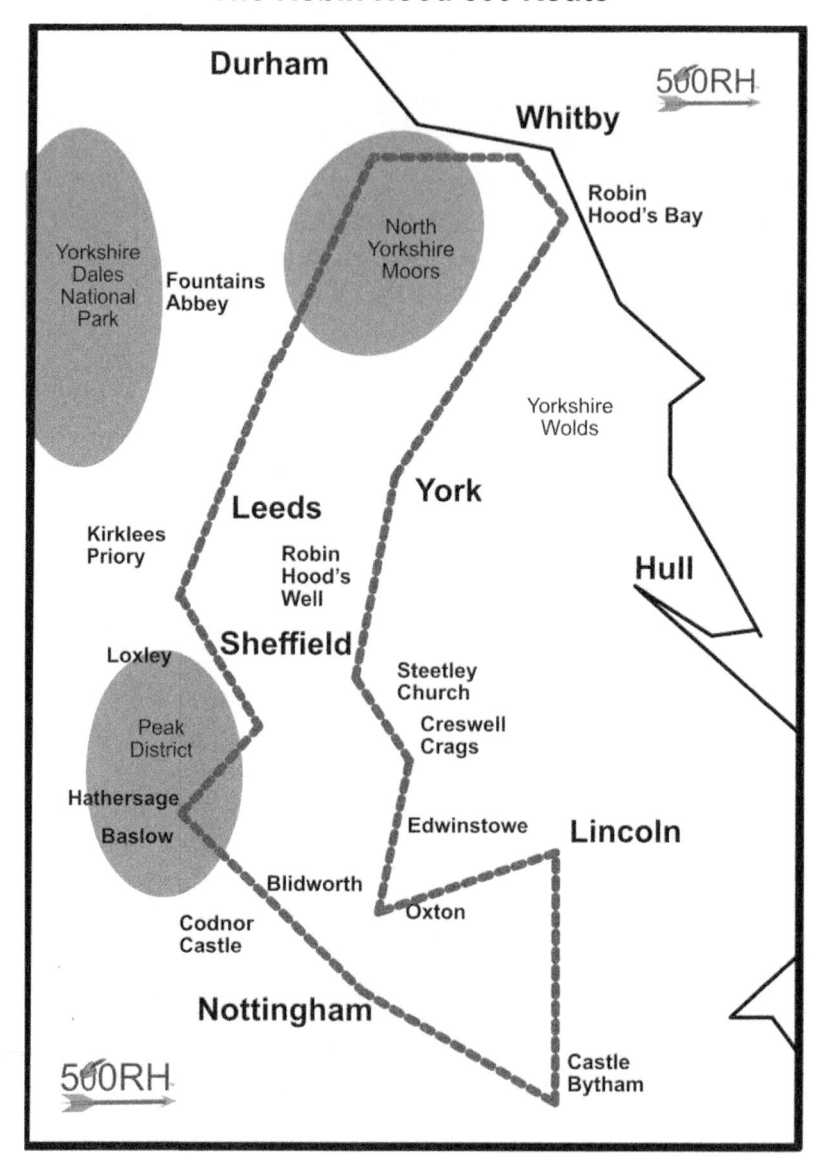

www.500RH.co.uk

Printed in Great Britain
by Amazon